MW01173321

DEADLY
JUDGMENT

O'HALLERAN SECURITY INTERNATIONAL, VOLUME 4

TJ LOGAN

DEADLY JUDGMENT by TJ Logan

Published by TJL Creative Works LLC, 2020

Copyright © 2020 TJ Logan

tjloganauthor.com

First edition: August 19, 2020

Paperback ISBN: 9798645318857

Cover Art:

Wicked Smart Designs

Editor: Chris Kridler

DEDICATION

Deadly Judgment **is dedicated to my five brothers:**
Mike, Jim, John, Mark and Matthew.

Like Emily O'Halleran, the heroine in *Deadly Judgment*, I was surrounded by five brothers who were equal parts irritating and amazing. I will admit, I wasn't always lovable, and I was a bit of a brat, sometimes a tattletale. In general, there were times I was an annoying pain in the butt. Though, in my defense, the odds were stacked against me. We could fight with each other, but no one dared messed with their sister. I always knew they would have my back when I needed them, and I would always have theirs. They were there for me when others let me down. As a result, I learned about trust and unconditional love from them. They were my heroes long before I knew what a hero was.

I love and respect each and every one of them and am proud to call them *my brothers*.

ACKNOWLEDGMENTS

To my amazing beta reader extraordinaire, Sally Kalarovich. She is the mother of extremely active triplets, works full-time for her family business, all while keeping a smile on her husband's face. She volunteers tons of hours at a local community theater: onstage as a performer, and offstage working with young performers. Even with all this going on, she still manages to eke out time to read through the many versions of my books as they are being written, then offers amazing and invaluable insights about the story development, characters, etc.

Sally, you are a very special friend. I love you and am so SO happy you came into my life. And not just because you're an amazing beta reader!

To my honey, Joel, you will forever be my person. I love you.

PROLOGUE

One year ago ...

E mily O'Halleran knew a third glass of wine was a sorry substitute for what she really wanted, but it was easier to get her hands on than the handsome and totally unattainable Mason Croft.

While internally debating the pros and cons of getting drunk, she glanced around her parents' big backyard. Family and close friends had gathered to celebrate the marriage of her brother, Jonathan, to the love of his life, Andi. Her new sister-in-law was awesome, if a bit intense, and Emily loved her like the sister she never had growing up.

Actually, she'd gotten pretty darn lucky on the sister front in the past couple of years. All three of her older brothers were now married to amazing, uniquely different women. Their large family was growing ever larger, and she couldn't be happier. Well, she could, but ...

Her eyes scanned the makeshift dance floor set up under

multiple strands of crisscrossing white lights. The weather was perfect, the slight chill to the night air signaling the end of spring.

Jonathan stood in the middle, holding his new wife as they chatted quietly to themselves, their precious baby daughter, Ashling, sleeping snugly between them. Her third oldest brother wasn't much of a dancer, but he never gave up an opportunity to hold Andi.

Beck, her oldest brother, had his long arms wrapped firmly around his wife, Gwen. Emily noticed how he was always watching her, touching her, whispering secrets in her ear that made her blush. He cherished her.

Caleb held Dawn, his hands spread across her butt. Oh, how her mighty playboy brother had fallen when he'd first laid eyes on his now wife. He said something to Dawn, and she threw her head back and laughed. They did that a lot.

She was very happy for her brothers. Really, she was. Really. But lately, their happiness seemed to illuminate her sense of melancholy. She longed for someone to love her the way her brothers loved their wives, and the way her father loved her mother.

Her job had given her a glimpse into the darkest side of humanity. She'd come to realize life was uncertain, which created a sense of urgency to live life to its fullest that grew with every case they worked.

Emily was surrounded by a big family she loved and who loved her. Yet, as she watched them on the dance floor, she felt desolate and profoundly alone.

She rubbed the ache in her chest. *Good grief, pity party much?* She walked over to the bar and held up her empty wineglass. "I would like another one of these filled with some of that, please." She pointed at the bottle of Darby's Purple Haze.

"Sure thing." The bartender took her glass and replaced it

with a clean one, popped the cork on the red blend and filled her glass to the midpoint.

"Here ya go." He winked and set it on the bar.

"Thanks." She smiled at him. He was good-looking but a definite player. She'd bet her favorite pair of leggings he never left a wedding without a bridesmaid or female guest on his arm.

Besides, she was only interested in one man. Tragically, he didn't feel the same way about her.

Emily turned and headed back toward her table. Halfway there, her heel caught in the grass, and her long dress tangled around her legs. She gasped. Her wine splashed over the rim as the ground quickly approached. Her eyes squeezed shut and she prepared for an embarrassing face splat when, suddenly, a strong arm circled her waist from behind and stopped her fall, lifted her and set her on her feet in one fluid motion.

"What the—" Her heart raced, as if she'd run a marathon. Which, yeah, that would never happen.

"I've got you." *Oh, that yummy, panty-melting voice.*

Emily closed her eyes, took a deep breath, then opened them and turned to face her savior, the singularly magnificent Mason Croft. Her brother Caleb's best friend. And the guy she'd had a serious thing for since the first time her eyes landed on him standing in her parents' backyard.

"Thanks. This dress is a menace." She emitted an awkward sort of snort-laugh. *Real sexy, Emily.*

"Are you okay?" Genuine concern softened his voice.

"I'm fine." Emily frowned at the empty wineglass she'd managed to keep hold of. She thought about getting a refill but decided against it. She needed to have her wits about her right now.

Mason accompanied her to a high-top table set up in a

darkened area near the edge of the festivities. She set her empty glass down among a few others.

"You sure you're okay?" He snagged a napkin from the nearby table and handed it to her.

"A little embarrassed but fine." She wiped the wine from her fingers and set the napkin next to her glass.

He reached up and tucked a hank of hair over her ear that had fallen from her up-do. She could've sworn his hand lingered, then he dragged it down her neck and over her shoulder before it fell to his side. Her entire body tingled at his touch and screamed for more. Why did he have to be so darned potent?

"Thanks," she mumbled as she reached up and haphazardly pinned it back in place.

"Having fun?" He stepped closer in the darkened space.

"Yeah. You?"

"Yeah, and the company's great." He smiled down at her.

Her mouth opened slightly, then she blinked, snapped it shut and turned to the dance floor. Away from his powder-blue eyes. "They're all so in love, aren't they? It almost hurts to look at them. Someday, I hope ..."

She gave him a sideways glance and cleared her throat to keep from spilling any more secrets. *Stupid wine.* Emily was such a lightweight. She knew better than to have more than one glass.

He curled his hand over her shoulder and brought her around to face him. "Someday, you hope what, Em?"

She hesitated, and he tilted his head to the side. "Tell me."

She marveled at the happy couples across the lawn. "Someday, I hope someone loves me like that and looks at me the way my dad looks at my mom, the way my brothers look at their wives. Like they are the single most important thing in their life."

Being this close to him and talking about wanting to be

loved was surprisingly painful. Emily was suddenly swamped with emotion. Her eyes burned, and she swallowed against the ridiculous urge to cry. She was *not* a crier.

"Hey, hey." Mason circled his arms around her and gently pulled her into him.

She pressed her cheek against his chest and wrapped her arms around him. Her eyes fell shut, and she breathed in his scent. She allowed herself to enjoy his embrace for what she knew would be a fleeting moment, then loosened her grip to step back.

His hold tightened, keeping her close.

Her brows drew together, and she looked up at him.

For a long moment, he looked down at her, then slowly lowered his face, giving her ample time to pull away. She did not, and the next thing she knew, Mason Croft's lips were on hers. And, oh, they were just as soft as she'd imagined them to be.

Emily threw her arms around his neck and fell heart-first into his kiss. His mouth moved over hers carefully, almost reverently, at first. She let out a little moan and nipped at his bottom lip. Wanting ... needing more. Everything about him and their kiss changed. Intensified. He drew her body tight against his. She raised to her toes in an effort to get closer still. His fingers speared into her hair—making a mess of her expensive up-do—then he angled her head and took the kiss deeper. Their tongues brushed across each other's as heavy breaths panted from her nose and across his cheek.

Joy rushed through her, and she poured it all into their kiss. It, *he*, was so much more than she'd ever dreamed, and she'd dreamt *a lot*. Finally, everything she'd hoped for with Mason appeared to be one step closer to becoming reality.

Laughter cut through the night. He broke their kiss and, hands on her shoulders, stepped back. It ended so abruptly, she almost lost her balance. He steadied her, then quickly let go and cast a furtive look around.

"Shit. I'm sorry, Em. That was a mistake. This—us—can't happen. You're Caleb's little sister. It wouldn't be right." He hesitated, then placed a soft kiss on her forehead, turned and walked away, leaving her standing alone in the dark with her heart cracked wide open, wondering what just happened.

CHAPTER ONE

Present day ...

The young woman fanned her trembling fingers across her belly, her nails jagged and ripped apart, dried blood caked on her hands. The butterfly-like flutters of life she'd begun to feel had stopped the day the man tossed her in this box and buried them alive. She couldn't even cry over her loss —the monster had robbed her of tears when he stopped giving her food and water. They just wouldn't come. Instead, she hummed a soft, now useless lullaby into the oppressive, never-ending darkness.

The monster—that's what she'd started calling him, but only in her head. Never out loud.

It felt like it had been years since he'd grabbed her, shoved her into a utility van, then jabbed a needle in her arm. When she woke up, she had a horrible case of cotton-mouth, a ferocious headache, and one of her wrists was chained to a ring screwed into the concrete wall of some old basement. What she wouldn't give to be back there now.

Her screams for help in the dank cellar had gone unanswered until nothing remained of her voice but a croaking, harsh whisper. All she'd gotten for her efforts to free herself from the sharp metal cuff was a torn and bloody wrist.

Whenever he walked across the floor directly above her, she'd held her breath as the old beams groaned, sending dust and splinters of rotted wood raining down. A bare bulb dangling high above would bounce and jerk on its wire, splashing light into the corners. A critter of some sort squeaked and scurried in and out of the shadows along the walls. She wasn't sure if it was a rat or an opossum. Either way, it had creeped her out. A continual *drip drip drip* came from somewhere in the far-right corner. The stench of wet wood, mold and decay permeated the gloomy space, accompanied by the smell of bleach that had burned her nostrils. At the time, she'd been worried about the health risks to her baby. In hindsight, the basement was certainly better than her current situation.

The monster had always worn the same thing whenever he came to see her. Long-sleeved T-shirt, jeans, gloves and old work boots. All black, all very generic, and all completely unidentifiable. A hideous, rubber Freddy Krueger mask covered his whole head. On those rare occasions when he did speak, his voice was garbled, like he was using some kind of device to alter it.

She'd pleaded with him over and over to let her go, had promised never to tell anyone about anything. Because, really, what could she say? She'd never seen his face, had no idea what his real voice sounded like, and she had no idea where she was or even how long she'd been there.

He had just laughed. The distorted, chilling sound from behind that damn mask would haunt her in death. Which shouldn't be long now. Once his laughter subsided, he would tell her good night, walk up the wooden stairs—twelve of them, she'd counted—shut off the lights, and lock the door.

The first few days he'd given her water and a hunk of bread three times a day. He would remove the handcuff long enough for her to use the filthy bathroom in the corner. She'd tried to escape once, but he'd grabbed her by the hair and tackled her before she even made it to the steps. After that, he was always careful to shackle her hands and feet together.

One day he'd shown up with a legal pad and two, sharpened number two pencils. Her immediate thought was to shove one through his neck and hope she hit an artery. Watching him bleed to death would've given her great joy. And to think, there was a time she couldn't bring herself to step on a spider.

As if he'd read her thoughts, a demonic chuckle had rolled from behind the mask and he'd waggled his finger in her face. "Ah, ah, ah. None of that now." Then he'd surprised her by tugging off his mask and smiling down at her.

Many times, as she'd sat alone in that godforsaken hellhole, she'd pondered what he might look like. Her muddled brain had envisioned a slobbering, hairy beast with gnashing teeth and beady eyes. In reality, he was none of those. He was … ordinary.

"You don't remember me, do you? How about when I said hi to you in the corridor and you just looked down your nose at me like I was nothing? Little Miss High-and-Mighty, thought you were too good for me." He'd stepped closer, face contorted, spittle flying. His anger grew with each word hurled her way.

Reality slammed into her, and any fragment of hope that he would let her go vanished. No sense wasting her dwindling energy pleading with him—her time was up.

She'd been forced to write her Last Will and Testament.

At only twenty-four years old, she'd never given a moment's thought to having a will. Weak from hunger, hand shaking with the effort to grip the pencil, she'd managed to scribble a few things down—a goodbye to her parents and boyfriend and a request that they name her unborn baby Tabitha. The last thing she remembered was scrawling her name across the bottom.

A dry, violent cough burned her lungs and yanked her painfully back to her current hell, trapped in a box.

Fresh air that had been filtering across her bare feet from a small opening had slowed to nothing. Every breath was now a struggle, becoming shallower with each attempt. It was becoming increasingly more difficult to stay awake, and bouts of delirium wreaked havoc with her teetering sanity. A bit ago, she'd imagined herself snapping upright in her own bed, relieved to discover this was all just a horrifying nightmare. She'd banged her forehead, hard, against the top of the box, a brutal reminder she was still trapped.

As she sucked in shallow, panting breaths, she could hear her boyfriend calling out to her, then his voice faded. Her father's silly jokes and her mom's laughter drifted through her foggy mind. She hadn't even had the chance to tell them they were going to be grandparents. Now it was too late.

"I'm sorry, Mommy. I'm sorry, Daddy." Her apology eked out like sandpaper scraping against the lonely, eternal darkness.

CHAPTER TWO

"Am I going to have to kick your butt?" Emily O'Halleran propped her hands on her hips, tilted her head back—*way* back—and glowered up at the man hovering in her office doorway. *Blocking my office doorway would be more accurate.*

"Because you know I won't hesitate to get up on a chair to do it." Not an idle threat either. She might only be five feet three and a half inches tall on a good day, but she'd grown up with five very large, annoyingly domineering brothers. She had no problem getting in his face.

"Sorry, Emily." Golden Bailey hung his head. His teammates called him Viking. Fitting because, seriously, he straight-up looked like one. His long, dark blond hair hung just past his shoulders, and at an impressive six feet eight, he was O'Halleran Security International's tallest operator. Heck, he was their tallest employee, period. He also happened to be their nicest, which explained his sheepish demeanor.

She worked for O'Halleran Security International's Pacific Northwest operation, known in the covert ops community as

OSI PacNW. They specialized in close protection, private security, national and international hostage retrieval, tracking, and cybersecurity.

The company was the brainchild of her oldest brother, Beck, a former FBI Special Agent who oversaw the entire operation from their main compound in San Francisco.

"You were supposed to bring *all* your documents in today, Golden. It's the only way I can get your Contractor Access Card updated in time for you to deploy with your team."

As the manager of deployment and logistics, she was responsible for getting their teams and all necessary support equipment into and out of what were usually hostile foreign countries. And it had to be done as quickly and quietly as possible.

The day after she was notified of her Top-Secret security clearance, Emily began doing massive amounts of research to ensure she had the best, most streamlined process in place to successfully deploy their personnel. She spoke with current and former NSA and CIA operatives and traveled to U.S. military bases and embassies all over the world. As a result, she'd established a network of powerful connections and had created a well-oiled process. As proud as she was of all she'd accomplished, she'd much rather be working in the field on domestic assignments.

Beck and Jonathan, *the big jerks*, wouldn't agree to it. Said she was too valuable to them working deployments. Emily called BS. For most of her life, she'd lived under the overprotective thumbs of her brothers. All because they blamed themselves for something that happened to her a bazillion years ago. *Stupid*. Heck, she didn't even have nightmares about it anymore.

She understood, sort of, and she loved them all very much for it. But it was a long time ago, and Emily was an adult now, not some clueless little girl. Was it too much to ask that they trust her to take care of herself? Their attitude pissed her off only slightly more than it hurt her feelings. Of course, she kept the latter to herself while falling back heavily on the former.

"My grandma was sick, so I flew down there to take care of her." Golden had been raised by his very sweet, staunchly religious grandma. He'd once said he would walk through fire for her, and Emily believed it.

"I had it all worked out. I would spend a few of my days off with her, fly home, go to the doc's office and pick up my forms, then bring them in to you. Then my flight was canceled, and by the time I caught a different one and got back, their office was closed."

Well, heck. Her hands slid from her hips.

"I'm sorry to hear about your grandma. Nothing serious, I hope." What kind of a hag would she be if she stayed mad at the guy for taking care of his sick grandmother?

"Nah, just a bad cold. But when you're almost ninety, a cold can turn into pneumonia just like that." He snapped his fingers, then wedged his hands in his front pockets.

"Do you need to be with her? Because I can pull one of the other guys in to take your place on the next op." All the operators thought she was a pain-in-the-butt nag with all her pre-deployment demands, but she wasn't completely heartless. And besides, it wasn't her fault the government required so dang much paperwork.

"Nah, she's good. Her younger sister, my great aunt, got there yesterday. She was going to be moving in with her anyway. They just moved up the timeline a few weeks." His grandma lived in a little two-bedroom villa Golden bought for her in a large retirement community in Florida. She knew this because he'd proudly shared pictures.

"I'm glad to hear it's nothing too serious." Emily blew out a bang-ruffling breath and shooed him away. "Okay, get the heck out of my office, you big knucklehead. I've got some butts to kiss if I'm going to get you deployed."

Her mind started clicking through all the favors she'd have to call in and hoops she'd have to jump through. First thing she'd do was call the doctor at home. Sure, it was Friday, and his office closed early, but OSI sent him a lot of business. Not to mention, he'd delivered all six of the O'Halleran kids.

"You're awesome, Emily." Golden tossed out one of his aw-shucks smiles as he clumsily patted her on the shoulder with one of his massive hands. "I owe you one."

As he walked away, she called out, "Yeah ... well ... bring me chocolate and we'll call it even." Emily shook her head and turned back to her desk.

"What do I get if *I* bring you chocolate?"

She didn't have to turn around to know that silky-smooth voice belonged to the very same man who'd nearly kissed her lips right off her face, right before soundly rejecting her.

Emily forced her feet to keep moving, using the time it took to round her desk to school her expression. God forbid she give away how mortified she was by how he'd ended what happened between them. Only then did she dare look at her next visitor.

"You get your butt deployed to Afghanistan, is what you get." *What a nice butt it is, too.* She plopped into her chair with a sigh and started shuffling papers. Maybe if he thought she was busy, he'd have the decency to remove his handsome albeit infuriating self from her office.

Her guest chair squeaked.

Her eyes rolled up to find him grinning at her. And what a beautiful sight it was—all those perfectly straight, brilliant white teeth framed by full lips she knew firsthand to be cushy-soft. It made her skin tingle in a not-welcome-any-longer sort of way.

His broad shoulders and tall, leanly muscled body overwhelmed the chair. One ankle laid atop the opposite knee, his fingers curled over it, just as casual as you please. Like he had every right to be in her office making her insides feel like an acrobat was doing tumbling runs.

She sighed. "Can I help you with something, Mason?" *Like, take your shirt off, maybe? No. Bad, Emily, bad.* "I have a lot to get done before I leave today, and I'm already running behind." She waved her hand over her cluttered desk.

"Got a hot date or something?" He tossed the words out as he glanced over at the rows of names and deployment dates printed neatly on her big whiteboard.

"As a matter of fact, yes, I do." Emily had started dating in hopes of exorcising Mason from her system. So far, it wasn't working worth a darn. Having to see him just about every dang day wasn't helping either.

"Oh, really." His eyes slid back to her. "Who's the lucky guy?"

Okay, so, here's the thing. Most people would look at him and think, *wow, that guy is one chill dude.* But she knew him, had spent what she now realized was an embarrassing amount of time watching him. Which is the only reason she picked up on the way his jaw tightened ever so slightly as he asked the question.

"What business is it of yours?" She tucked her pen over her ear and took a sip of her favorite tea, which was now —*blech*—tepid.

"Just curious." Elbows on the arms of the chair, long fingers threaded together, he settled his hands atop his very toned, ridiculously flat midsection.

Okay, maybe she'd ogled him in the gym a time or two as well. *So sue me.*

"Do your brothers know?" Mr. Snoopypants asked.

"How the heck should I know? And anyway, it's really

none of their business who I date." Though her brothers had argued that fact. Vehemently. Ad nauseam.

"You going out with that Richie guy again? He's an accountant or something, right?"

"His name is Richard, and he runs the flight desk at the naval base."

"Whatever." He waved it away. "Has he been properly vetted?"

"Has he been … You can't be serious." Her indignation grew, which was never a good thing where Emily was concerned. "I'm not hiring him for a job. I'm having dinner with him."

Whoa. Wait a second.

"How the heck do you know his …" Her eyes widened, and her mouth dropped open. Her giant pink mug with the words *Don't stress meowt* on the side hit the desk with a dull *thunk*. Tea sloshed over the edge.

"Wait a darn minute. Have you … have you been *spying* on me?" She flew right past indignant straight to seriously pissed off.

He chuckled. Which ticked her off even more.

"Emily, everyone in this town knows you. You're like the damn Princess of Whidbey Cove." He grumbled the last part under his breath. "You can't honestly think no one would notice you going out with some strange dude."

"Pfff. Don't be absurd." She rolled her eyes and sat back in her chair. *Princess of Whidbey Cove. Ridiculous.* "Richard is not the least bit strange. And people, including you, should get a life and stay the heck out of my business. I am a grown woman who is capable of making her own decisions. Thank you very much."

"Oh, trust me, Em. I am very well aware you're a woman. Don't ever doubt that." His deep voice tumbled across her desk, wrapping around her like a studly blanket, and, like a caress, those striking blue eyes of his traveled over her hair, her face.

To avoid being sucked in by those gorgeous peepers, Emily broke their gaze, yanked her pen from over her ear and flipped open a random folder on her desk. She reminded herself—for what had to be the gazillionth time—of his painful words to her after sharing the hottest kiss of her life. Not that she'd ever forget. They were indelibly etched in her memory.

"I'm sorry, Em. That was a mistake. This—us—can't happen. You're Caleb's little sister. It wouldn't be right."

"That was a mistake." Who knew four words could hurt so much?

She'd rocketed to the heights of euphoric joy, then nose-dived into a deep, crushing heartache. Until that moment, she'd harbored a silly fantasy that they would be great together. Now she had to accept that that's all it would ever be—a young woman's ridiculous fantasy.

"Mason, unless you need me for something, I have work to do." She couldn't deal with this right now.

"Listen, Em, about what happened—"

She held up one hand without looking at him as she scribbled a useless note on a piece of paper with the other.

"Uh-uh, not talking about that." Immature? Possibly. Critical to her peace of mind? Most definitely. "You made yourself abundantly clear, Mason. You're not interested. Got it. That horse is dead. You can stop beating it."

Emily tucked her hurt feelings into the same place she'd been shoving them since she was little and didn't want to give away how left out she always felt being "the only girl," "the baby sister."

His foot dropped to the floor, and he bolted up from the chair with a growl. His big hands covered hers, and he leaned in close. Like, nose-to-nose close.

Emily focused on his large, capable hands completely covering hers. One had a long scar straight across the knuckles that she'd never noticed before.

"Emily, look at me."

She took a deep breath, braced herself with a look of indifference, before lifting her chin.

"Don't for one minute think that kiss didn't mean anything to me. That I don't still feel your lips against mine. That I can't still taste you. It's just that—" He certainly seemed sincere, but she refused to open herself up to being hurt and disappointed again. Instead, she fell back on her characteristic sarcasm.

"Sure. Whatever. If you say so," she mumbled under her breath. Then she dragged her hands free and sat back in her seat. He smelled so flippin' good, she couldn't think straight when he was so close.

"Emily-y-y-y." He dragged out her name in a frustrated growl.

"Mason, it's fine. Really." She leaned on the arm of her chair—oh so blasé. As if this conversation wasn't tearing her up inside.

No. Emily was done with that. She'd allowed herself one week after the *mistake* to wallow in misery. During that time, she'd eaten what had to have been several pounds of chocolate, cursed at her television when her favorite show was preempted, again at her pantry when it was empty of chocolate—pretty much everything, really. She'd also blubbered so many tears into her pillow, she thought she might have to replace it. All done without witnesses, thank you very much. She'd learned a long time ago that tears were a potential weakness to be exploited.

"After much thought and reflection, I realized you were right. I've moved on." At least, she was trying to. "I'm dating and having a great time." Okay, so *great* might be a bit of an exaggeration. "I assumed you would do the same."

Even if the thought of seeing him with another woman made Emily want to gouge her own eyes out. Or maybe the other woman's ... Nah, that wouldn't be right. *We gals have to stick together and all that.*

He straightened to his full six feet one inch, and his hands fell to his sides.

"So you really like this guy? This ... Richard?" He spit the name out like it was an offense to his taste buds.

Richard was thirty-five, nine years older than her. Decent-looking, nice, intelligent, and attentive. Heck, they even graduated from the same college, for Pete's sake. They'd had fun the few times they'd gone out. Unfortunately, there was just no spark—that intangible *something* just didn't exist between them. Not like the way she felt about ... *No, no, nopity, nope, nope. Not going there.*

"This will only be our third date, Mason. At this point, we're just having fun, hanging out, getting to know each other." No way was she telling him the truth. That she couldn't stop thinking about *him* long enough to give any other guy a fighting chance.

CHAPTER THREE

Heavy metal music crashed off the concrete walls. The perfect complement to Mason's piss-poor mood. Sweat poured off him, and he grunted as he landed a vicious right hook followed by an uppercut, then a strong round-house kick. He finished off his *opponent* with a jumping front kick just as his best friend, Caleb O'Halleran, and his K9 partner, Jake, walked over.

"*Sedni.*" Caleb gave Jake the command for *sit,* which the Czech shepherd followed immediately.

Caleb lived in San Francisco with his wife, Dawn, and his dog. He used to be a Tactical K9 Specialist on the Bureau's Hostage Rescue Team until some pretty awful shit went down with Dawn and her sister. That's when he left the team to work with Beck at OSI's headquarters in California.

"Dude, whose face are you visualizing?" Caleb shouted over the music as he grabbed the remote and clicked off the old boom box. He stepped up to the heavy bag and stopped it from swinging.

"No one in particular." *Your sister's new boyfriend.* "Just trying to get in a decent workout."

Mason hated keeping things from him, but he couldn't risk letting on how much it was killing him that his best friend's baby sister was dating some other dude. That would lead to questions about why Mason cared so much. Questions he wasn't prepared to answer.

"Right. If you say so." Caleb parked his ass on one of the plyometric boxes. "So what's the deal with this guy Emily's dating?"

Okay, so I guess we are *talking about this.*

"Don't really know much about him." Other than he worked at Naval Station Whidbey Island, a few miles up the road, and that Emily was *having fun* while *getting to know* him.

What exactly does that entail? He quickly derailed that train of thought. There lay misery.

"Hmmm ..." Caleb hesitated, then his eyes lit up, and a treacherous smile slowly spread over his face.

"What the hell is that look?" Mason asked, knowing he wasn't going to like the answer.

"You guys are friends, right? So *you* should ask her about him." Caleb tapped the remote on his leg with one hand, scratched behind Jake's ears with the other. "If I do, she'll just accuse me of interfering in her life."

"Because you *are* interfering in her life." Sweat burned his eyes, and he turned to wipe his face on his shoulder.

"Come on, man. You—"

"Not happening." Mason shook his head.

He cared about Emily—too much—and it seemed disloyal to talk about her personal life with her brothers. Or anyone else, for that matter. Contrary to the way they treated her, she was a very strong, *extremely* independent woman who could take care of herself. It was one of the many reasons he was so drawn to her.

Caleb rose and tossed the remote back onto the shelf. "Dude, when you transferred up here from San Fran, I kinda hoped you'd keep an eye on her. You know, make sure she stays out of trouble."

Like that was even possible. Emily was as headstrong as she was smart. Sneaky, too. Once she set her mind to something, she was as tenacious as a hungry dog with a bone.

"I'm not going to spy on your little sister for you. And we both know the reason I transferred was because Jonathan needed my help." The O'Halleran brothers individually could be intimidating. As a group, they were a force to be reckoned with. Lucky for Mason, he'd grown up taking care of himself and knew how to hold his own.

"I know you care about her." Caleb tossed him a towel.

Mason caught it as his heart skipped a beat. *Christ.* Had his best friend figured out he was hung up on his kid sister? He and Caleb had been through so much together, and the O'Hallerans were the family he'd never had growing up. He didn't want to risk losing all of that by pursuing a relationship with Emily. What if they didn't work out?

But what if we did? He shook off the thought as he'd done many times before.

"Of course, I care about her. She's your kid sister and, yes, a friend." He played it cool and used his teeth to loosen the laces to his gloves. Saying it out loud was a good reminder to himself.

Unfortunately, his friendship with her had changed since the wedding. She seemed more guarded around him now. Which he fucking hated. It was his own damn fault—he never should've kissed her, but he couldn't help himself. She'd looked so sad and, in typical Emily fashion, tried to hide it. All he'd wanted to do was chase the shadows from her eyes. Now that he'd had a taste of her, he couldn't stop thinking about her. Knowing he could never have her was like a stone in his gut.

"Is that all? She's just ... a *friend?*" Caleb pierced him with a look Mason couldn't decipher.

"What are you getting at?" He wedged a glove under his arm and tugged his hand free, did the same with the other one, then tossed them in his bag on the floor.

Caleb hesitated, then clapped him on the back. "You know what? Never mind. I know you care about her and would never let anything happen to her."

"I would protect Emily with my life," Mason proclaimed without a second's hesitation.

"Yeah, I know you would. You were there for Beck when he needed you, and you almost got yourself killed saving Dawn and Luna." Caleb's jaw clenched, the rage still simmering just beneath the surface of his laid-back exterior.

A little over a year ago, Caleb's wife and her younger sister had been taken hostage by a maniac cult leader. Mason was part of the OSI team that went in after them. He'd ended up taking a bullet to the chest during the op.

"Thanks to you and Dawn, I'm still alive." Mason rubbed the gnarly scar on his chest. "The risk you both took for me ... I'll never be able to repay either one of you for what you did."

Dawn was an amazing doctor and just as fearless as Caleb. Had she and Caleb not braved their way through gunfire to get to him and triage his wound, Mason was absolutely certain he would not be here today.

"Dude, you look like you're about to kiss me, so I'm gonna leave now," Caleb joked. "I'm headed back out to the folks' place. I dropped Dawn and Luna off earlier. They were anxious to see Mom and Dad and spend some time with Andi and Ashling."

Andi was married to Jonathan O'Halleran, who ran OSI PacNW. She left her job as an interrogation tactics specialist with the National Security Agency to manage special field training for OSI. They had a beautiful, spirited two-year-old daughter named Ashling.

Even though Jonathan was his boss, he treated Mason more like family than an employee. Sometimes that was good, great even. Other times, not so much. The O'Hallerans were a meddlesome bunch. Oh, sure, their snoopiness came from a place of love, but Mason had never had anyone care much about what he did or didn't do, who he did it or didn't do it with. He was still getting used to the attention.

"Kemne." Caleb gave Jake the command for *come,* and the dog moved to his side. "I'll see you at Mom and Dad's for dinner later, right?" he asked as he walked backward away from him.

"Not sure yet if I can make it. I've got a few things to do." He reached down and snagged his water bottle from his bag.

Truth was, it was becoming more difficult to be around Emily without wanting to drag her to another dark corner and pick up where they'd left off.

His best friend stopped and tilted his head as if thinking, then one side of his mouth twitched up.

"My sister might bring her boyfriend," Caleb taunted in a singsong voice. "Could be a good chance for us to grill him about his intentions toward her."

Mason stifled his reaction even as his teeth ground together. Would Emily really bring the guy around her family already? She'd have to know her brothers would put him through the wringer.

"Like I said, I've got a few things to do." He shoved his arms in his hoodie and tugged it over his head

"Dude, you are so full of it. You've never turned down a chance to eat my mom's cooking." Caleb plastered on an innocent look. "Besides, you wouldn't want to hurt her feelings, would you?"

"You are such a dick, you know that?" Molly and

Michaleen O'Halleran were two of the most amazing people he'd ever met. Mason would take a hammer to his own head before hurting Caleb's mother.

"See you at dinner." His friend flashed a triumphant smirk, then turned and, whistling, strolled away with Jake close at his side.

CHAPTER FOUR

"Richard, I am so sorry, but I'm not going to be able to hang out tonight." What did it say about her that she was actually relieved to have an excuse to break their date? "I completely forgot one of my brothers was going to be in town with his family, and my folks invited all of us to dinner at their place."

She'd been passing herself coming and going lately. Two teams had to be deployed to opposites sides of the world at the same time, with very little advance notice. And there was a lot more to it than what they showed in the movies. You couldn't simply stuff a bunch of armed-to-the-teeth warriors onto a plane and fly them willy-nilly into a foreign country. There were manpower and gear requirements to be assessed, foreign operatives that needed to be given a heads-up, palms to be greased, and so *so* much more.

All that combined with Richard's fluctuating duty schedule and the night classes he was taking to get his master's made it tough to find time to get together. Probably for the best, since they had different expectations for their ... friendship.

"Sounds nice. Must be great having your family around." Richard was in the Navy, and he'd once mentioned how he wished he could see his family more often.

"Look, Richard, I'd invite you to join me, but my family can be a bit ... overwhelming. Not in a bad way," she rushed to say. "It's just that, well, we've only known each other a short time, and we're not really *dating* dating, and I don't want them to get the wrong idea and ... Criminy, I am really screwing this up."

"Emily, relax. I wasn't fishing for an invite." He chuckled, then turned serious. "I get it. I really do."

"Thank you." She wedged her phone between her shoulder and ear and shoved her laptop in her bag. "I wish I could offer you more, but I'm just not there."

"Yet?" His tenuous hope filtered through the phone.

"I'd better finish up here if I'm going to make it to my folks' before all the food is gone. My brothers are like a pack of hungry hyenas." Like a big fat chicken, she avoided his one-word question.

She'd been very honest with him from the beginning about not being interested in anything serious. He'd also been upfront about wanting more, when and if she ever changed her mind.

"How 'bout let's do this. Once things quiet down with your family, drop me a text and we'll figure something out," he suggested.

"Thanks for understanding." *Darn it.* He was such a good guy. Not for the first time, she cursed Mason Croft and his irresistible allure.

"This is me, being respectful of your desire to just be friends. But Emily, you should know this about me—when it comes to something I want, I am a very patient man, and I don't give up easily. Enjoy your time with your family, and we'll talk soon." The line went dead, but his declaration hung in the air.

"Why can't I fall for a guy like him?" Emily grouched as she tossed her cell phone on her desk and flopped back in her seat with a heavy sigh.

"A guy like whom?" Her sister-in-law Andi stood in the doorway, booted feet planted apart, her very toned arms folded over her chest. With her dark hair cut short with choppy bangs and oozing all that confidence, she was stunning. From her lofty five-foot-ten-inch height, she observed Emily in that spooky, all-seeing way of hers.

Jonathan's wife was like a human lie detector. She also happened to be a warrior badass of the first order who could take down most of the guys on the teams. Heck, she'd been the one to save their mom and Ashling when a senator's crazy, rogue aide kidnapped them. That toughness and inability to concede defeat had finally gotten Jonathan to pull his head out of his butt long enough to see what a perfect match they were.

She exposed it to very few people, but her sister-in-law had a huge heart and loved Emily's brother and niece with an unrivaled fierceness. Their journey to happiness had been paved with heartache, but they came out the other side as a family, each of them stronger for having the other in their life.

"Earth to Emily." Andi leaned her head to the side and looked at her. "A guy like whom?"

"Oh, just this great guy who likes me but whose feelings I can't return because I'm stupidly hung up on someone else." She planted her elbow on the desk and propped her chin in her hand.

"Why don't you just tell Mason how you feel?" Andi stepped in and settled her hip on the corner of Emily's desk. "It is so obvious you guys have the hots for each other."

"Only to you and your wizardly ways. And only one of us has the hots." Emily didn't bother trying to hide her feelings around Andi. The woman's ability to see through bullshit was matched only by her ability to keep a secret.

Andi snorted as she picked up the family photo sitting on Emily's desk. "Yeah, right. After that kiss at our recep—"

"Wait? What? How ...?" Emily stammered and lurched forward in her chair and whispered, "You saw that?"

Andi's dark brows rose, her chin lowered, and she looked at her like, *seriously?*

She groaned. "Does Jonathan know? Please tell me he doesn't know. Because if he knows, for sure Beck knows. And if Beck knows, then Caleb knows. And, oh man, if Caleb knows, then—"

Her sister-in-law's gusty laugh cut through Emily's panic.

"Get real. All Jonathan cared about that night was us getting to the hotel so we could ... Well, suffice to say, he wasn't paying much attention to you or Mason. Or *anyone,* for that matter." Her eyebrows danced up and down. "If you know what I mean."

"Ew. Gross. Enough. Stop." Emily scrunched her face and covered her ears. "That's my brother you're talking about." She lowered her hands in time to hear Andi laugh again. "It's great hearing you laugh. Even if it is at my expense." When her sister-in-law first arrived in Whidbey Cove, she never laughed. She was guarded and kept everyone at arm's length—until their mom and dad wore her down. She never stood a chance against them and all their boundless warmth and unconditional love.

"Thanks. I love having something to laugh about. And I love being a part of your family." She gave a little cough and, as if realizing she'd shared too much, became fascinated by the back of the picture frame.

"Hey." Emily gave a friendly swat to Andi's knee. "It's your family now, too."

"Yeah. It is, isn't it?" A soft smile lit her face, and pride glowed within her huge brown eyes.

"Okay, so I'm sure you didn't come in here to talk to me about my nonexistent love life."

"You're right, I didn't. I was wondering if you've gotten confirmation on that support equipment for Team Two?" And just like that, Andi moved on to business.

In their world, *support equipment* could mean anything from food and water to weapons and other required ordnance. In this case, Team Two was in need of a vehicle capable of going off-road in what would likely end up being swampy terrain.

"Hang on a sec." Emily turned to her laptop, logged in to her encrypted account and discovered she had one hundred and three brand-new, unread e-mails. *Ugh*. She skimmed her cursor down the list until she found the right one, then clicked on it.

"I have a CIA contact down there who's been working this for me." She spoke as she scanned the guy's e-mail. "Looks like they're good to go. I'll send a secure message to Sherm with the coordinates for where they can pick up their new ride."

Tyrone Jefferson, nicknamed Sherm because he was built like a Sherman tank, was the leader of OSI PacNW's Bravo Team. He was a former Navy SEAL who served with Jonathan.

"Damn, you're good," Andi said.

Big whoop, so I can send an e-mail. Where's the excitement in that?

She finished dragging the e-mail to the appropriate folder, and her eyes locked on a familiar name in the subject line of one of her unopened e-mails. Brows pinched together, she clicked on it.

She gasped at the photo included with the case file. "Oh my God. I know her."

"You know Pamela Westcott?" Andi slid her hip from the desk and moved to look at the screen over Emily's shoulder.

"We lived in the same dorm at U Dub for a couple of years until I moved to a place off campus." She enlarged the photo. "Her room was down the hall from mine."

U Dub was what the locals called the University of Washington.

Andi recited details of the case as Emily stared at Pamela's photo.

"About six months ago, she was snatched out of a parking lot in broad daylight. Two months ago, some Olympic National Park personnel and volunteers were performing fire mitigation—clearing brush, removing old trees, that sort of thing. They found her grave about two hundred yards from the Mount Rose Trailhead. Medical examiner said she was alive when she was buried and that she was approximately three months pregnant." As if the weight of her words was just too much to bear, Andi lowered herself into the guest chair.

"Oh my gosh, how horrible." Emily silently mourned the life of a bright young woman and her unborn child, cut short by violence. "I'm assuming we were brought in to assist with the investigation because they haven't caught the person responsible?"

"Correct. The perp knew where all the cameras were located and planned accordingly. He wore all black, had the hood of his jacket pulled over his head, hunched to keep from giving away his height, and kept his back to the cameras. He appeared to be heavy-set in the video, but my guess is he padded himself up to hide his build."

"Hold up." Emily looked at the address of the parking garage, then back at Andi. "This is right next to the campus."

"It is." Her sister-in-law gave her a questioning look. "Does that mean something to you?"

"I walked through it more times than I can remember. It's right across from two of the larger dorms and the student union. Everyone uses it as a shortcut to the library and football stadium. How is it possible no one saw anything?" The three-story structure was well lit and patrolled by campus security at night.

"Because people don't pay attention to their surroundings." Andi grumbled something about smartphones sucking people's brains out and making them stupid. "Sorry, it just irks me when I see people with their noses buried in their damn phones all the time." Not surprising from a woman with a love-hate relationship with technology. A woman who proudly owned more than one T-shirt emblazoned with the words *Too bad stupid isn't painful* on the front.

"The son of a bitch walked right up behind her, locked his arms around her and tossed her in a van." Andi shook her head. "She had her earbuds in, and by the time she realized he was there—"

"It was too late." Emily's brothers had drilled situational awareness into her from a young age. Had she ever thanked them? Doubtful. She'd probably accused them of being overprotective jerks.

"The Mason and Jefferson County Sheriff's Departments, along with the National Parks Service and the FBI, had been working the case, but they had very little to go on. Then, two weeks ago, Pamela's parents find an unmarked manila envelope in their mailbox. Inside was her handwritten Last Will and Testament. That's when the Feds jumped in."

"Wait a minute. Wasn't there a serial killer several years ago who made his victims write their will before he killed them? Is that who they think this is?" Emily was in middle school at the time. It had been all over the news until one day it just wasn't. She'd assumed the guy died or was caught.

"Who the hell knows?" Andi tossed up her hands and dropped them back into her lap. "In typical bureaucratic bullshit fashion, it's taking them forever to get anything done. Dumbasses have been tripping all over each other comparing dick sizes, fighting over who has jurisdiction, worrying about breaking the fucking rules." Contempt poured from Andi as she shook her head. "Pardon my French."

"Pretty sure that's not French," Emily said. "And you know I'm surrounded by guys who cuss all the time, right?"

"Yeah, well, now that Ashling is repeating everything she hears, I'm trying to be better about it." Andi took a deep breath and blew it out. "Anyway, the first thing Jonathan did when we got the case was request copies of the bureau's files on the Last Will and Testament Killer. We should have those soon."

"How did we end up with the case?" Not just anyone could call up and hire them.

"Seems Pamela's folks have some well-connected friends. One of them got in touch with Jeffrey on their behalf," Andi said.

Jeffrey Burke was the crazy-powerful head of the National Security Agency, the NSA, and Andi's former boss. Most of OSI's assignments were funneled to them by him. A person could not have a better ally or a worse enemy.

"If anyone can find who did this, it's OSI," Andi said. As an autonomous organization, OSI had the unique and enviable flexibility to work outside the lines. Pamela's case couldn't be in better hands.

"And, since I'm part of OSI, I want in on this case," Emily added.

Andi shoved up out of the chair. "If it was up to me, I'd say, hell, yeah."

Unfortunately, it wasn't up to her. Jonathan was in charge of assigning personnel to domestic investigations. And he still treated Emily like she was the same little girl who got snatched from the park by a stranger. Didn't seem to matter she was twenty-six, not six.

Andi got to the doorway, stopped and, hand on the frame, looked back at her. "Listen, I know your brothers can be a bit overbearing—"

"Understatement of the year," Emily groused as she crossed her arms.

"It's only because they love you and worry about you." Andi's tone held an underlying strain of sympathy for Emily's frustration.

"Jonathan loves *you,* and yet, you're out there, kicking butts and taking names."

Andi responded in her usual direct way. "I'm better trained and have a lot more experience than you."

True. But that didn't mean Emily wouldn't do some investigating of her own. After all, what's the worst that could happen?

Eyes narrowed, Andi stepped back into her office and pointed at her. "Emily Marie O'Halleran, I recognize that look."

"What look? There's no look." *Shoot!*

"That look you get when you've set your mind to something."

"I have no idea what you're talking about." Darned Andi and her uncanny ability to read people. To keep from giving anything else away, Emily turned to her computer and busied herself with e-mails.

"Okay, have it your way. But you'd better hope your

brother doesn't find out that you're snooping around this case."

Emily turned, mouth open, ready to beg her sister-in-law not to snitch on her, but Andi spoke first.

"See you at Mom and Dad's later, Nancy Drew." Andi smirked and walked out of her office.

CHAPTER FIVE

M ason yanked his keys from the ignition, shoved the door open and stepped out of his big truck. He gave himself a minute or two to take in Michaleen and Molly's expansive, incredibly beautiful home, surrounded by dense woods on three sides. A warm and inviting golden light shone from the large windows. The emotional epicenter of the entire O'Halleran family, it exuded warmth, love and—for him and Molly's many other strays—acceptance.

What Mason had as a kid could never be classified as a *home*. More like a place to store his few belongings, an address to keep the school off his mom's back. See, Vera May Croft liked to have a good time, which usually involved vodka, or scotch, or beer … Pretty much anything with alcohol in it. She also had a knack for attracting all the wrong kinds of men. Mean ones. Ones who liked to hit. Her. Mason. Didn't seem to matter.

As far back as he could remember, Mason had been putting himself between his mom and some abusive prick. Not like he could just stand there and do nothing while she got knocked around. Eventually, the guy would either pass out, leave, or he and his mom would head into the bedroom to *make up*.

Mason would take off, head to the old airfield on the edge of the small central Texas town he was trapped in. There was an old rickety shed at the far end of the short runway where he kept a sleeping bag, camp lantern, and some basic provisions—granola bars, bottles of water. Knowing good grades were the only thing that would get him out of that crappy town, he would do his homework, then settle back, arms bent, fingers laced under his head, and look up at the stars peeking through the holes in the roof. Some people counted sheep to fall asleep. He would count the days until he was old enough to leave that sad, desperate place.

His unwelcome stroll down memory lane was interrupted by laughter flowing from the open windows. *Shit*. He scrubbed his hand down his face, shook off the oily residue of memories. It had been a long time since he'd thought about all that crap. Yet another reason he couldn't be with Emily. She deserved better than a guy with his shitty history.

Mason headed up the wide, bluish-gray flagstone walkway. He raised his hand to knock on the massive wooden door, but it swung open.

"Ha! I knew you'd show up." Caleb stood there, beer in hand, shit-eating grin on his face.

"Shut up," Mason grumbled as he stepped inside.

His friend laughed and shut the door, then yelled over his shoulder, "Mom, look who decided to grace us with his presence."

"Have I mentioned recently how much of a dick you are?" Mason shook his head.

"Yeah, I think you have."

A moment later, Molly O'Halleran rounded the corner from the kitchen, her arms loaded with a large platter stacked high with uncooked burgers, steaks, and hot dogs. A big smile spread across her face. She handed the tray to her son and turned to Mason with open arms. "It's so good to see you."

"Hey, Mrs. O." He bent slightly to return her hug.

The woman might only be a couple of inches over five feet, but she embraced you with the intensity of a burly offensive lineman. And *she* decided when the hug ended. Not you.

He looked up and saw Caleb standing there with a stupid grin on his face and flipped him off. The guy had managed to penetrate Mason's loner façade back when they were on the Hostage Rescue Team together. As one of the HRT's two Apache pilots, Mason supported all the teams. He and Caleb worked an extended op together, and their friendship just sort of grew from there.

"You're just in time—Michaleen just fired up the grill." She turned to retrieve the tray from her son.

Caleb lifted it out of reach. "I got it."

"Thanks, sweetie." She patted him on the arm and turned to Mason. "While he takes that outside, would you mind helping me with something in the kitchen? It'll only take a minute."

"Absolutely. Ladies first." He bowed slightly and swept his arm out, then followed her to the massive kitchen. "Okay, put me to work."

"Actually ... I fibbed. Just a little bit." She crinkled up her nose, held her thumb and forefinger about an inch apart. He'd seen the exact same look on her daughter's face.

"I really just wanted a minute to chat with you, to see how you're doing?"

Mason was momentarily taken aback. His own mother had never even cared.

"Me? Actually, I'm doing great." Arms crossed, he leaned back against the counter. "I just closed on the place up over the hill. Guess that means we're going to be neighbors."

Thanks to the generous salary he received from OSI, he

was able to buy the old four-bedroom, two-and-a-half-bath farmhouse with the big wraparound porch. The roof was a nightmare, the steps leading up to the porch—even the porch itself—were rotted, and he was pretty sure there was a family of raccoons living somewhere underneath. The yard was overgrown with weeds and wildflowers, and that was just the outside. But it was tucked away in the middle of ten acres of beautiful land. Fir, spruce and pine trees wider than he could wrap his arms around hid the property from the road. He planned to do as many of the repairs and renovations himself as possible. He would hire the major stuff out, like the new roof, plumbing and electrical.

Mason's first real home.

"You bought Mr. Landers's property?" She glanced out the window with a look of concern. "Hmmm ..."

And just like that, his old insecurities roared to the forefront of his mind. Trailer trash Vera May's feral kid, running around town begging for odd jobs so he could buy groceries. Always careful to hide his latest bruise or cut. Wearing secondhand clothes that never quite fit his tall, lanky frame. By his junior year in high school, he'd filled out, added some muscle to his height. Suddenly, he had the attention of all the girls who'd wanted nothing to do with him the year before. Which made all the guys want to kick his ass. A few tried, but once word got around that he'd become proficient in a couple of different forms of martial arts, they pretty much left him alone.

"Is there a problem with me living there?" He straightened from the counter.

"Absolutely not. Don't be ridiculous," she lightly scolded him.

Mason was convinced Molly had some sort of magical ability to see what was going on inside people's heads. It was unsettling to a guy who had a lot he didn't want people to see.

"At one time, Emily had talked about buying that old place," she said.

Mason imagined Emily arranging her furniture in the large front room or painting the kitchen her favorite color. Was she still hoping to purchase the property? *Shit.*

"We offered to help her with the down payment, but she insisted on saving up enough money to do it herself." Molly cast a sardonic look his way. "In case you haven't noticed, my daughter can be very stubborn."

"Really? I hadn't noticed." He chuckled.

"She hasn't mentioned it for a few years, so maybe she gave up on the idea."

"Well, hell. Sorry. Heck." Caleb had warned Mason about his mother's dislike of cussing in her house. "The Realtor never mentioned there was another person interested in the property. If I'd known she—"

"Listen, don't you worry about Emily. She'll be fine. You just enjoy this exciting time." She patted his chest just over his heart and looked him in the eye. "Everyone deserves to have a place they can call home. I'm just tickled to death you've decided yours is here in Whidbey Cove."

Mason felt the warmth of that statement all the way to his heart.

"Thanks, Mrs. O." He gave her a quick hug, then stepped back.

"Come on. Let's go eat." She tipped her head toward the door leading out back. "I'm starving, and my husband grills the best burgers in town."

CHAPTER SIX

The man looked up and down the quiet street, then scanned the nearby neighbors' homes. All were dark, except Mr. Davies' place. The old man always left a lamp on in the front window. Said bad guys wouldn't want to risk someone might be awake inside. *Right.* Like a fucking lamp was going to keep someone from getting inside.

As a kid, he'd taken it as a personal challenge to prove Davies wrong. His neighbor would shit if he knew how many times he'd roamed around in his house while he slept upstairs. He even knew where his valuable coin collection was hidden. It would've been so easy to bash his bald head in.

A light rain began to fall, bringing with it a convenient dense fog. He pulled up his hood and, keeping to the shadows, dodged from bush to bush, rushed across the damp grass and up the steps to the back of the house. He'd removed the bulb from the porch light months ago. Made it easier for him to come and go undetected by the neighbors.

She would be asleep by now, doped up and passed out from the morphine. The old bat was bedridden and had become his responsibility after suffering a massive stroke. It was a real pain in his ass. He could've dumped her in a nursing home, but he had special plans for her.

He toed off his muddy boots, then picked them up and headed upstairs, careful to avoid the squeaky one—old habits died hard. He crept to her door, set his boots down in the hallway, and quietly swung it open.

Mist rose from a diffuser perched atop the tall chest of drawers, filling the space with the scent of camphor, euca- lyptus and menthol. Thick carpet silenced his approach as he moved to her bedside.

A small lamp cast a warm glow over her pale face. She was flat on her back, mouth gaping open. The loose skin on her neck undulated with each gurgling snore. Dead to the world. *Well, not yet, anyway.* Soon, though. Very soon.

He leaned down and whispered close to her ear. "Hello, Mother."

Her forehead crinkled, and her eyes moved behind closed lids. Anymore, her eyes and some facial muscles were the *only* thing she could move. He waited until her features relaxed, then neatly arranged her blankets, making sure she was tucked in nice and tight. He walked out and pulled the door shut with a whisper.

At the far end of the hall, he slipped a key into a new deadbolt with ease and stepped into his childhood bedroom. He clicked on the light, confident the dark blanket over the window offered him the privacy he required. A quick scan of the room confirmed everything was just as it had been for years. He'd never liked people messing with his things.

Mocking him from atop his dresser was a ridiculous little gold, plastic trophy he'd won in a seventh-grade math compe- tition. God, he despised that fucking thing, but he kept it to help fuel his hatred of her. She never allowed him to partici- pate in sports. Said he wasn't good enough, that no one would want him on their team. Actually, she said that about most everything. A couple of ribbons from lame elementary school spelling bees were pinned to a bulletin board next to some movie ticket stubs. Horror and slasher films were his favorites, his escape. The gorier, the better. Posters of his top four—*Saw, Friday the Thirteenth, Halloween, Silence of the Lambs* —still covered the wall behind his bed. Colors faded, their edges curled with age, the images still managed to stir something deep within him.

He dropped his keys atop the dresser and stepped into his closet. After dragging the door shut, he flipped the light on and blinked a few times until his eyes adjusted.

He set his muddy boots to the side. Rubber gloves were next. He peeled them off and shoved them in one of the pockets of his black jeans. Next, he stripped off all of his clothes, the padding around his mid-section, and stuffed them in a black, plastic trash bag. He wedged the bag into the back of the closet to be destroyed tomorrow. No big loss, really. The clothes he used for his extracurricular activities were always bought from secondhand stores, which were great. A city the size of Seattle had a ton of them, so he never had to go into the same location twice. And most didn't have the budget for security cameras. *Convenient.* One of his favorite things about them was that the she-beast occupying the bed down the hall would staunchly disapprove of him wearing someone else's cast-offs. *Appearances matter, don't you know?*

He turned to switch off the light, and his gaze fell upon the stack of old newspapers perched high atop the shelf. He stretched up and slid a few from the pile. With a quick puff of air, he blew away the dust coating the clear, plastic cover. He smiled down at the headlines—*Last Will & Testament Killer Claims Fifth Victim, Last Will and Testament Killer Terrorizes Community,* and *Who Is the Last Will & Testament Killer?* He'd made sure he had at least one copy of every newspaper covering the story. After a last light stroke of his hand over the plastic, he gently returned them to their spot.

Buck naked, he walked into his connected bathroom and tugged the chain on the light above the mirror. He craned his neck to the side for a better look at the three long, angry scratches running down the right side of his neck. A slow smile crept across his face. Weak from hunger, her once bright eyes glazed and sunken from dehydration, this one had struggled right up until he shoved the needle in her arm. He kinda liked it when they fought back—it livened things up a bit. Made it more fun. He'd suspected she'd be a handful the first time she glanced his way as she left the large auditorium classroom.

Smarter than the others, she was more cautious, aloof. Kind of a bitch. He'd followed her to the coffee place and asked her to join him for a cup. She'd looked at him like he was scum and said, *"No, thank you. I'm married."* As if that meant she was safe, untouchable, better than him somehow. They all acted like they were better than him.

He thought back to how she looked earlier. Three feet below him, eyes closed in a drug-induced slumber, her thin arms crossed over her chest. His latest victim resting peacefully in the simple, pine box.

It had taken him five trips, over the course of two weeks, to haul all the pre-built sections up to the isolated spot and conceal them under some thick, thorny underbrush. He'd picked a location not far from the other one, but deeper into the woods, where it was unlikely anyone would stumble across it. Even if they did, nothing would lead back to him. He'd pieced it together the night he took her there.

After a last long look at her, he'd dropped the lid on top, unconcerned about securing it. Unnecessary, really. A thousand pounds or so of dirt and rock would be more than enough to keep it shut nice and tight.

Shovelful after shovelful, the hollow thud of dirt clumps and rocks had hit the wood, echoing dully around the remote wooded area. He was careful not to block the PVC breathing pipe near her feet. *Don't want the fun to end too early, now, do we?*

The full moon had glowed bright overhead when he'd scattered pine cones and needles, sticks and rocks over the freshly turned earth. He'd maneuvered a large, rotted tree limb over the grave to disguise the pipe sticking about six inches out of the ground. He always spray-painted them dark brown and black, but the lichen-covered branch would provide additional camouflage.

He'd dragged the filtered beam of his flashlight over the entire area to ensure he'd left nothing behind. Shovel in hand, he'd leaned close to the opening of the pipe and whispered, "Enjoy your nap, beautiful. I'll be back in a few days."

CHAPTER SEVEN

Mason's eyes tracked Andi, her forehead scrunched in thought as she roamed the strategy room, her long legs eating up the space like a caged cheetah. She'd stand directly in front of the large screen mounted on the wall, concentrate on the images, turn and pace away, then find her way back to the screen again. Jonathan had once told him she did her best thinking on her feet. Her record of success was impressive as hell, so, hey, whatever worked.

The strategy room was exactly what it sounded like—the place where every single aspect of new and ongoing cases and operations was discussed, plotted and planned. It, along with the state-of-the-art communications center and deployment supply depot, were located underneath the main operations facility, in what everybody called *the cellar*. The only way to access this floor was via a secured elevator that required a two-step process to operate. A magnetic card had to be swiped through a reader, which then activated the retina scanner. All very high-tech and all created by Caleb.

The only other way out of this part of the facility was via a four-inch-thick steel door that led into a half-mile-long tunnel that dumped out into the dense woods surrounding the property. Calling the O'Hallerans a careful bunch would be a dramatic understatement. A limited number of personnel had access to the tunnel. Mason was honored to be one of them.

The Pacific Northwest branch was located in the small town of Whidbey Cove, Washington, near Deception Pass. A one-time logging town with a small fishing marina, it was nestled in some old growth woods along the dark and tumultuous waters of the Puget Sound. The San Juan Islands loomed a short ferry ride away, like eons-old sentinels shielding the coastline.

OSI had bought an old shut-down lumber mill secluded in the middle of a couple of hundred acres of sloping terrain and giant trees. Land that once held tall stacks of milled timber had slowly been reclaimed by the surrounding woods, the perfect landscape for their multiple obstacle courses, shooting range, training facility, and covert ops headquarters.

Mason smoothed his hand over the surface of the table taking up the center of the spacious room. Michaleen O'Halleran had created it out of a vertical slab taken from the center of an old, downed tree found right here on the property. Infinitely wise and an all-around stellar human being, the senior O'Halleran was the exact opposite of the men Mason's mother had consorted with.

He and Golden sat on one side of the table. Across from them were the O'Halleran twins, Mathias and Killian.

They were so similar, yet so completely different.

Killian was a neat freak. His dark hair was always kept short, combed back off his forehead, and he was always dressed like he had a hot date. He was also very open about his love for the ladies.

Mathias, on the other hand, was more of a jeans and T-shirt kinda guy, with hair on the shaggy side and a chin that always sported a bit of scruff. He was referred to as *the quiet twin* and was much more private about his dating life than Killian.

They finished each other's sentences, were able to communicate with a look, and no one dared come between them.

Every face in the room held varying degrees of sadness, anger and determination. Mason focused his attention back to the large flat screen at the far end of the room and the last known photo of Pamela Wescott, taken by her boyfriend the day they found out she was pregnant. Smiling, hopeful, she had her whole life ahead of her. A short time later, she disappeared, and it all came to a tragic end. Next to it was a photo of the handwritten will delivered to her parents.

Jonathan moved from where he stood at the end of the table and touched an icon at the bottom corner of the screen. Pamela's image disappeared, replaced by another woman. With light brown, shoulder-length straight hair and hazel eyes, she had a strawberry-colored birthmark running down the right side of her neck.

"This is our latest victim. Her name is Sandra McMahon, twenty-six years old, married, no children. Last seen alive twenty-three days ago, when she left home to go to her night class at U Dub. They found her about five hundred feet from where Pamela had been buried. Here's the thing"—he looked at his brothers—"she used to live here in Whidbey Cove."

Mathias and Killian glanced at each other, then leaned forward, eyes narrowed, concentrating on the photo.

"Sandy Edmonds?" They spoke in tandem. They did that a lot. Some kind of eerie twin thing.

Jonathan bobbed his head. "McMahon is ... was her married name."

Mathias dragged his gaze from the photo. "Does Em know yet?"

"Not yet." Jonathan tucked a hand in his front pocket. "We only just got this last night."

"Wait." Mason held up his hand. "Emily knows San—"

"Sandy?" Emily stood in the doorway, arms loaded with a stack of brand-new, unwrapped tactical pants. Brows furrowed, she slowly moved across the room, each step taking her closer to the screen.

"Why are you looking at a picture of Sandy?" She regarded the photo with concern.

"Emily, you shouldn't—"

"Jonathan!" she snapped, and plastic wrap crackled as her arms tightened around her load.

Her older brother gently set his hand on her shoulder. "I'm sorry, Em. Sandy's dead."

"Dead?" Her voice was softer than Mason had ever heard before, and her eyes remained locked on the screen.

"Yes." Jonathan didn't bother to mention she was found by a bunch of kids who'd snuck into the park after hours, looking for a place to party. One of them had been gathering up wood for an illegal bonfire and tripped over a pipe sticking out of the ground. Curious, they started digging, got a couple of feet down and found the coffin.

Her lips rolled in, she turned her back to the group and faced the screen. Mason was so tuned in to her that he noticed how her shoulders stiffened, the way her chin wobbled and twitched, how her throat moved up and down, the tension in her face. Unshed tears glistened in her beautiful green eyes.

Every single person in the room tensed, shifted in their seat. It's a lot to expect a bunch of alpha types to just sit idly by while someone they cared about suffered. Hell, if he didn't think she'd slug him, Mason would stomp over there and wrap her in his arms, his friendship with Caleb be damned.

Killian must've had the same idea. He made a move to

stand, but Mason gave a quick shake of his head. Emily's brother opened his mouth as if to argue, glanced at her back, then grumbled and stayed put.

Emily was a very proud woman. She would hate thinking anyone, especially her brothers, felt sorry for her. She worked hard to make everyone think she was tough, impervious to heartache. Of course, he knew otherwise. He'd seen that brief flash of hurt in her eyes when he referred to their kiss as a mistake. She'd tried to hide it with a dismissive, *Yeah, you're right,* but it would haunt him forever knowing he was the one who'd caused it. Especially since what he'd said was a huge pile of bullshit.

She blinked a few times, swallowed hard and, by the time she turned around, any hint of sadness had been wiped away. Except in her eyes. The usual mischievous twinkle was dimmed.

Their eyes connected, as they so often did, and he reached over and rolled the seat next to him back from the table. Emily wasn't typically included in these briefings, but good luck trying to kick her out now. He rose and took the bundle from her arms and set it on the floor against the wall.

After they were both seated, she turned to him and mouthed the words, "Thank you."

Mason laid his hand over hers where she gripped the arm of the chair. He stroked his thumb back and forth over her cold, tight knuckles. She looked at him from the corner of her eye, then slipped her hand free and laid it on her lap.

Jonathan, to his credit, said nothing. He flashed to another picture and continued with his briefing. "This is Sandy's will. It was delivered via bike messenger to her husband's office a week ago."

"Hold up. A week?" Killian, the *cocky twin,* chimed in. "Why the hell did it take so long for us to get it?"

"Because the Feds and locals still have their heads up their asses," Andi said in her typical succinct fashion.

Mason appreciated that. You always knew where you stood with her.

"Let's just say the communication between the FBI and local law enforcement is lacking." Jonathan speared his wife with a look. "I can assure you, it won't happen on another OSI case."

She responded by blowing him a kiss, then dropping into a chair. One corner of her husband's mouth twitched, and he lowered himself into the seat next to her. She was the only person on the planet who would dare pull shit like that with the former SEAL.

"The courier service uses a night drop where people can leave deliveries for the next day." He leaned his elbows on the table, threaded his fingers and tapped his thumbs together.

"Cameras?" Golden asked as he flipped through the briefing notes in front of him. Jonathan had pulled him in to work this case after the doctor screwed up his paperwork, preventing Viking from deploying with his team.

"Yes, two," Jonathan said. "They were both out of commission at the time our perp dropped off the package."

That set them all off, and they spoke over each other.

"Of course, they were," Mathias said under his breath.

"Unfuckingbelievable," Killian added, not-so-under his breath.

"Why bother having them?" Golden asked the most obvious question.

Andi just growled, "Dumbasses."

Jonathan glanced at his notes. "They cleared the husband. His alibi checked out."

"Any other suspects?" Mathias started flipping a pen through his fingers.

"Not at this time."

For the next half hour, Jonathan continued sharing details

of the investigation. He refreshed their memory about the Last Will and Testament Killer from twelve years ago. How they'd found eight women dead after they were buried alive. And how they'd never caught the killer.

Mason snuck occasional glimpses at Emily. She'd grabbed a legal pad from the stack in the center of the table and had been scribbling copious notes. Not once did she interject or ask any questions. Atypical of her assertive and inquisitive nature. Occasionally, she would look long and hard at Sandy's will. A couple of times, she tilted her head as if seeing something there.

"Emily, were you still in contact with her?" Mason asked.

"Not really. We lost touch when her family moved away. Let's see ..." Eyes on her notepad, she tugged on her bottom lip. She did that whenever she concentrated or was worrying about something.

"We were about fourteen at the time. So I guess it's been about twelve years since I've actually spoken to her." She looked at Jonathan. "When she moved back to Seattle about two years ago, we reconnected on social media and exchanged cell phone numbers. After everything that happened with Gwen, and then Dawn and Luna, Beck thought it would be a good idea to scrub our online profiles."

No surprise there. Her family was big on privacy and security. Social media was one of the surest ways to jeopardize both of those.

"Unfortunately, I forgot to transfer her number to my phone, so it was lost. If I had, maybe—"

"What? 'If you had,' what?" Mason swiveled his chair to face her. "She wouldn't have been grabbed? She'd still be alive? That's crap, and you know it."

He turned back to the group. Their mouths hung open in shock. No doubt they thought he was an asshole for talking to Emily that way. But here's the thing: They didn't know her like he did. They had no idea how much she appreciated people being straight with her—not always trying to shield her from ugly truths.

"The one thing we haven't discussed is the fact both of our victims were students at U Dub, and they both have a connection to Emily," Mason said to the group before turning back to her. "I'm not at all comfortable with that."

Jonathan's phone vibrated on the table. He picked it up, read the screen, then tucked it in his pocket. "We've received the electronic copies of the FBI's files on the Last Will and Testament Killer."

He checked the time, then stood. "Why don't we take a break, grab something to eat, then we'll meet back up in an hour to start digging into them. Andi, I'll have you work your magic on the witness statements while the rest of us dig into the case notes, coroners' reports, etc."

"You got it," his wife responded.

"Okay, I'll clear my schedule for the rest of the day." Emily grabbed her cell phone off the table and lifted her hip to tuck it in her back pocket.

"That won't be necessary, Em." Jonathan switched off the flat screen. "If we have any other questions for you, we'll let you know."

"Excuse me?" She slowly rose from her chair.

Uh-oh. Mason recognized that tone of voice.

Mathias, Killian and Golden, who'd been playing rock-paper-scissors to decide who would pay for lunch, must have picked up on it, too. Because they halted in their tracks on the way to the door and became stone silent.

Andi's eyes shifted back and forth between her husband and sister-in-law. Not a sound whispered around the room as everyone held their breath in anticipation of Emily's imminent explosion.

Jonathan beat her to it. "You know the drill, Emily. You're

not an investigator. You're in charge of deployment logistics. That is where I need you." He gathered up his notes, unfazed by her glare.

She slapped her hands on the table and leaned forward.

"Sandy was my friend, Jonathan." Her voice continued to rise with each word. "And I knew Pamela—"

"And that is *exactly* why you're staying away from this investigation." He'd mirrored her stance.

Emily straightened, drew back her chin and blinked at Jonathan's forceful tone. He'd obviously never used his command voice on her before. Grown men had been known to shrink from it. Not Emily.

"You cannot be serious?" Her hands went to her hips. "You're cutting me out of this investigation?"

"You were never *in* this investigation. And yes, I am serious." Jonathan tucked the file under one arm and curled the other behind Andi's waist and pulled her to his side. "This is for your own safety, and you know it."

"I have to agree with him, Em." Mason's instincts were telling him she was too close to this thing. And he'd learned a long time ago to listen to his gut.

Emily's hands fisted at her sides, and she turned her ire on him. "No one asked you, Croft."

"It's done," Jonathan said.

Emily turned back to her brother, arms crossed, her hip cocked out.

Jonathan pointed at her. "And you can stop looking at me like you're going to put snakes in my bed again."

As soon as they cleared the doorway, Mason stepped up and set his hand on her shoulder. "Em, I'm sorry, but—"

She shook him off. "Save it. Okay?" She grabbed up her packages and, just short of the door, stopped and looked back at him. "You have zero standing to say anything about what I do or don't do with my life."

CHAPTER EIGHT

E mily slammed her office door and dumped the tactical pants on the table in the corner. She stomped back and forth, grumbling into the silence, chewing on Jonathan's words.

"*You were never in this.*" She deepened her voice and stuck out her chest, mimicking him. "Like it or not, big brother, I am in this."

And who the hell did Mason think he was, interjecting like that? He had always been her staunch advocate, sticking up for her with her brothers, trusting that she had a brain and knew how to use it. He'd disappointed her more than he'd pissed her off. And that was saying something.

Emily thought about Sandy and was hit by a massive wave of sadness. She couldn't believe she was gone. But there was no doubt the woman smiling in that photo had been her childhood friend. The birthmark on her neck was unique. In third grade, Emily had beaten up a boy for making fun of it.

When the Edmonds family lived in Whidbey Cove, she and Sandy had been inseparable. Her mother used to say, "*You never saw one without the other.*" They'd spent hours together having impromptu dance parties, doing each other's hair, giggling their way through sleepovers. Emily would complain about her bossy brothers, and Sandy lamented about her parents not letting her have a kitten. Didn't seem to matter that she was allergic.

To hell with Jonathan. And to hell with Mason. She was not going to be relegated to the sidelines on this case.

She rushed to sit behind her desk, logged into her laptop and pulled up the picture of Sandy's will from her case file. Eyes narrowed, she expanded the view and re-read it again and again, concentrating on every curve of every letter of every word. There was something there, something familiar teasing just along the edge of her memory. But what?

A knock on her door broke into her thoughts.

"Come in," she called out, somewhat distractedly.

The door swung open and Dawn's younger sister, Luna, blew into the room with a big smile and all the energy you'd expect of a nineteen-year-old on spring break. Except, instead of heading to a sunny beach in Florida and partying with her contemporaries, she chose to spend her vacation working for OSI.

"Hey, Emily. Christina asked me to bring these files to you." Luna handed them across the desk to her.

A genius with computers, Luna had a patent pending on a device she created that was currently being field-tested by some of OSI's teams. The tiny sensor was placed behind the operative's ear using a super-strong adhesive. It tracked their physical location via GPS, monitored their vital stats—heart rate, body temp, hydration levels—and sent the data back to the Ops Center. Definite brainiac.

"Thanks, Luna." Emily tossed them on the desk and turned back to the will taunting her from her large monitor.

Luna turned, hesitated, then pivoted back. "Is everything okay?"

"I'm not sure." Her finger and thumb pulled on her bottom lip.

"Anything I can do to help?" Luna asked.

Emily forced her gaze away from the screen and turned to her visitor.

"Actually, there might be." Maybe a fresh set of eyes would help. Especially if those eyes belonged to a certain brilliant teenager. "Take a look at this."

Emily grabbed the remote, clicked a button, and the large flat screen on the wall came to life. A couple of keystrokes later and the will appeared.

Luna's eyes lit up like a kid at a carnival, and she hustled over to stand shoulder to shoulder with her.

"Is this from that new case they're working on?" She scrutinized the document as she spoke. "I heard it's a pretty bad one."

"Yeah, it's pretty bad." She wouldn't burden Luna with the details. Thanks to that sicko cult leader in Montana, the kid had been through enough. Last thing she needed to have rattling around in that big brain of hers were the horrid details of Sandy's death.

"Okay, so, what am I looking for?" Luna asked.

"I wish I knew. There's just *something* about it that seems familiar, yet I can't figure out what it is."

"Are we sure it's her handwriting? Maybe someone forged it?" Luna cast her a quick sideways glance, then returned to studying the document.

Emily shook her head. "No, according to the notes in her case file, her parents and her husband confirmed it was Sandy's handwriting."

A forensic graphologist, a handwriting specialist, would be consulted for confirmation.

Luna stepped closer to the screen, tilting her head to the side. "Most of it is printed, but there are some cursive letters mixed in as well." Her head swiveled to Emily. "I guess that's pretty common, but—"

"Hold up—" Emily's hand flew up as a flash of memory scorched through her subconscious, then just as quickly it vaporized into nothing. Her hand dropped to her side. "Damn, never mind."

"What? Did you think of something?" Luna asked, excitement sparkling in her cornflower-blue eyes.

"Whatever it was, it's gone now." She sighed and plopped into her chair. "Crap, I just know I'm missing something."

"Ya know, whenever I'm having trouble with a program, I find a change of scenery helps."

"Yeah, maybe you're right." She glanced at the clock on the wall. "Think I'll go out and grab some lunch. Want to join me?"

"Thanks, but I ate already," Luna said.

Emily logged out of the system, shut down her laptop and the large flat screen. Before they stepped out of her office, she touched a few buttons on the keypad next to her door to set the alarm, then turned off the light and shut the door.

"How's Gary?" Luna asked.

Gary was Emily's cat. Yes, she was aware it was a weird name for a cat, but in her mind, he looked like a Gary. She'd just recently found out he was a snowshoe breed, a distant cousin of the Siamese. He had the distinctive white triangle between his eyes that continued over his cheeks and down to cover his chest. The rest of him was a mishmash of black, dark brown, and a sort of gray color. He had huge blue eyes that would turn black as night when he was ready to pounce. Gary could be kind of a jerk—approaching anyone who came over to her place and rubbing along their legs, meowing to make them think he really wanted their attention. The minute they gave it to him, he would hiss and spit at them, then turn and saunter away like *they* were the problem.

"He's living his best life, as usual. Sleeping twenty hours a day—none of which happen to be at night, of course." Too many times to count, she'd awakened from a dead sleep to the distinctively horrifying sound of him gacking up a hairball or food he'd inhaled. She would bound out of bed as if someone had poked her with a cattle prod and run around in the dark trying to figure out where he was. Hoping she didn't step in it. The ugly bruise currently marring her shin was proof of her inability to see in the dark.

Luna laughed. "I really wish I could get him to like me."

"Yeah, I get that from a lot of people." Gary had only ever warmed up to Emily. *Not true,* she reminded herself. To her great dismay, he seemed beyond infatuated with Mason.

"So how are things going for you?" Emily asked as she locked her office door.

"School is ... well, school. Oh, I'm working on a couple of refinements to a new program." Luna went on, excitedly chattering on about source code text and structured query language as they headed down the hall.

Far as Emily was concerned, the kid might as well have been speaking French.

CHAPTER NINE

E mily admired the beautiful, giant oaks lining either side of the street. Their thick branches, weighed down with fresh green leaves, arched overhead, shading the pavement and framing the little white church sitting at the end. The scene would have been tranquil—if not for the black hearse parked in the circular driveway and the row of reporters and camera crews crowding the sidewalk.

Garish television vans with their antennas raised high overhead selfishly took up the prime spots in the small lot. The mourners parked wherever they could find room— patches of grass here and there, bumper to bumper along the sides of the narrow roadway.

Emily pulled into the first spot she could find and made her way down the sidewalk. She waited for a car to pass, then hurried across the street, staying as far away from the press as possible. Her mom, dad and, to her surprise, Beck and Gwen stood at the top of the steps. No one had told her they would be flying in from California.

Then again, Emily hadn't exactly been all that *available* lately. She'd snooped in the OSI case file and read the details of her friend's death. Seeing the crime-scene photos and reading the autopsy report, learning about what Sandy had endured, had been devastating. She had just needed some space to try to process it all. If that was even possible.

She'd reached out to Sandy's parents to express her condolences for their loss. To let them know she was available if they, or her husband, needed anything. Ridiculous, hollow words to someone who'd just lost an only child, a soul mate. And in such a horrific manner.

You can do this, Emily, she told herself and headed up the steps.

"Hi, honey." Her mom stepped forward, gave her a hug, then stepped back so her dad could do the same.

"How ya holdin' up, kiddo?" her dad whispered close to her ear.

"I'm fine, Dad." He held her at arm's length and looked her in the eye. "Really. I promise."

Her big, warmhearted father narrowed his eyes at her, then nodded once. He knew her well enough not to press.

"My turn." Gwen stepped around him and gave Emily a sympathetic smile. "I am so sorry about your friend."

Emily refused to lose it in front of everyone. Instead, she pulled her sister-in-law in for a hug and, okay, she might've held on a little longer than usual.

When they finally released each other, Gwen's eyes glistened with unshed tears. Even after everything she'd been through, Beck's wife had such a kind heart. She hurt whenever someone she cared about was in pain. Today, she'd decided that someone was Emily.

Then it was Beck's turn to test Emily's resolve. Fortunately, her oldest brother sensed her unease and cut his hug short to check the time. "We'd better get inside. Everyone else is already here, saving seats for us."

He clasped his wife's hand, placed the sweetest kiss to her

temple, and they walked inside. Her dad wrapped an arm over her mom's shoulder, the other over Emily's, and led them into the little church.

Three rows from the front, Killian stood in the aisle, looking very sharp in his suit and tie. She glanced down the pew at the rest of her family. She rarely saw them when they weren't wearing T-shirts, tactical pants and boots. She had to admit, they all looked great.

Emily braced herself for another round of hugs and concerned looks, then took a seat with her mother on one side, Gwen on the other. As if they knew she needed them close.

People continued to shuffle in as the organ quietly played in the background. Along one side of the sanctuary, afternoon sunlight streamed through three towering, elaborate stained-glass windows, sprinkling the pews and everyone in them with a rainbow of colors. She turned her attention to the altar, where the glow of several candles flickered across a large photo of Sandy set on an easel. Beside it, the closed, gleaming white coffin sat, seemingly perched atop a cloud of multicolored, freshly cut lilies. Their light scent filled the small church, softening some of Emily's grief. Her friend would have loved everything about this.

As if brushed by a cold breath of wind, the fine hairs on the back of her neck lifted, and her spine stiffened. She casually checked her surroundings. Most of the rows were full. People sat on folding chairs along the outer walls, stood in the back of the church and spilled into the vestibule. Not one of them was looking her way. Yet she could've sworn someone was watching her.

You're being ridiculous. It was just the intense emotions of the day messing with her nerves.

"Can I see that?" She pointed at the funeral program in her mom's lap.

"Of course, honey."

Sandy smiled up at her from the front cover, looking so much like she did all those years ago, yet so different. Emily flipped it open and scanned the various readings and hymns, then turned to the back page. Beneath a Bible verse was a photo of Sandy sitting on her husband's lap, heads together, with the sun setting behind them.

Emily closed her eyes, collected herself, then opened them. As she swallowed hard against the emotions striving to escape, she vowed to find the person responsible.

CHAPTER TEN

Not the least bit concerned about being discovered, the man walked right up the steps and into the vestibule of the church. Colored contacts, a set of bushy eyebrows, and thick-framed glasses helped shroud his eyes. Age spots on the back of his hands, latex prosthetic jowls, bulbous nose and dangling earlobes helped, too. To top off the look, he'd worn an oversize brown suit with a couple of mothballs in one of the pockets and leaned heavily on a cane.

He was getting so good at disguising his appearance that no one even looked his way. He was just some old geezer there to pay his respects.

As he waited to go into the sanctuary, he noticed the group in the row less than fifty feet away. Big, broad-shouldered, powerful-looking guys with an I-am-not-one-to-be-fucked-with look about them sat next to their wives or girlfriends or whatever.

And *she* was there, too. The reason he risked being here.

Who would've ever thought his mother would be responsible for him meeting the woman he planned to spend the rest of his life with? Funny the way things happened sometimes.

A lady in front of him noticed the group, too. She pointed, then turned and whispered something in the ear of the older woman with her.

He strained to hear but to no avail.

She wasn't the only one buzzing about them. A couple of uniformed cops stood next to two guys in bad suits and cheap ties, watching people as they entered.

The younger of the two in uniform leaned close to his partner and spoke out of the side of his mouth. "Did you see the O'Hallerans come in?"

The man made his way closer and, under the guise of signing the guest book, eavesdropped.

"Yeah." His partner stole a look around. "I guess someone high up called OSI in to find out who's murdering these women."

Well, well, well.

"Makes sense," the other cop said. "I hear the O'Hallerans have resources we don't. What I wouldn't give to work for an outfit with their reputation."

Fucking loser cops. The awe in their voices was nauseating. No one was *that* good.

One of the rumpled suit guys stepped in front of them, his back to the room. He pointed a finger close to their faces. "Would you two keep your fu—" He cast a quick glance over each shoulder. "Take your positions, and keep your mouths shut."

Properly scolded, they both lowered their chins and stepped into the sanctuary.

They had to call in reinforcements. His chest swelled, and he smirked as he made his way inside. He stopped at the end of a row with an empty spot. Everyone practically fell over themselves scooting down to make room for an old man. He gave a small, grateful smile and, as an added touch, groaned as he lowered himself to sit. *I should've been an actor.*

He craned his neck, desperate for a peek at the front row, where the girl's family sat. The mother sniffled into a wad of tissues, her husband's arm over her shoulder as he did his best to console her. The grieving husband, shoulders slumped, tie crooked, stared straight ahead. Dude looked like he'd been through hell. No doubt they'd looked at him first for his wife's murder. *Boo-fucking-hoo.*

When he'd seen on the news that they'd found her, he was pissed someone had ruined his fun. The timeline was his to control, and that had been taken away from him.

He shrugged internally. *Eh, she was probably dead a day or two after I left her there anyway.* He'd stopped feeding her about two weeks before he buried her, which wouldn't have been enough to kill her. Not having water for as long as she did is what would've caused her body to shut down. That's the part he'd been cheated out of—listening to them hallucinate and cry out for their mommies and daddies was one of the best parts. No one had ever cried for him.

The organ music stopped, and when he looked over at the preacher making his way to the altar, his eyes, once again, landed on *her*, tucked safely in the middle of her family. They all seemed especially concerned, casually sneaking peeks her way. He guessed that was to be expected when you were friends with the victim.

He'd stumbled upon that helpful little detail when he was standing in line at his favorite coffee place, waiting to order. The dearly departed had been in front of him, yammering on and on to someone on the phone. He was just starting to tune her out when she mentioned a very familiar name.

"Mom, you're still in touch with Mrs. O'Halleran, right? Do you think you could get Emily's phone number for me? It's unlisted, and I'd really love to reconnect with her. I've missed her."

At first, he was sure he'd imagined the whole thing until she started asking questions about how the O'Halleran family was doing, were they still living in the same house in Whidbey Cove. She'd ended the call when the barista called her name, and that's when he'd decided she would be next. When he saw her there again and asked her to join him for a coffee, the bitch had sealed her fate by turning him down.

His gaze slid back to Emily. He'd always been drawn to her, couldn't *not* look at her. So much so, she almost caught him watching her. He lowered his chin and observed her from under his big brows until she turned away. One side of his mouth lifted in triumph. She had no idea how close he was.

CHAPTER ELEVEN

Contact me on my cell. Mason read the note printed on the small whiteboard affixed to Emily's closed office door. He cursed under his breath, then looked up and down the hall as if she would magically appear simply because he wanted her to.

Ever since he found out she'd accessed Sandy's file, he'd been trying to talk to her. Calls to her cell phone went to voice mail, and she had yet to answer any of his text messages. She'd closed herself off. Not just from him, but from everyone. It wasn't like her to avoid, well, anything. Emily had a *damn the torpedoes, full speed ahead* approach to life.

Dammit, he really needed to see her with his own eyes.

He grabbed the dry-erase marker and left a note: *Please call me. Mason,* then jogged down the hall and straight to Christina's desk.

OSI's office manager was Emily's best friend. If anyone could tell him where she was, it would be Christina. She had this mysterious way of knowing everything that went on around OSI.

She looked up from her paperwork, her typical smile firmly in place. "Hey there, Mason. What's up?

"Do you know where Emily is?" His fingertips drummed against the counter.

Christina looked at them, then at him. "She's at her friend's funeral. Did you—"

"Shit. That's today? How could I forget?"

"You've been pretty focused on other things lately. Give yourself a break, would ya." She scribbled something on a piece of paper, tore it from the pad and handed it up to him. "Here's the name of the church where the service is being held. If you leave right now, you can probably just make it."

"Thanks, Christina. You're the best." It was true. Jonathan said many times how lucky OSI was to have her.

Mason didn't know much about her story—she rarely talked about herself. But Jonathan had briefly mentioned she'd gone through some pretty bad shit. You'd never know it from being around her. She was one of the perkiest, most positive people he'd ever met.

"Yeah, yeah, yeah. Get out of here." She shooed him away with a flick of her wrist and got back to her paperwork.

A few slightly bent traffic laws later, he jogged across the parking lot and up the steps of the church. He managed to sneak in just before they closed the doors. Some folks standing at the back shifted over so he wouldn't end up blocking the aisle.

He spotted the O'Hallerans immediately—not an easy bunch to miss. Mason's focus naturally centered on Emily. His body relaxed as he drank in her profile—the straight nose and rosy cheeks dusted with freckles, her noble, delicate chin, the way her wavy, auburn hair brushed her shoulders whenever she moved her head. God, it was so good seeing her. Without him realizing it, she'd become a very big part of his everyday life, and he'd missed her.

He took in each of her brothers and noticed their usual hypervigilance.

Killers often showed up at the funerals of their victims. Some lingered around the edges, latching on to any tidbit of grief. Others were more brazen and would insert themselves right into the middle of the mourners, reveling in the friends' and family's emotional torment, gloating internally at their superior intelligence over law enforcement.

Speaking of, a couple of uniformed cops from the Seattle PD were stationed on either side of the altar. Another two stood like sentries in front of the closed main doors. Probably to keep that pack of press buzzards from getting inside and intruding on the service. Two more guys he recognized as detectives huddled together in the back corner. They were part of the task force that had been working the murder cases since the beginning. Decent enough guys, but they just didn't have the resources, reach and, mostly, the flexibility that OSI had.

Caleb, his arm over Dawn's shoulder, turned and spotted him. His friend tipped up his chin in the direction of a man hovering behind a large pillar. Mason casually scanned the church until he had the guy in his sights. He was probably in his late thirties, early forties, just under six foot, a bit heavy-set, hair disheveled. His eyes darted over the crowd, then he slipped behind the column, only to lean out and do it again.

Mason tensed, prepared to make a move.

An older woman approached the man and placed her hands on either side of his face to gain his attention. His entire demeanor calmed. She raked his hair from his eyes, took his hand and led him to a couple of empty chairs by the wall. He sat next to her and began to slowly rock back and forth.

Mason gave Caleb a subtle shake of his head. Emily must've noticed, because she glanced over her shoulder and did a double-take. As if surprised to see him there. They stared at each other until everyone seemed to fade into the background, leaving just the two of them. She looked so damn sad, her usual sass and brightness dimmed. Mason hated that she hadn't asked him to come with her to the service. But why would she?

A woman began to speak from behind the pulpit. Emily blinked a couple of times and, their connection broken, slowly turned back to the front.

About forty-five minutes later, the ceremony ended with the pastor inviting everyone to join the family in the fellowship hall for some light refreshments. Taking that as her cue, the organist began playing quietly, and everyone stood and waited for Sandy's family to exit. Her father cupped her mother's elbow, helped her stand, and they started toward the aisle, then stopped. Instead of following his in-laws, Sandy's husband had taken the four wide steps up to stand in front of his wife's coffin. The pastor gently laid a hand on his shoulder, nodded once to Sandy's parents and they, along with various aunts, uncles and cousins, streamed out of the sanctuary.

Mason moved into the vestibule and waited for the O'Hallerans. The complete and total look of desolation on Sandy's husband's face rattled around in his head. What would it feel like to lose someone who meant that much to him?

His mom died of an overdose a few years back, though he'd lost her to drugs and alcohol long before that. He never knew for sure who his dad was. Hell, the closest thing he had to a father was Henry "Hank" Ward, a sixty-five-year-old, ornery as hell Vietnam vet who would probably outlive everyone. Hank's genius was well-disguised behind a gruff, surly exterior. Everything Mason knew about flying, which was a lot, he learned from that man.

He'd been a beat-up, scared kid the night Hank found him

huddled in that nasty old shed at the end of the airstrip he owned. When he noticed Mason's black eye, rather than calling the cops or worse, sending him home, he'd fed him a can of soup and some homemade biscuits. Said only a dang fool would sleep in that rat-infested shack, then showed him a little room next to his office—a storage closet, really.

"You can clean this out, if'n ya want. That way, the next time you feel like you need a break, you can take it in here." He'd tossed Mason's bedding onto the floor and walked off muttering, "Can't have some fool kid dyin' of rabies on my property." The old man didn't know it, but he'd saved Mason's life that night.

Emily stepped into the vestibule and gave him a small smile. As he looked into her soft, green eyes, the truth hit him with the power of a jet blast. Her—*she* was his weakness. Losing her would destroy him.

CHAPTER TWELVE

E mily and Mason worked their way down the row of easels in the church's fellowship hall, four of them in all. Each one held a collage of photos: Sandy in her high school cap and gown, with her husband on their wedding day, the two of them with their dog.

Her steps slowed, and she bent at the waist. It was a photo of her with Sandy when they were about eight.

"Sometimes, when it was raining outside, we would play in my room with our Barbies for hours and hours. I can still remember their names." She pointed at the doll in her friend's hand. "Sandy named hers Lizzie, after a character she liked on TV." Then she pointed at her own doll. "Mine was already named Midge. I liked it, so I kept it."

She slowly straightened.

"Midge," she said, almost to herself.

"Em, what is it?" Mason cupped her jaw with his hand. He'd been keeping quiet vigil at her side since she walked out of the sanctuary.

She blinked a few times and looked up at him. "Why didn't I think of that before?"

"Think of ... wait ..." He hesitated. "Wasn't that the name of the friend Sandy mentioned in her will?"

"Yes, it was." Emily thought back to the moment in her office with Luna. "That first day, when I found out about Sandy, I stood there looking at that thing for the longest time. I *knew* there was something familiar about it. I just couldn't put my finger on what it was."

"You think she meant you?" The whole time, his thumb continued to gently stroke across her cheek.

"I'm not sure, but it would seem like a huge coincidence. It's not like Midge is a very common name." Emily felt a sudden urge to rush back to the office to get another look at Sandy's will. "Maybe she was trying to tell me something."

"You've got great instincts, Em. If you think there's something in that will, then let's go back and take a longer look." It was like the man could read her mind. Which would be bad. Very, very bad.

"That's not necessary. I can do it myself. I'm sure you've got stuff to do." As much as she loved the idea of spending time with him, she also knew it wasn't good for her emotional health.

"I know it's not necessary. I *want* to help you," he insisted.

Sensing her family's approach, she took a small step back, and Mason's hand dropped to his side. No sense giving everyone the wrong impression.

Her mom, who never missed a thing, looked back and forth between them. Thank goodness, she kept whatever she was thinking to herself. She pulled Emily in and held on tight, bringing the comforting, sweet scent of roses that always hovered around her.

She stepped back to make room for her father, but not before giving her and Mason another quick look. Then she winked at him.

Oh, good grief.

Her father stepped in and draped one of his big arms over her shoulder. "Beautiful service, wasn't it?"

"Very," Emily said.

The rest of the family strolled over just as her father released her.

Mason turned to Jonathan. "Emily and I were just—"

"We were just talking about how nice it is to see how many people cared about Sandy." She gave him a long, pleading look.

"Uh, yeah. It must give the family some solace." He turned to her. "Emily, how about some punch?"

"Sure. Sounds good." Mason's hand warmed her lower back as he guided her through the mourners to the other side of the room.

The ladies of the church auxiliary had set up two tables. One held a punch bowl, cups, coffee, tea, and water. The other was lined with an array of finger sandwiches, various platters of cheese and crackers, cut-up fruit, and vegetables with dip. There were even trays of assorted cookies. All the things you'd find at any party. Emily found it all very surreal.

"Here ya go." Mason handed her a napkin and little plastic cup of punch.

"Thank you." She turned to take in the crowd. "It really is nice to see so many people here."

"Huh-uh. Nice try. You want to tell me why you didn't want Jonathan to know about the name?" He crossed his arms over his chest and pinned her with a look only Mason could manage. A look that said, *I'm not moving until I have the truth*.

"If you must know, I want to make sure there's something to it before I talk to Jonathan." Growing up, she'd always been accused of being impulsive in her decision-making, too emotional. Not completely untrue. As a result, she'd learned to keep things to herself until she was absolutely certain her opinions couldn't be easily dismissed.

Mason turned away to grab a cup and, without warning, the feeling of being watched crawled over her skin. She whirled around, and punch splashed over the lip of her cup and soaked the napkin underneath. Heart pounding, she scanned the room. Folks mingled about, eating their snacks, sipping their beverages, perusing photos. Muffled conversations were accompanied by the occasional soft chuckle here and there from folks sharing fond memories. Not one person looked her way. Not a single one. No menacing evil eyes glared from afar.

"Emily?" Mason stepped closer. "What is it?"

"What? Oh ... it's nothing."

He waited. *Darn it.*

"You're going to think I'm losing it."

And still, he didn't move. In addition to being one of the most compelling men she'd ever met, he also possessed monk-like patience. Quite opposite from Emily.

She sighed. "Okay, fine." Voice low, she said, "I keep getting this weird feeling someone is watching me. First in the church, then just now."

Mason shifted to surreptitiously survey the room, then lifted his cup to hover in front of his lips. "Did you notice anyone? Maybe someone quickly averted their eyes when you looked their way or something?"

She pivoted toward him. "You believe me? I mean, you don't think I'm crazy?"

"Emily, you are a lot of things—argumentative, frustrating, bossy—"

"Hey! I—"

"—gorgeous, but you are not crazy."

It meant so much to her that he believed her. That he didn't dismiss her. And he also managed to distract her from her near-panicked state.

"You think I'm gorgeous?" She decided to steer clear of his other, less than complimentary personality assessments.

"Now you're just fishing for compliments." He took a sip of his punch and watched her over the rim of the cup. Gosh, she loved his eyes.

For the first time since finding out about Sandy, Emily smiled, really smiled. "Thank you."

"For what?" He finished his drink and tossed the empty cup in a nearby garbage can.

"Just ... for being here." She lifted one shoulder. "For keeping me company and making me smile. For believing me."

How the heck was she supposed to get this guy out of her system when every time she was around him, he seemed to burrow deeper.

"What can I say? I love seeing you smile, and I really hate seeing you sad."

Dang it. Why did he have to be her brother's best friend? And why should that matter to him so much? Unless ... Was it just an excuse? Was she nothing more to him than his friend's annoying kid sister? No, she refused to believe that. The kiss they'd shared was way too hot to have come from a guy who didn't care on at least some level. Something else factored into his decision. But what?

"Hey, you two." Caleb clapped Mason on the shoulder. "We're all headed back to the house. You guys coming?"

"I need to swing by the office." She shifted her purse strap up her shoulder.

"How 'bout you, Mason?" Caleb turned to his friend.

His best friend, Emily reminded herself.

"I've got a couple things to finish up at work, then I'll swing by."

"Hey, I've got an idea." Her brother turned and signaled Mathias over. "Emily, grab your car keys."

Several women—and a couple of men—tracked Mathias with a great deal of appreciation as he strolled over. Her brothers all had that effect on people. For Emily, who was short, a bit curvy through the hips, and somewhat average-looking, it was super annoying.

"What's up?" he asked.

"You rode here with Killian, right?" Caleb asked, and their brother nodded. "Perfect. You can drive Emily's car to Mom and Dad's."

Emily and Mason spoke over each other.

"I can drive myself," she said.

"Sounds good," he said.

She shot him a dirty look. He smiled. *Big lug.*

"It's settled. Your keys, Emily." Caleb held out his hand. When she just glared at him, he added, with exaggerated sweetness, "Pleeease."

"Give me one good reason why I can't drive myself." She had to concentrate to keep from stomping her foot. *Grrrr.* Her brothers could be such frustrating pains in the patoot.

Caleb put his face close to hers and spoke quietly. "I can give you two—Sandy and Pamela. Look around you, Emily. Remember why we're all here? Do I really need to remind you of your connection to them?"

Crud. Emily valued her independence and hated that he made sense. Still, her stubbornness would not let her concede defeat just yet.

"I also have to go to my place to feed Gary, since he's all of a sudden decided to be picky about what and when he eats." Good thing she loved that weird old cat so much because he could be a fussy pain in the butt sometimes. "I don't want to inconvenience Mason."

"It's no problem. If you'd like, I can talk some sense into Gary," Mason offered. "He does like me better than you, after all."

"I can manage, thanks. And that is not even close to being true." Although it kind of was.

"You sure? I really don't mind." He gave her a smug grin that somehow managed to be incredibly sexy at the same time.

"Yes, I am quite sure." Emily rolled her eyes and shook her head, then realized the rest of her family had gathered around and now stood watching them.

Dawn and her mother each held a hand over their mouths, trying to hide a smile and doing a poor job of it, by the way. Her dad made zero effort to hide his. Gwen giggled, and Andi had an *I told you so* smirk on her face. All five of her brothers stood there, arms crossed over their chests like a row of bouncers at a nightclub.

"Why are you all staring at us like that?" She looked at Mason. "Why are they all staring at us like that?"

"Oh, no reason." This from her mother, who had a grin on her face and her right hand over her heart.

Uh-oh. She'd seen that look on her mom's face before—back when she'd decided Andi and Jonathan should be together. At the time, Emily had enjoyed watching her brother squirm. Now that she appeared to be the next target of her mom's matchmaking, she realized she didn't much like it. Considering Mason's declaration, she was going to have to set her mother straight about the futility of that exercise.

"I agree with your brothers, by the way," her father said. "I refuse to let one more member of my family become a victim. And, young lady, if that means your wings get clipped a little until we find who's doing this, then so be it." Edict proclaimed, he kissed Emily on top of her head, took his wife's hand and left.

After the horrible things that happened to Gwen, Dawn and Luna, then their mom and Ashling, their dad and Beck had circled the O'Halleran wagons. She loved that about her family. No one, *no one* messed with the O'Hallerans and got away with it.

Mathias held out his hand and wiggled his fingers.

Emily dug through her purse and pulled out her keys. She worked her Jeep key from the cluttered ring. "Here, and you better be careful with my baby, or I might have to hurt you."

She might be stubborn, but she wasn't stupid enough to jeopardize her personal safety.

"Thanks, sis." He tucked it in his pocket and turned to Mason. "I know I don't have to tell you how important she is to this family."

"No, you don't." He straightened, and his wide shoulders drew back. "She will always be safe with me."

"Uh, hello." She waved her hands in front of their faces. "*She* is standing right here."

"See you at Mom and Dad's." Her brother tweaked her nose like she was a little kid. She swatted his hand away. He chuckled and strolled over to meet Killian and the rest of the family waiting by the door.

Mason tilted his head to the side. "That really bothers you, doesn't it?"

"That my brothers treat me like a child? Yeah, it bothers me." What did she have to do to prove to them she was an adult?

"I don't know if that's true, but if it's any consolation, I don't think of you as a child." His warm gaze traveled over her face. "Not even a little bit."

"If you say so." Emily turned to throw her cup away and bumped into an older gentleman. She instinctively reached out and grasped his upper arm to keep from knocking him down. "Oh, my goodness. I am so sorry. Are you okay?"

"Oh, I'm just fine, dear." Hunched over slightly, he gave her a small smile.

"Are you sure?" She looked at Mason, then back at him.

"I'm certain. You have a lovely day." He turned, slowly made his way to the door at the side of the room and followed a group of folks out.

Emily stared in his direction for the longest time. There was something odd ...

He watched her from where he'd parked down the street. She floated down the steps like a lithe fairy. Her dark red hair and fair skin glowed in the bright sunshine.

It was so sweet, the way she'd worried about hurting him.

His breath hitched at the memory of her touch. He'd taken a huge risk, getting so close to her, especially with that big guy watching over her like a junkyard dog. But he couldn't help himself. It had been totally worth it to prove he could get to her whenever and wherever he wanted.

The guy with the tactical pants was still bird-dogging her, standing way the hell too close. Who was he to her? A boyfriend? The logo on his shirt would seem to indicate he worked for OSI. If so, the muscle-head could present a problem, get in the way of his plans.

"If it becomes necessary, I'll deal with him, and he'll never see it coming," he muttered to the empty space around him. It would have to be done the right way, lest he bring the heat of OSI down on himself.

He lowered his binoculars and looked at his reflection in the rearview mirror. "No biggie. I'm good at eliminating problems." After all, brains always won out over brawn.

They crossed the parking lot and headed toward a shiny, black, jacked-up truck. *Figures.* The guy opened her door for her, then grabbed her around the waist and lifted her up into the passenger seat.

The man seethed. That would not do. Emily was his.

CHAPTER THIRTEEN

"How you holdin' up?" Mason shot Emily a quick sideways glance before looking back to the road. They were stuck in stop-and-go traffic on Interstate 5. At this rate, it would be an hour or so before they made it to the ferry that would take them across to Whidbey Island. After that, they still had a forty-minute drive to Whidbey Cove.

"I'm okay. I just can't stop thinking about Sandy and Pamela and what they must've gone through." She turned her body to face him, her folded legs drawn up onto the seat.

"Don't do that to yourself, Em." He set his hand on her knee. "Right now, let's concentrate on figuring out who's doing this and why. Okay?"

She scrubbed her fingertips across her forehead. "You're right."

With a last gentle squeeze, he moved his hand back to the steering wheel. Though he would love nothing more than to leave it right where it was.

"Okay, so you've scoured their case files. What are your thoughts?" he asked.

"I knew both of them, but did they know each other? Had

their paths ever crossed, even in the most peripheral way?"

"We find that out, and it'll help us narrow down who the real connection is." Though he had little doubt it was Emily.

"All three of us went to U Dub, though at slightly different times. I think that's where we should start. See if we had the same classes. Then we'll need to strong-arm a copy of the class lists from the admissions office. They're pretty persnickety about protecting student records."

"Rightfully so. But I'm confident OSI has enough pull to make that happen." Hell, one phone call from Beck or, God forbid, Jeffrey Burke, and the head of student admissions would be falling all over himself to satisfy their request.

"Ya think?" One side of her sexy mouth kicked up, exposing an adorable dimple.

He grinned. The return of her energetic sparkle was a welcome sight. Even in the midst of all this turmoil, she still had the ability to make him smile. Taking her mind off her friends' death and giving her something else to concentrate on had worked.

They spent the next half hour or so brainstorming until Emily started yawning.

"Why don't you lean back and get some rest?" The shadows beneath her eyes indicated she hadn't been sleeping well yet in no way diminished her beauty.

"You sure you don't mind?" She yawned again.

"Nah, go for it. The button is on the side of the seat. And here, cover yourself with this." He reached his arm around to grab his denim jacket from the back.

Her seat hummed as it reclined, and she practically disappeared when she burrowed herself under his coat. As her eyes drooped shut, he could've sworn she mumbled, "Mmm, smells like you."

God, what this one spirited woman did to him. Without realizing it, she'd wrapped herself around his heart. He'd been a fool to think he could be around her and not want her. He could request a transfer back to the San Francisco operation. Maybe if he didn't have to see her practically every day, he could forget about her. *Right, like that could ever happen.* And was that really what he wanted? Hell, no, it wasn't.

The other option was to risk his friendship with Caleb and, by default, with the entire O'Halleran family. Perhaps even jeopardize his career with OSI. He loved the people he worked with, loved knowing what they did was vitally important. But good pilots were always in demand—and he was a damn good pilot. The part that was like a punch to the gut would be losing his connection with the O'Hallerans. Was he willing to risk it all for a chance at happiness with Emily?

They finally cleared the traffic and made it to the ferry terminal. He drove down the ramp and straight into the belly of the large white and green ferry. A guy in an orange vest directed him to pull up close to the car in front of him, then Mason shut off his engine.

The ride only took twenty minutes, most of which he spent watching Emily sleep. Once she'd conked out, she hadn't moved. At all. He wasn't used to seeing her be so still for such an extended period of time. She was always a whirling dervish of energy and movement. He reached over and carefully skimmed her long bangs from her face.

He dragged his eyes from her at the sound of chains clanking and car engines firing up.

Emily stirred, blinked a few times, then took in her surroundings. She looked up at him and smiled. Her cheeks were flushed from sleep, her hair an adorable mess on one side.

"Nice nap?" He tightened his grip on the wheel to keep from picking her up and dragging her over onto his lap.

"Mhmm." Emily raised the seat, and his coat slid to her lap.

Ferry personnel tugged long, thick ropes to the front as the ferry approached the dock. The powerful engines reversed, churning up murky water and slowing their approach until the boat was nestled between the tall sets of pylons. Once it was secured, the ramp was lowered to the deck with a banging sound of metal against metal, and cars began driving off the ferry.

"You can just toss that into the back." With a boot on the brake, he pressed the *start* button, and the big engine roared to life.

She got to her knees, shifted to face the back and leaned through the space between the front seats. Framed in his rearview mirror, her perfect butt wiggled as she wrestled his coat onto the hook over the door. It took every shred of self-control he had not to stroke his hand along one perfect cheek. Chore complete, she turned, plopped back into the seat and put on her seat belt.

"I'm sorry I fell asleep on you." She stretched like a little cat, then flipped the vanity mirror down.

"Not a problem. You obviously needed it," he said.

"Good grief," she grumbled as she tried to fix her hair.

"What's wrong?"

"Oh, just that I look like I have a bird's nest on my head." She continued torturing her hair into submission.

He couldn't take it anymore and reached over and took hold of her hand.

"Stop." Mason was well aware of the fact that she had a love-hate relationship with her hair. He happened to love it.

Emily turned to him, mouth open—no doubt ready to protest him telling her what to do. Instead, she simply smiled, flipped the visor up and lowered her hand to her lap.

"What's that smile for?" He put the truck in gear and pulled forward. They bumped over the ramp and headed up the long road that traversed the center of the island.

"You really don't care, do you?" Her voice held a note of confusion.

"About what? Your hair?"

She nodded.

He hesitated, thought carefully about his answer. "We're friends, Emily. Stuff like that doesn't matter to me."

Her smile faltered, and her shoulders sagged ever so slightly. She looked out her window and said, "Good to know."

She dug through her purse and pulled out her cell phone. A few swipes and taps and she put the phone to her ear. She listened, sighed, then tapped the screen again before dialing a number.

"Hey, I just got your message." She listened a moment. "Yeah, I ... wait, how did you know I was at Sandy's funeral?" Her brows drew together. "I did? Huh, I guess I don't remember telling you."

She talked a few more minutes about the service and how nice it was.

"I'm sorry, tonight isn't good. I'm heading over to my folks' place." Her tone stiffened, along with her posture. "Yes, Richard, I'm aware that's the same reason I used last time. And yes, I'm fully aware you're still waiting to hang out again. Things have just been really ... hectic lately."

She snuck a sideways peek at Mason before turning toward the window and lowering her voice. "I'm sorry, but ... my mind isn't in the right place for this conversation."

Mason's jaw clenched tight.

"Okay, thanks. Bye." She pressed the screen.

"Everything okay?" Attention on the road, he forced a light easiness to his tone. He already hated the guy for the simple fact he was spending time with Emily. But if he was pressuring her in any way ...

"Yep." She tucked the phone back in her purse, grabbed a

little tube of something and popped it open. She swiped it across her full lips, making them dark pink and shiny and filling his truck with the smell of strawberries. *Just fuckin' great.* Now, whenever he smelled strawberries, he would think of her.

Recognizing the stubborn set of her chin, Mason changed the subject.

"Caleb told me that he and Dawn have been talking about starting a family." His friend, a former lady's man, was crazy in love with his wife. It's no wonder he'd want to have children with her.

"Really? That's awesome!" She perked up and shot him a big, toothy grin. "I know I'm biased, but I think my nephew and nieces are the most precious, gorgeous kids ever."

Mason never gave it much thought, but he had to admit Ashling, Alice and Rian were pretty damn cute.

"Alice is a lot like you," he said.

She had her father's dark hair, but her mossy-green, mischief-filled eyes she shared with her aunt and grandmother. Mostly, it was her personality that mirrored Emily's. The little girl had a way of finding trouble, which certainly kept her mom and dad on their toes.

"Beck told her they would consider getting her a puppy. Of course, all she heard was *get a puppy* and has been relentless in her efforts to remind them. Serves him right for being such a control freak his whole life," she said.

"Do you want kids?" *What the hell?* Where had that come from?

Emily's head pivoted his direction, and she looked him dead in the eye. "As soon as I find a man who loves me as much as I love him, yes, I'd love to have kids." She slowly faced front. "What about you?"

"I've never given it much thought." One shoulder lifted and fell.

"Forever the bachelor, huh?" she teased.

"If you say so." Truth was, he never *let* himself think about starting a family. Unlike Emily, he didn't have amazing examples of what parenting should be like. His childhood had been messy, dark, and filled with pain and a looming sense of despair. What if he turned out to be a shitty parent like his mom?

He turned onto the drive leading to the OSI compound. Lofty trees on either side cast long shadows and blocked out the waning sunlight. There weren't any overhead lights along this stretch of road to draw unwanted attention.

Folks in Whidbey Cove knew about the facility, but they had no real idea what OSI did there. They would have to have some serious sleuthing skills to find out.

His headlights flashed across the front of the large building, where a few cars were parked near the entrance. From the outside, it looked like what it was, an old lumber mill renovated for office use. Mason knew otherwise.

Guarded by a state-of-the-art security system, it housed technology so advanced, even the military didn't have access to it yet. Personnel were on site twenty-four seven, three hundred and sixty-five days a year monitoring the compound and teams operating around the world. Mason could practically feel the two sets of eyes that had locked on his truck the second it turned onto the access road.

He pulled into an open spot and shut off the engine.

Chin down, Emily said, "I think you'd be an amazing dad." Then she opened her door, hopped down and rushed to the entrance. Leaving him sitting there—her words pinging around inside his brain.

He caught up to her as she entered her passcode into the keypad, then bent to allow the retinal scanner to do its job. The door buzzed, she yanked it open, and he followed her in.

She blew right through the unoccupied reception area and headed toward the elevator.

She stopped and spun back to him. "Mason, I'm—"

He put his hands on her shoulders to keep from plowing into her.

"Sorry." Her throat moved up, then down before she stepped back, out of his grasp. "I'm going to my office to look at the will. I'll let you know when I'm ready to leave." She whipped back around and started to walk away.

He caught her hand. "That's not how this is going to go, Emily."

Her brows flew straight up to her hairline. "I beg your pardon?"

Oops. Poor choice of words. She hated being told what to do. Said she'd been bossed around her whole life and was over it.

"What I meant was, I was hoping we could take a look at it together." He pressed the elevator button.

"Don't you have other stuff to do?" She tugged her hand, and he reluctantly relinquished it. *Shit.* He really needed to stop touching her.

"No, not really." There was always stuff to do, but he was curious to see if she'd find something in the will.

"Fine. Whatever." The elevator door whispered open.

They stepped inside, and Mason pressed the button for the top floor. He stood next to her. That damn strawberry scent filled his head as he watched her reflection in the door. She rooted around in her purse. Her hair would fall forward, and she would swipe it back behind her ears with a huff.

The elevator dinged, and the door opened to the executive level. The space never failed to take his breath away. At one end, a wall of stacked stone framed a massive fireplace with cubbies of precisely arranged firewood on either side. A big, dark leather sofa, a couple of big chairs and a giant, handmade wood coffee table, courtesy of Michaleen, gave the space a homey feel. Not what you'd expect for a feared spec-ops organization.

Jonathan had offered Mason an office up here, but he'd declined. He liked being accessible to the guys on the teams, so he'd chosen an office in the workout facility. It wasn't nearly as fancy as the ones up here, but it was all he needed. Besides, he spent as little time in it as possible.

"A-ha!" Emily's overloaded keychain jangled as she yanked it from the depths of her big purse.

"What all do you have on that thing?" Hard to believe she'd ever have trouble finding that monster.

"Let's see ..." One by one, she named everything: "Pepper spray, keys to the workout facility, keys to this building, keys to my office, a spare key to my Jeep, a lucky rabbit's foot I got when I was twelve." She gave him a very serious look. "You can never have too much luck." Her inventory continued. "Another can of pepper spray, just in case, and a charm with a picture of Gary."

"What about that one?" He tapped a large, silver, heart-shaped locket.

"It was my grandma's." Her footsteps slowed to a stop. She palmed the antique piece, pressed the bezel, and it flipped open. "It's a picture of her and my grandpa when they were young."

"She's beautiful." Mason leaned in for a closer look, then turned his head to Emily. "You look like her."

"So I've been told." She rushed to add, "That I look like her, I mean. Not that I'm beautiful."

"Well, you are beautiful." Mason couldn't stop himself from stepping into her personal space.

"Are you teasing me?" Her head tilted back, and she narrowed her eyes. "Never mind. Don't answer that."

I, Sandy McMahon, do hereby write this, my last will and testament.

To my husband, Roger, sweetheart, please know I loved you and cherished every day of our life together.

Daddy and mommy, carry me protectively in your heart. I am sorry. I hate causing you this much pain and heartache.

Please remember me with nothing but happiness and everlasting love for you all.

To my dear friend, Midge, I remember when we were six years old and met for the first time. Since then, only you have held the key to all my childhood secrets and I can't believe you didn't share them with anyone. I love you and have missed you.

Please do not be sad. My life has been incredibly happy, filled with nothing but amazing family, great and special friends and more love than any girl could ask for.

I will miss you all and I love you all and I wish for you nothing but happiness.

CHAPTER FOURTEEN

Emily quickly unlocked her office and led Mason inside. She flipped on the lights, rushed around behind her desk and dropped her big bag on the credenza. She leaned over and booted up her laptop.

"Can you turn that on for me, please?" She pointed toward the flatscreen on the wall.

A moment after it hummed to life, Sandy's will appeared. Side by side, they took a moment to read it to themselves.

> I, Sandy McMahon, do hereby write this, my last will and testament.
>
> To my husband, Roger, Sweetheart, please know I loved you and cherished every day of our life together.
>
> Daddy and mommy, carry me protectively in your heart. I am sorry. I hate causing you this much pain and heartache.

Please remem*ber* me with *noth*ing but h*app*i*ness* and ever*l*asting love for you all.

To my dear friend, Midge, I remember when we were *six* years old and met *f*or the first time. Since *t*hen, only you have held the key to all my childhood secrets and I can't believe you didn't share them with anyone. I love you and have missed you.

Please do not be sad. My life has been incredibly happy, filled with nothing but amazing family, great and special friends and more love than any girl could ask for.

I will miss you all and I love you all and I wish for you nothing but happiness.

"Any luck?" he asked as he continued staring at the hand-written note.

Emily's eyes widened, and her hand went to her forehead.

"Oh my gosh. How did I miss that?" She turned, snatched a note pad and pencil from her desk. She flipped to a blank page and frantically started scribbling letters.

"Miss what?"

She didn't answer him, just kept scratching away.

"Emily ..." He placed his hand gently over hers. "Miss what?"

"The code," she said.

"Code?" He looked back at the will. "What code?"

"When we were little, all my brother's friends would hang out at our house. They always acted so cool, with their secret handshakes and boys-only clubs." She shook her head. "It was super annoying, so Sandy and I decided to make up our own private code."

"So you think there's a message hidden in there for you?"

"Why else would she mention the name Midge? And here, where it says *childhood secrets* ..." She tapped the eraser-end of the pencil on the screen. "I really think she was trying to get my attention."

"How would she know you'd ever see this though? You said yourself, you hadn't spoken to her in years."

"Hmmm ..." *Good question.* Her brows crunched together, and she tugged on her bottom lip. "Her aunt and uncle still live in Whidbey Cove." She scratched a couple more letters on the pad. "Maybe ... maybe one of them heard we were working on Pamela's case and mentioned it to Mr. and Mrs. Edmonds, then they said something to Sandy?"

"I guess that's possible." He looked over her shoulder. "What have you got so far?"

Emily had written a long line of random letters across the page.

"As many times as I've read her will, I cannot believe I didn't notice this earlier," Emily chastised herself.

"Take it easy, Em." He rubbed his hand up her tense back, then curved it around the back of her neck. "That was a long time ago."

"Yeah, I guess. Hang on a sec." She slipped from his grasp, dropped the notepad next to her keyboard and sat. Energy snapped inside her, indicating she was close to a discovery. "I'm going to type these out, then put them up with the will."

Mason continued to study the document.

Emily tried to ignore the dark smudge marring one corner and along a good portion of one crumpled edge. She knew from studying the forensic report that it was Sandy's blood. The autopsy photos revealed injuries around her wrists, consistent with being handcuffed or shackled. Which would explain the dried blood they found on her hands. They'd also found skin underneath her fingernails but were waiting to hear back from the lab regarding a DNA match. Aside from tiny injection sites at the base of her neck and her left biceps, and some bruising on her upper arms, there were no other marks on her. And, thank God, there were no signs of sexual assault. The person doing this seemed to get his kicks in other ways.

She couldn't imagine what Sandy and Pamela must have endured in the days and weeks before their death. Those last awful moments, scared, alone, trapped and waiting for death to claim them.

"Here we go." A row of letters appeared on the screen, above the will.

Emily pushed back from her computer and stood.

"How does this code of yours work, anyway?"

"See how some of the letters are printed and some are in cursive?" She waved her pencil over the screen.

He looked closer. "You're right. I hadn't even picked up on that."

"That was the whole idea. People often write with a mixture of print and cursive. We decided our code would be all the cursive letters."

"Words hiding in plain sight. Simple, yet effective. And pretty damn clever."

"Exactly. So, if I'm right, all of the cursive letters should translate into a message. We just have to figure out what it is."

"Did you write them in order or jumbled?"

"In order. After all, we were only like seven or eight when we came up with it." And they'd thought they were so clever.

BRNEYESPSYCHCLASS
BRNHAIRSIXFT

It only took a couple of minutes to pull out the most obvious words—*eyes, psych, class,* and *six.*

"Oh my God." Emily gasped and clutched his arm. "Mason, I think it's a description of her killer. I think *brn* stands for brown, and *ft* means feet. So, if you add those to the rest, you get *brown eyes, brown hair, six feet.* And *psych class* could mean he was in her class? We have to get a copy of her class schedule."

"I texted Beck from the ferry and asked him to work on that." His phone pinged in his pocket. He tugged it out, checked the screen, then swiped his finger to answer it.

"Hey, Beck? Already?" He looked down at her. "Yeah, she's right here. Okay, hang on." He tapped the screen. "You're on speaker."

"Emily, I'm letting you listen in on this because you'll just snoop through the file anyway." Beck's deep voice filled the space. "I got ahold of the dean of admissions. He was a little pushed out of shape, being pulled away from a staff cocktail party and all. When I stressed the urgency of my request and tossed out Jeffrey's name, he decided it was in his best interests to abandon his martini and cooperate."

"That's great, but I'm surprised you even bothered to contact him." OSI could've accessed the university's system and gotten what they needed without a soul knowing they'd been there.

"If he hadn't been amenable to my request, I would have gone around him."

"You got both Pamela and Sandy's?" Mason asked.

"Yeah. I got Emily's, too. Pretty impressive class load, sis," he added, a hint of pride in his voice.

"Thanks." Her cheeks warmed, and Emily cut a quick look at Mason. Her family knew she had a double major in business management and psychology, but they had no idea she'd taken all graduate-level courses.

"Why don't you go ahead and send what you have to me via e-mail and we'll take a look at it." Mason picked up his phone from the desk.

"You guys on your way to Mom and Dad's?" Beck asked.

"Actually, your sister came across something I think you all should see. Can you pull the team together and have them meet us at the office in an hour? You and Caleb should probably be here, too."

"What's this about?" Beck asked.

"I think it's best if Emily fills you in when you get here." Mason's eyes never left hers.

"All right. I'll pull everyone together, and we'll meet in the strategy room. See you then." Beck hung up.

"What did you do that for?" She knew they all had to be a part of this decision, but it was so annoying.

Mason tucked his phone back in his pocket. "What are you so worried about?"

She lifted one shoulder and avoided eye contact.

"Look, Em, I get it. You don't think your brothers take you seriously, that they're dismissive of you or whatever. But this"—he tipped his chin toward the screen—"what you've discovered, it's important and needs to be shared with the team."

Why would he have to be the one person on the planet who *got* her? Who understood her so completely?

"You want to know the truth?" she asked.

"Always."

"Because they'll thank me, pat me on the head and send me on my way. They will cut me out of this investigation, and I can't ... I *won't* let that happen. This is too important to me, Mason."

"How about if I make you a deal?"

She drew back her chin. "What kind of deal?"

"We'll talk to your brothers about adding you to the team."

"Really?" She smiled.

"However, you have to promise that you will not, under any circumstances, go off on your own to investigate."

She opened her mouth, but he put a finger to her lips.

"That is nonnegotiable, Emily." His eyes tracked his finger as it gluided across her mouth, causing a funny tingling sensation in her belly. "It's for your own safety. Can you agree to those terms?" Legs braced apart, he folded his arms against his wide chest. All alpha male and unyielding.

"What if I get a lead and there's no one around? Am I supposed to just sit on it?" Emily couldn't give in too easily. She had a reputation to uphold, after all.

"You call me. If I'm not available, then you call one of the other guys." He relaxed his posture and propped his butt on the edge of her desk. His long legs stretched out and crossed at the ankles.

"You're not trained for field work. Yes, I know your brothers taught you how to shoot and fight. But here's the thing. The person doing this is smart, and he covers his tracks. We don't know enough about him, which makes him that much more dangerous. Not to mention, you are connected to both victims."

Yeah, that little detail on its own was enough to make her think twice about going rogue.

"Em, you don't honestly think your brothers do anything alone, do you?" He didn't wait for her answer. "They don't. They understand how important it is to have someone at their back. It's what being part of a team is all about."

"I got it. I got it. Don't go it alone." *Sheesh*.

"I have your word?"

"What? You wanna pinky swear or something?"

He lifted his hand and extended his pinky toward her.

"Are you serious?" She let loose an aggrieved sigh and hooked her little finger with his. "Fine. Yes, you have my word."

"Good." He released her finger. "Now, you've got an hour before they get here. That should give you enough time to do what you need to do."

"Well, thanks for *that* anyway," she grumbled. "What are you going to do while I pull this all together?"

"I'll just hang out here and return a few emails, if that's okay with you." He grabbed his phone and settled into her guest chair.

"Knock yourself out." Emily turned to her desk and started building her pitch.

She needed to be prepared for any argument her brothers might have. Because, no matter what Mason might think, convincing them to ignore whatever danger she might be in was going to be a giant uphill battle. Like climbing the Matterhorn in the dead of winter kind of battle.

CHAPTER FIFTEEN

A n hour later, Beck, Caleb, Jonathan, Andi, Mathias, Killian and Golden strolled into the strategy room and joined Mason and Emily around the large table.

"Okay, what have you got for us?" Beck got them started.

Emily looked over at Mason, which pleased the hell out of him. He gave her a quick wink and a nod—a silent *you got this*. Because she did.

Her shoulders drew back and, with a click of the remote in her hand, the will popped up on the large screen. A second click of the remote highlighted each of the coded letters in bright yellow.

"I believe Sandy left me a coded message in her will." Her opening statement got everyone's attention.

Emily spent the next fifteen or so minutes explaining the code and its origins. She clearly and concisely presented her evidence and laid out her reasons for being a part of the investigation. She was a true professional. A fucking rock star, and Mason was so damn proud of her.

"And you're sure about this code?" Beck asked.

"Yes. Positive." She looked at each of her brothers. "Look,

I get it. You guys worry about me, and that's cool. But ... I am not that defenseless, little six-year-old kid who climbed into a car with a stranger."

Tension rippled around the room as every single one of the O'Hallerans shifted in their seats, their muscles visibly bunching.

"What the hell?" Mason sat forward, his forearms on the table.

"We were all there in the park that day, Emily. When you got in that car and he drove away with you ..." Beck hesitated, shook his head. "If we'd been paying attention, that never would've happened to you. That's on us."

The rest of the brothers mumbled their agreement.

Emily bolted up from her chair. "You guys are a bunch of idiots! The only one to blame is the man who grabbed me." She dropped back into her chair and crossed her arms. "Twenty years, and you guys are still carrying that around. It's just dumb."

"She's right, ya know." Andi pierced each one of them with a look. "You guys were just kids. You can't blame yourselves for some perv trying to snatch your little sister. You should be proud of the fact she managed to get away from the guy before anything truly awful happened. Her instincts told her something wasn't right, and she acted on them. It is long past time to let that shit go. Because all you're doing is hamstringing her ability to reach her full potential."

"Thank you." Emily smiled at her sister-in-law.

Mason took advantage of the lull in conversation. "What happened to the guy who grabbed you?" He was confident the O'Hallerans had kept tabs on him.

"He got twenty-five years and was sent to Washington State Penitentiary. I wasn't the first child he grabbed." She turned back to her brothers. "But I was the only one who got away."

"Jesus." Mason sat back and tried to absorb this new information. No wonder they were so overprotective and hypervigilant where she was concerned. A need for retribution burned through him, and he wanted to scoop her up and promise her nothing bad would ever happen to her again.

For the first time since entering the room, Mathias spoke. "About four months after the guy went to prison, the prosecutor called our folks to let them know he'd been stabbed to death in his cell. Good riddance. Piece of shit."

They were the harshest words Mason had ever heard from him.

"Amen," Andi added.

Killian squeezed the top of his twin's shoulder.

"Anyway, back to the matter at hand," Emily said. "Am I on the team or not?"

For the next several minutes, they broke down the pros and cons of her request. Though everyone would have a say about her being added to the team, ultimately, the decision was up to Beck and Jonathan. Beck, because he owned the company, and Jonathan, because he was her immediate boss. As much as anyone could actually *be* the boss of Emily.

Mason turned to find her tugging on her bottom lip. He wrapped his fingers gently around her wrist and lowered her hand.

"I say we give her a chance."

Beck scrubbed his hand over his face, tapped his fingers on the table for a moment.

Finally, he said, "You can be a part of the team." He leaned toward Emily and pointed. "But you do not, I repeat, *do not* do anything on your own. I am dead serious about this, Emily. If you do, I will pull you from this team so fast, you won't remember ever being a part of it."

EMILY'S INSIDES RELAXED, and she breathed easily for the first time since Mason called to arrange the meeting.

"Thank you, Beck." She looked around at her new teammates. *I've got teammates!* "Thanks, all of you."

"Congratulations, Emily. Now, if we're done, I'm going to rescue Christina from our daughter." Andi rose from her chair. "I had no idea a twenty-three-month-old could get into so much mischief."

"I'll come with you." Emily turned to Beck. "Is Alice here, too?"

"She stayed at the house with Rian and her mommy. She's fascinated by her baby brother and is very protective of mommy these days. Speaking of, I'm going to check in on my beautiful bride." He grabbed his cell phone and dialed. "Hey, baby. How are things there?" His voice softened, then faded as he moved to the corner of the room.

Caleb was in the other corner, smiling and chatting with Dawn on the phone.

Hands laced together behind his head, Killian lounged back in his chair. "I don't know if this facility can withstand Alice and Appleseed at the same time. Those two are scary enough on their own. Put them together and it's like two tornadoes coming together and combining their strength."

Emily's mom and dad had planted a tree when each of their six children were born. They carried on the tradition by planting pear trees for Beck's two children and an apple tree for Ashling. Her Uncle Killian had been calling her Appleseed ever since. He could be very sweet, when he wasn't being a pain in the butt.

"Ain't that the truth? Ashling started walking at nine months, and our life hasn't been the same since." Jonathan chuckled as he pushed up from his chair.

Andi wrapped her arms around his waist and tilted her head back. "And I wouldn't have it any other way."

"Nor would I." He tucked his hands in her back pockets and kissed her.

Beck, Jonathan and Caleb had all found their person and had never been happier. Her eyes strayed to Mason. What if he was her person but he refused to accept it?

"Aaand, that's my cue." Killian bounded up from his chair.

"Can you still give Emily a ride out to Mom and Dad's?" Mathias looked over at Mason. "I left her Jeep there and rode back here with Killian."

"No problem," he said. "We need to stop by and take care of my buddy Gary first."

"The key is on a hook by the back door." Mathias turned to Emily. "Welcome to the team, sis." He gave her a quick peck on top of her head.

Emily wasn't too crazy about everyone making plans on her behalf. But if it meant spending more time with Mason, then she would let it pass. And how pathetic was that?

"Yeah, welcome, Emily." Golden smiled.

Killian gave her a long look, then walked up to her, planted a big hand on each of her shoulders and looked down at her.

"You're not in this alone, Emily. We've all got your back. Always have. Always will. Don't ever forget that. You got me?" There was a seriousness to him she'd seldom seen before. Then he mimicked his twin with a kiss to the top of her head and walked out with Mathias and Golden.

She watched him leave, then glanced around the room at Beck, Caleb and Jonathan. A lump tightened her throat. Killian was right. There had never been a time in her life when they hadn't had her back. Hadn't always been there for her. They could be annoying and overbearing, heavy-handed sometimes, but she could not imagine her life without every single one of them.

"Hey, you okay?" Mason bent his knees to see her face.

Gah. Why did she have to love so much about the stupid man?

"I'm good, thanks." She turned to Andi. "Let's go see my niece."

Her sister-in-law gave Jonathan a last kiss. He pulled his hands from her pockets, rubbed her butt, then let her go.

"Jonathan, Caleb, and Mason, could you stick around a minute?" Emily hesitated at Beck's request.

"Come on, Emily." Andi circled her arm through Emily's. "Let's leave these guys to their little hen party while we go see my precocious, perfect child."

CHAPTER SIXTEEN

They were five feet from the door of Emily's townhouse and Mason could already hear Gary yowling on the other side.

"Uh-oh. Someone doesn't sound happy," Mason said.

"He's never happy." Her keys jiggled in the lock. "I'm coming. I'm coming."

It swung open and there sat Gary, yelling up at them as if they'd wronged him somehow. The beep of the alarm added to the noise. Emily flipped on the light and took a step toward the touchpad. The cat decided that was the perfect moment to wrap himself around her legs. She stumbled. Mason reached out for her, but she managed to keep herself from falling.

"You did that on purpose, didn't you?" She glared down at her cat and entered the code. The beeping stopped. The yowling did not.

"What's the matter, buddy? Is Emily being mean to you?" Mason scooped him up and cradled him in his arms like a fur-covered baby, then scratched under his chin. Which he knew to be his favorite spot. The cat's eyes drooped shut in ecstasy, and he started to purr. And drool.

"See, told you he likes me best." Mason rubbed his nose against the soft fur on Gary's head.

"Whatever." She rolled her eyes and walked toward the kitchen.

He followed and waited as she poured fresh water in a bowl, then grabbed a plastic container of dry cat food from the pantry. The second the first kibble bounced off the bottom of the ceramic bowl, Gary morphed into a multi-colored, wriggling, spitting ball of let-me-down-now.

"Okay, okay, relax." Mason set him on the floor in front of his food.

He began to crunch away and, even as he ate, he somehow managed to voice his displeasure. About what, who the hell knew?

Mason liked the old grouch. Probably because he reminded him of Hank. A comparison his old friend would not appreciate.

"I'll be right back. I want to change clothes before we head to Mom and Dad's. Help yourself to something to drink." Emily waved her hand toward the fridge, then headed down the hall. A few seconds later, he heard the sound of a door closing.

He stared after her, imagining her stripping down to her bra and panties. He blew out a breath, stretched his neck side to side. His feet tingled with the need to march over there, throw the door open and fill his eyes with the sight of alabaster skin he knew would be tinged with a warm peach glow.

Gary stretched up on his hind legs and put his front paws on Mason's thighs. Blue eyes glared up at him and, with an odd combination of a growl and a meow rolling up from his throat, his needle-like claws appeared and slowly began to dig into Mason's jeans.

Before the little beast could get a good grip on his flesh, he reached down and picked him up. "Was that a warning, buddy? Don't worry, I'm not—"

"Are you talking to my cat?" Emily stood, wide-eyed, grinning at him.

His gazed trekked the length of her. She had changed into a pair of black leggings with a sleeveless, purple shirt that fluttered at her hips. Her green eyes flashed like sunlight through an emerald. Little toes with nails painted the color of her shirt peaked out of her flip-flops. *So damn cute.*

"Of course, I was." He turned to Gary. "We were having a nice little chat, weren't we, buddy?"

Emily snagged her keys from the counter, setting Gary to yowling again.

"He knows we're leaving." Emily grabbed a couple of kitty snacks from the pantry, then stood in the middle of the kitchen. "Sit."

Gary's eyes never left the hand with the treats as he grudgingly did as ordered. Only then did she set them on the floor and stroke her hand down his back. He inhaled the snacks as if he hadn't just scarfed down a half bowl of food. Hunger satisfied for the moment, he stuck his nose in the air, dismissed them with a petulant whip of his tail before moving to *his* chair, where he commenced grooming himself.

"No parties while I'm gone, mister." Emily gave him a last scratch behind his ears, turned on the lamp next to him, set the alarm and locked the door behind them.

"You can't see anything through these damn things." Mason looked up at the tall, thick hedges lining either side of her walkway. "Ever thought about trimming them down a bit?"

"Of course, but I'm not tall enough. I talked Mathias and

Killian into doing it for me next week." She grinned. "It's going to cost me a case of their favorite microbrew, but it's totally worth it."

"With the three of us working, it shouldn't take long."

Emily quickened her steps to stand in front of him. "You don't have to do that."

Mason stopped to keep from plowing her over. "I know." Then he stepped around her and resumed walking.

He was fully aware of her reluctance to accept help—she was a proud, determined woman—but she would just need to set that aside in this instance. He pressed a button, and his headlights flashed and the horn beeped twice.

"Greeeat," she said with forced enthusiasm.

He opened the truck door, lifted her up and set her on the passenger seat.

"You know I *can* get in by myself, right?" She dragged her seat belt across and clicked it.

"Yep. Sure do." He liked having an excuse to put his hands on her. He closed the door, then moved around to his side, slid behind the wheel and fired up the big engine.

She turned to him. "Thank you, by the way."

"For what?" He gave her a quick look before turning back to the road.

"For understanding why I need to do this. And again, for being here."

"You're welcome." Mason was exactly where he wanted to be.

CHAPTER SEVENTEEN

Mason and Emily approached the stately, red brick building that housed the University of Washington's Psychology Department. He pulled her to a stop at the base of the wide front steps.

"You follow my lead, okay?" He bent his knees to bring them eye to eye, but hers were fixated on the main doors. With the tip of one finger, he gently turned her face to him. "Did you hear what I said, Em?"

"Yes. Sheesh." She rolled her eyes in that adorable way of hers. "I heard you the first five times you told me," she grumbled before she charged up the steps like a conquering warrior.

He tossed up his hands and shook his head, then rushed to catch up with her. "You're off to a pretty shitty start to this whole following-my-lead thing."

"Sorry. It's just that ... he's out there"—arm outstretched, she indicated the general area—"and every minute that passes is more time for him to grab his next victim. If he hasn't already."

"And that's why we're here, following up on one of the

clues Sandy left. But there's a right way and a wrong way to do this. Charging in there and hammering the guy with a million questions is definitely the wrong way. Okay?" Mason understood her impatience. His urgency level had multiplied ever since they discovered that Emily, Sandy and Pamela, at different times, all took the same psychology class, taught by the same professor, Dr. Reginald Tompkins.

"You're right." She lifted the strap to her bag over her head so it hung across her body.

"Wait ... did you just say I was—"

"Shut up." She jabbed her small fist into his abs, then gave it a little shake.

He grinned, kissed her knuckles, then threaded his fingers through hers.

To say Beck and Jonathan weren't thrilled about adding their sister to the investigation would be a massive understatement. But when Mason told them his plan for staying close to her, they relaxed a bit. When she found out just *how* close, she would probably kick up a fuss. *So be it.* Ensuring her safety was worth a little bit of a battle with her. A small part of him looked forward to it. Going toe-to-toe with Emily was always a kick.

He hauled open one of the large, heavy doors and they stepped inside. *Holy shit.* Mason gawked at the incredible space. Hanging in the center of a coffered ceiling, a massive wrought iron and milk-glass light fixture cast the space in a soft glow. An inlaid medallion with four compass points in gold dominated the lobby floor.

"This way." Emily tugged on his hand. Her rubber soles squeaked on the terrazzo as they crossed to a wide marble staircase bordered by a beautiful, carved wooden banister. Decades' worth of students making their way to and from class had worn a slight dip into the surface of each step. The lobby had an elegance and richness about it not typically found in academic buildings.

"Smell that?" She closed her eyes and dragged in a deep breath through her nose. "It's orange oil—they use it to clean the wood. I only know that because I was here late one night and asked the janitor, James. We chatted for a bit, and he told me he'd been working here for forty-three years. Can you believe that? Said he put his son and daughter through college right here at U Dub." She smiled. "He was so proud, his face lit up when he talked about them. He retired a year later and moved to Florida with his wife. The guy they hired to fill his position ended up being friendly, too. Heck, everyone who worked here was friendly. I always felt safe. Which is probably why I'm having a hard time wrapping my head around the idea that one of them could be the animal who's killing my friends."

That was Emily—she never met a stranger. Outgoing, open and honest. Not a fake bone in her smokin' little body. Whether talking to a janitor or a four-star general, she was the most *real* person he'd ever met.

"You're pretty special, you know that?" He wrapped an arm around her shoulder and pulled her into his side.

A beautiful flush stained her cheeks. His compliment, like all others, seemed to catch her off guard.

"Oh, well, thanks." Instead of stepping away, she curved her arm around the back of his waist and leaned into him. He didn't hate it.

"Professor Tompkins can't be the one doing this. He's only a few inches taller than me and walks with a cane," she said.

"Yeah, I had one of the guys in the cellar pull his background." The tech guys worked in the communications center, a secured room down the hall from the strategy room. "Unless the person doing this has help, which I don't think he does, then he has to be strong enough to lift someone, move them from a van to wherever he keeps them, then again when he carries them to wherever he's going to bury them."

Emily shivered.

Mason rubbed his hand up and down her arm and tightened his hold. He didn't bother to ask if she was okay. Because, of course, she wasn't.

Tompkins's office was midway down the wide hallway. A frosted glass window took up the top half of the door, so they could tell the lights were off inside. A barely legible syllabus, scrawled in black marker, was taped to the center. On the wall next to the door was one of those engraved nameplates that slid in and out.

She glanced at her watch. "One forty-seven. Dr. Tompkins's office hours don't start until two. He dislikes them so much, he refuses to show up even one minute early. He used to call them his *complaining and pleading hours*. Said students only ever came in to complain about a grade or plead for a chance to improve a grade."

"Here, let's wait over here." Mason headed toward a wooden bench directly across from the door and they sat. "Sounds tough. Did you like him?"

Her shoulders lifted and dropped. "He was a bit crotchety, but his bark was worse than his bite. I learned a ton in his class, and I think he kinda liked me. Not that he'd ever admit it."

Of course, he liked her. Who wouldn't love Emily?

Love? Mason sat back and stared at the office door. The word knocked around in his head, then wiggled its way to his heart. He looked down at Emily—the confident set of her shoulders, her proud chin, the way she chewed her bottom lip as she typed a note into her phone, and a powerful sensation burned in his blood. *Mine.*

Try as he might, he could no longer deny, at least to

himself, that she was meant to be his. He was as sure of it as he was that his eyes were blue. She filled a part of him he never knew was empty and made him want things he never knew were missing. Now was not the time for him to share his epiphany with her. Not when women were being killed—women close to Emily. Too close.

"Mason?" She bumped her shoulder against his.

"Yeah?"

"You okay?" Her look of concern warmed him. "Where did you go?"

"Just thinking about the case."

No more denial. No more excuses. How did the saying go? The heart wants what the heart wants? And Emily was worth risking it all. *Guess it's time to have a chat with Caleb.*

Eyes narrowed, she hesitated. "Aaanyway, while you were spaced out, I asked what we're doing after this?" She dropped her phone in her bag and started talking at a hundred miles per hour. "First, I think we should go check out the parking lot where Pamela was taken. Then we—"

"Emily—" Mason tried to interject.

"—should go talk to Sandy's mom and dad and her husband. After that—"

"Emily!" He actually had to raise his voice to cut her off.

She jumped. "Jeez-Louise, dude. Chill."

"Yes, I agree, we should go check out the parking lot. I also think we should talk to Sandy's family and Pamela's," Mason said. "But—"

"But what? You said you agreed with me.

"I do. *But* I think we should call them and arrange to meet them tomorrow or the next day." Mason hated to chase her triumphant smile away. "They've had to bury someone they love, suffer through the horrible details of how she died, then were forced to answer a million painful questions. Sandy's husband and Pamela's boyfriend were even considered suspects for a short time. I'm sure they're tortured by thoughts of what happened, and their emotions are very raw." He curved his hand over her knee. "If we're going to add to that, don't you think we owe them the courtesy of a phone call?"

She blew out a breath. "Of course. I should've thought of that." Her shoulders sagged, and she leaned her head against his shoulder. "I just want to catch this guy so badly."

"We all do, Em. But these things take time, patience and teamwork." He would continue to hammer on that last part to ensure she followed Beck's orders about not going off on her own.

Irregular footsteps approached, accompanied by the rhythmic thump of a cane and the jingling of keys.

Mason immediately recognized Dr. Tompkins, professor of psychology, from the photo in his file. He had a white, closely trimmed beard and mustache and a receding hairline of equally white close-cropped hair. Atop his head sat a pair of round, black-framed glasses. He even wore a tweed, three-piece suit and tie with a … Mason looked closer … *Is that a pocket watch?* This guy was a living, breathing incarnation of Sigmund Freud. Mason had little doubt it was intentional.

They rose from the bench, and Dr. Tompkins turned their way.

"Ms. O'Halleran?" He squinted, then yanked his glasses from atop his head and slid them on. "What are you doing here? I thought you graduated?"

"Hey, there, Dr. Tompkins. Yes, I graduated a few years ago." She turned to Mason, her hand on his arm. "This is Mason Croft. We were hoping you might have a few minutes to chat with us."

"What is it you'd like to discuss? Certainly you're not here to complain about a grade." One side of his mouth twitched in what Mason guessed was an attempt at a smile.

Emily chuckled. "No, I'm not here about a grade. Would you mind if we discuss this in your office?"

He looked from Emily to Mason over the top of his glasses, then turned and shoved his key in the lock. The door swung inward with a low squeak. He flipped up the light switch, and the overhead fluorescents flickered on. There were stacks and stacks of bulging file folders, three-ring binders and loose papers covering every inch of horizontal surface.

He hooked the ivory handle of his cane on the edge of his desk and lowered himself into his high-backed leather chair. Centered on the wall behind him was a framed, black-and-white photo of Sigmund Freud. The similarities were uncanny.

"Well, don't just stand there. Come in. Come in."

CHAPTER EIGHTEEN

E mily and Mason navigated their way around teetering stacks of God-knows-what on their way to two wooden chairs in front of Dr. Tompkins's desk. *Seems some things never change.*

Mason picked up the pile from her chair and added it to the one from his chair. He lifted the whole thing, then turned around, searching for a place to set them. He managed to find a spot near the corner, squatted down and placed them carefully on the floor. Hands out in front of him, ready to stop it from tipping over, he slowly backed away.

Dr. Tompkins looked at her. "He's a nervous one, isn't he?"

She could only laugh at the idea of Mason Croft being nervous about anything.

Mason sat down and got right to it. "Dr. Tompkins, we're here to talk to you about a couple of your students."

"Let me guess—Ms. McMahon and Ms. Wescott." He yanked off his glasses and absently wiped them with a tissue.

"Yes, sir. We're conducting an investigation at the request of their families." Mason said.

"Such an awful thing." He shook his head.

"Would you mind answering a few questions, sir?" Mason asked.

"I already spoke to the police, so I'm not sure I'll be much help. But fire away." He put his glasses back on and tossed the tissue in a small garbage can.

Emily remained quiet and let Mason do all the talking. She was determined to prove she could do this—that she could be an investigator. And if sitting here, keeping her mouth shut got her there, then so be it. But holy moly, was it tough.

She watched in awe as Mason, in that level yet intense way of his, coaxed answers from the professor. They learned that both Sandy and Pamela used to go to the same coffee shop. More than once, they'd both brought him a cup of his favorite dark roast.

When it became obvious there was no other new information to be gained, Mason stood. Emily did the same.

"Thank you for your time, Dr. Tompkins." He reached into his back pocket and pulled out a white business card. "If you think of anything else, please give us a call."

The professor rose from his chair and reached out for the card. He flipped it over, then looked at Mason. "The only thing on here is a first name and phone number."

"That's correct." Mason offered no explanation, just cradled her elbow in his hand and steered her toward the door.

Emily looked back over her shoulder. "Thanks very much, Dr. Tompkins."

They were just crossing the threshold when he called out. "Wait!"

They stopped and turned back to him. Head down, he rubbed his fingertips across his troubled brow.

Mason and Emily stood quietly, giving the older man time to gather his thoughts.

"My eight thirty class had just ended. I was at the front of the room, and a group of students walked past. I overheard one of them say something about a man who always seemed to show up wherever she was. She seemed very worried." His hand lowered to the desk, and he finally looked at them across the cluttered space. "It was Ms. Wescott."

A rush of excitement sizzled through Emily, and her heart thumped like a bass drum in her chest. Had the killer been stalking Pamela? What about Sandy?

"How could I have forgotten that?" He thumped his knuckles on his desk blotter.

"Did she happen to mention what the man looked like or where she saw him?" Mason was the picture of calm, as if the professor hadn't just dropped a verbal bomb in the middle of the room.

Dr. Tompkins thought for a moment, then shook his head. "By the time I looked up, they had already walked out the door."

"If you didn't look up until they were out the door, how can you be sure it was her?" Mason pressed gently.

"Her voice had a very distinctive lilt to it. Like a soft Southern accent."

"Pamela grew up in Tennessee." She'd once shared that with Emily, when they happened to be in the dorm study area at the same time.

"Do you know any of the people she was talking to?" Mason continued. "If they were male or female? Or maybe how many were in the group?"

"Young man, I teach four classes every day, with over one hundred students in each one. A veritable sea of indistinguishable faces with glazed-over expressions staring back at me. Remembering all their names is close to impossible." He turned to Emily. "Present company excluded, Ms. O'Halleran. *You* were quite memorable."

Oookay. What exactly did he mean by that?

"What I can tell you is that I only heard women's voices. That's not to say there wasn't a man in their group. I'm sorry I can't remember any more than that."

"You've been extremely helpful. Thank you, sir." Mason reached across the desk to shake his hand.

Emily did the same. "Thank you so much, Professor Tompkins. Take care."

He carefully lowered himself into his chair. Emily would never forget the look on his face as she pulled the door shut —sadness about what he'd remembered and regret that it had taken him so long.

She and Mason took the stairs back down to the lobby, then walked outside. The late afternoon sun speckled through the rustling dark green leaves of the oak trees dotting the landscape around the building.

"Mason, do you—"

"Hold that thought until we're in my truck, okay?" His demeanor remained relaxed, even as he regarded their surroundings with the experience of a trained warrior. Her brothers always had the same look about them.

She leaned close and whispered, "Do you think someone is watching us?"

"I always think someone is watching me. It's safer that way." He held her hand, and they walked to where he'd parked.

How difficult it must be—not knowing who you can trust. Always being on guard, anticipating the next attack. What would cause a person to live that way?

Without thinking, Emily lifted their joined hands and kissed his knuckles. He looked down at her, the heat in his electric blue eyes undeniable. Then he returned the favor and placed a lingering, warm kiss to her knuckles.

Her breath halted, and her insides lit up like fire crackers in a metal bucket.

Like it or not, Mr. Croft, there is definitely something between us.

Mason helped her into the passenger side, then jogged around and climbed in. He pivoted toward her, one arm draped over the steering wheel, the other along the back of the seat. "Okay, shoot."

"Do you think the guy Pamela was talking about is the one who killed her?"

"I don't know. Maybe." Mason watched a guy walk past, and not until he was out of sight did he look back at her. "Seems like a pretty huge coincidence that she goes missing after being worried about a guy stalking her."

"She talked about him to people in her class. Maybe she described him to one of them." Emily thought back to the case file she'd reviewed. "Her classmates have already been questioned, but maybe we'll get lucky and this new information will jog their memories."

"Let's check out the parking garage, then we'll head back to the office to make some calls before it gets too late." He straightened in his seat, secured his seat belt and pulled away from the curb.

"My mom mentioned Sandy's parents are staying with friends up near Whidbey Cove. I guess the stupid reporters wouldn't leave them alone." As if losing their daughter hadn't upended their lives enough, they were forced to flee their home by a pack of jackals. And for what? The next big headline? Disgusting.

Mason reached over and gave her hand a tiny squeeze. His touch calmed her instantly.

"Why don't you give them a call to see if we can come by sometime tomorrow to talk with them." He removed his hand to grip the steering wheel. "Unless you'd like me to do it."

He is so sweet.

"No, I can handle it. I've already spoken with them once." It hadn't been easy, but she'd needed them to know how terribly sorry she was.

"Assure them we won't take up much of their time," he said.

The muffled sound of ringing had her grabbing her bag from the floor. She set it on her lap and rummaged through it until she found her phone—at the bottom, of course.

"Hey, Mom. What's up?" She listened, nodded. "Uh-huh. Yeah, actually, that's perfect. We were hoping to speak with them." Emily turned to him with a thumbs-up. "Sounds good. We'll see you then. Love you, too."

She dropped her phone into her bag.

Mason pointed at her tote. "You know, if you cleaned some of the stuff out of that thing, you wouldn't have such a hard time finding stuff."

"Excuse me, but not all of us are neatniks like some people I know. And by *some people,* I mean you."

"What did your mom have to say?" His lack of denial said it all.

"Sandy's parents and husband will be at Mom and Dad's tomorrow afternoon. They want an update on the investigation, and Jonathan thought they might be more comfortable at our parents' house."

"Everyone's more comfortable at your folks' house. You're lucky to have them." He pulled into the entrance of the large parking structure.

Emily watched him as he navigated his way to the fourth floor. He never talked much about his childhood. Whenever she asked Caleb about it, he told her to ask Mason, that it was his story to share and no one else's.

"Who did you have, Mason?" *Shoot.* She hadn't meant to say that out loud.

He pulled into a spot on the fourth floor and shut off the engine, then turned to her. Tires squealed on the slick cement, and a car horn beeped twice from somewhere in the large structure. His jaw jumped, and Emily was sure he was going to tell her to mind her own business.

He finally responded. "It's not a pretty story, and I don't think—"

"Sorry. Never mind. I shouldn't have—"

"Stop." He took hold of her hand and laced his fingers with hers. "I don't have any deep, dark secrets or anything. I just think we should focus on this right now." He indicated the lot around them. "Then I'll happily tell you anything you want to know. Deal?"

Relieved she hadn't overstepped, she smiled. "Deal."

They climbed out of the vehicle, and she followed Mason until he stopped by the spot numbered four hundred and ten.

"We know Pamela's kidnapper parked his van in this spot." He looked up, then pointed toward one of the corners. "And that is the camera that captured the video. Which means"—he moved about a half dozen steps away and looked up at the camera again—"right about here is where he grabbed her."

"Emily?" A voice called out from near the open stairwell.

Mason put himself between her and the sound of footsteps, and she flattened her hands on his back.

"Emily? Is that you?" No, it could *not* be him.

She leaned to the side and blinked a few times. "Richard?"

If it was possible, Mason got taller and his shoulders expanded. With her hands on him, she could feel the tightening of the muscles along his back.

"Emily, who is this guy? Is he bugging you?" Richard tried to look around Mason, but he was having none of that.

"I think the bigger question here is, who are you?" Mason's voice held a lethal edge she'd never heard before. And, man oh man, was it sexy.

Wait a minute. Focus! Emily pinched his waist.

He looked over his shoulder. "What the hell was that for?"

"You know darn well who he is." She slammed her hands to her hips.

Mason pointed at Richard. "Don't. Move." Everything in his tone made it clear something bad would happen if he didn't follow his orders.

He swung around and stepped right into her personal space. Close enough that her breasts brushed against his chest.

One side of his mouth rose very slowly, and his voice went all low and gravelly. "You know you're going to pay for that later, right?"

Ho-ly moly. Emily gulped. Her nipples beaded, and she was pretty sure her panties melted right off her body. His attention dropped to her chest and lingered. His eyes slowly rose up to meet hers, and the other side of his mouth lifted into a full, wicked smile.

Richard cleared his throat. "Hello. Excuse me."

She suddenly remembered they weren't alone—and wished they were.

"Move." She put a hand on Mason's chest and tried to shove him back. Of course, the big galoot didn't move a muscle.

He leaned down, putting nose to nose. "Ask. Nicely."

"Please move." Emily gave him a saccharin smile. "Before I introduce my knee to your family jewels."

"Okay, what the hell's going on here?" Richard's voice took on an edge.

Mason turned back to him, and Emily tried to step

around him. He looped a finger through the belt loop at the back of her jeans and reeled her in. Then he draped one arm around the front of her shoulders and held her there, so her back was along his front.

What kind of game was he playing?

She made the introductions, then said, "Mason and I are—"

"We're getting a copy of Emily's transcripts. She's thinking of taking a couple more classes to get her PhD. Isn't that right, Em?" He cocked his head to the side and smiled down at her.

"Um, yeah, that's right." *Duh.* Of course, she shouldn't tell him the real reason they were there. She had so much to learn about being an investigator.

Richard looked at Mason's arm around Emily, then at her.

"Is he the real reason I haven't heard from you?" Richard tipped his chin up at the man holding her.

CHAPTER NINETEEN

Mason liked hearing Emily hadn't been in touch with the guy. However, he did not like Richard's tone, and he sure as hell wasn't happy with the way he was looking at her. Like she belonged to him.

"We work together." She wiggled herself free of his hold and shot him a dirty look. "What are you doing here? I thought your classes were at night."

"I was just, uh … I was meeting up with a buddy of mine. He lives not too far from here." Richard jammed his hands in his front pockets.

Mason called *bullshit* on that.

"Oh, does he go to school at the U?" Emily asked.

"Nah, he's a guy I met through work." He took hold of Emily's hand. "Can I talk to you for a minute? Alone."

Her head whipped around, and she gave Mason an incredulous look. "Did you seriously just growl?"

Had he? Probably.

"Don't be ridiculous." But if the guy didn't take his hand off her, Mason was going to have to hurt him. Badly.

"Right." She rolled her eyes, pulled her hand free and

pointed up at him. "You, relax. We'll be right over there." She indicated the red car on the other side of his truck.

Before he could say anything, Richard cupped her elbow to lead her away.

Mason's teeth ground together.

They were about five feet away when he barked out, "That's far enough."

He could close the distance between them and take the guy down in less than five seconds. But any further, and he wouldn't be able to eavesdrop.

Emily looked at her watch. "Richard, I only have a few minutes before I need to leave. What was it you wanted to talk about?"

"Are we done, Emily?" He waved his finger back and forth between them. "You and me?"

"Richard, there is no—"

"I know you said you weren't interested in anything serious, and I respected that." He gave Mason a side-eye, then turned his back to him and lowered his voice. "But, if you would just try, I think we could have something pretty great."

She snuck a peek at Mason. "Look, I've got some stuff I need to work out. Until I do, I'm not ready for anything serious. With *anyone*. I told you all of this the first time we went out. You said you understood."

"I guess I thought you might start having feelings for me, like I do for you."

"I'm sorry." She put her hand on his forearm. "I think you're a great guy, and I'm sure the right woman is out there just waiting for you to find her."

"Well, I think you're making a huge mistake." Richard lowered his voice and yanked on her wrist.

"Ouch." Emily tried to twist it free. "Richard, you're hurting me."

Mason saw red. In three long strides, he closed the space

between them. Just as he reached out to grab Richard by the scruff of his neck, the guy let loose with a sound reminiscent of a squealing pig, collapsed to his knees on the pavement, then fell to his side in the fetal position. Holding his crotch, face red and sucking in breaths, he looked like he was about to puke. Emily stood over him, rubbing her wrist.

"Holy shit, Em." Mason blinked a few times. She'd actually taken the guy down.

"What the heck is wrong with you?" She scolded Richie-boy like he was a child.

"You okay, honey?" Mason held out his hand. "Let me see."

"It's fine." But she held her arm against her.

"Please?"

Emily blew out a heavy breath.

"Okay, but don't freak out." She thrust out her arm. Her small wrist was bright red and would likely be bruised before the end of the day.

"Son of a bitch." Mason started to reach down to finish what she had started, but she stopped him with a hand on his shoulder.

"I told you not to freak out. It's fine. I just bruise easily."

Richard coughed a few times, then managed to make it to his knees.

"Don't call me again, Richard." With that, she whipped around and walked back to the truck. "Can we go, Mason?"

"Yeah, honey. I just want to have a word with our friend here." He grabbed the key fob from his pocket and unlocked his truck.

"Fine. Whatever. Just … don't hurt him." Emily muttered something about men being idiots as she climbed up inside and slammed the door. Mason could just imagine her in there fuming to herself.

He squatted down, forearms on his knees, next to

Richard, who was taking deep breaths and rubbing his crotch.

"Give me your phone." He wiggled his fingers in the guy's red face. "Unless you want your balls permanently wedged in your throat."

Richard slipped a fancy new smartphone from his pocket.

"Now, delete Emily's number and every text message between you. Go ahead. I'll wait."

Richard cursed under his breath but turned his phone on.

What the hell?

Emily's smiling face was his background photo. Mason snatched the phone from him.

"Hey!"

"On second thought. I think I'll take care of it myself." He made a mental note of the guy's number, then wiped out everything he had in the cloud and reset the phone to its factory settings.

"Now I'm going to have to start all over again," Richard whined.

Mason didn't really give a shit. Considering what he really wanted to do to the guy, wiping out his phone was letting him off easy. And it was the only way to ensure he no longer had any contact information for Emily. He would also suggest that she change her number, just in case the guy had written it down somewhere.

"Okay, asshole, here's how this is going to go. You're done with her. You got me? If you see her out in public, you go the other direction. You don't call her. You don't show up at her house. Nothing. If you do, I'll find out about it, and I won't be happy. And, trust me, you do not want that. Do we understand each other?"

"I understand just fine." He cast a last longing look toward the truck.

"Good." Mason stood, then grasped Richard's elbow and

helped him up. "She got you pretty damn good, didn't she?" He couldn't help but smile.

Richard didn't respond, just turned and hobbled away.

Mason watched him head toward the stairwell and out of sight. What was he doing in the parking garage? And on this level at the exact time they happened to be there?

Before heading back to his truck, he pulled out his phone and called Jonathan.

"Hey, Mase. Did you guys talk to the prof?"

"We did. We'll fill you in when we get back. I'm actually calling for another reason." He let Jonathan in on their little tête-à-tête with Evans.

"I'll have the tech guys do a deep dive into the asshole. If he's ever so much as dropped a wad of gum on the sidewalk, we'll find out about it."

"Sounds good." Mason remembered the bruise on Emily's wrist and wanted to chase down the asshole and pulverize him.

"I cannot believe that son of a bitch put his hands on her." Jonathan's voice always got especially low and deadly-sounding when he was angry. "I knew I should've checked the bastard out before their first date. But Emily is so damn prickly about that sort of thing. Doesn't help that my wife agrees with her."

"Yeah, she values her independence, and I respect that. If it's any comfort, she took him down like a champ. It was fucking glorious. You guys taught her well," Mason said.

"Hey, you've had a hand in that, too. That training you've been doing with her has been invaluable." One of Mason's jobs at OSI was working with operatives on hand-to-hand combat, knife skills, grappling and martial arts. Emily had approached him several months ago about training with him, and he'd jumped at the chance to have a legitimate excuse to spend time with her.

"She's a natural. And growing up with all you guys taught her the value of situational awareness." Mason would argue that most women instinctively excelled over men in that area. "I'm really proud of her."

He started walking back to the truck.

"Uh-huh. So, you ready to admit you care about her as more than just a friend?"

Mason's steps faltered. Was he that obvious? And did Jonathan actually sound like he was cool with the idea? He took the last few steps, opened the door and slid in behind the wheel.

"We'll see you in a couple of hours." This was not a conversation he wanted to have over the phone, with Emily close enough he could smell her strawberry lip gloss.

"Yeah, you care about her. See you soon." Jonathan's knowing laughter rolled through the phone as Mason ended the call.

CHAPTER TWENTY

The man paced the large dining room floor, his anger growing with each step until it consumed him. Anger at his mother for his shitty childhood and the life her illness now forced upon him. Intense, burning anger at the man who dared touch Emily.

He scooped the blue and white vase from the center of the massive table, drew back his arm and hurled it at the china hutch. The priceless eighteenth-century antique crashed through the front, destroying his mother's precious tea cup collection.

His arms flew up to cover his face as etched glass and porcelain exploded outward. Shards nicked his forearms, dusted his hair and, like rough-cut diamonds, littered the Persian rug.

He pounded up the stairs and threw open his mother's bedroom door. It banged against the wall. A painting rattled and dropped to the floor, where its heavy, gilded frame splintered into pieces. His eyes flashed across the expanse of the large room. Fury propelled him closer to the woman in the bed. He stood over her, breaths sawing in and out, hands clenched with the need to strike.

"Who the hell does he think he is?" His frantic pacing resumed in earnest. "Acting like she belongs to him. Putting his hands on her."

He knotted his fingers in his hair and gave a sharp tug. When that didn't work, he smacked his palm repeatedly against the side of his head. The pain usually helped him regain his focus, settled him. Not this time.

He charged over to the bed, grabbed his mother's bony shoulders and shook her. Her thinning gray hair fluttered about, and her jaw flapped.

"This is your fault! You're the reason I haven't been able to be with her!" Spittle flew. Droplets landed on her forehead, her cheek.

Her voice, saturated with its typical burning criticism, whispered through his agitated and confused mind. *You're not good enough for her. She deserves to be with a real man, not a wimp like you. She would just laugh in your face.*

"Shut up! SHUT UP!" Blinded by rage, he snatched a pillow from the other side of the bed and held it against her face. His fingers dug into the down filling as he pressed with all his weight.

She didn't fight him, didn't cry out for him to stop. Yet, in his mind, her ridicule continued. Slowly, the voice began to fade, and his body relaxed one muscle at a time. He straightened and lifted the pillow from her face. It slipped from his grasp and dropped to the floor with a soft *thump*.

Shoulders slouched, breaths easing, he cocked his head to the side and stared down at the emaciated, lifeless shell of the demoness who'd made his life miserable. He waited, expecting to feel remorse or regret. He felt neither. For the first time in his life, he felt … tranquil. She could never hurt him again.

"Phew. Guess I lost it for a second there. Didn't I, Mother? Well, it *was* kinda your fault." He shrugged. "Oh, well. Sleep tight. Don't let the bedbugs bite." He snickered, gave her a last look, then turned and pulled the door shut behind him, falling back against it with a burst of air.

For a few minutes, his mind raced through different scenarios, then he shoved off the door and let himself into his room. He would deal with her later.

In the bathroom, today's persona—Jerry, a visiting home-care provider—stared back at him from the mirror. He'd met the real Jerry when they'd happened to share a couch at some little coffee shop on campus. The guy was taking a study break before he headed to work at a nursing home. A real talker, Jerry went on and on about how much he hated his job. But he needed the money for tuition, so he put up with all the "smelly old people." That's when inspiration had struck.

Jerry had gotten up to take a leak, trusting a man he'd just met to keep an eye on his backpack. It had been almost too easy to grab the uniform polo shirt—nametag and all—and transfer it to his own bag. His new friend had returned from the bathroom, and they'd said their goodbyes and gone their separate ways.

"Dumbass move, Jerry." He dragged the choppy, dark-blond wig from his head and dropped it in the sink. He sighed as he scratched his scalp, then pulled the light green shirt over his head and tossed it on top of the wig. Slowly, he peeled off the latex nose and wiped away any lingering remnants, then it joined the rest in the sink.

Freshly showered, he wrapped the towel around his waist and moved to his dresser. He slid open the top drawer, and the large manila envelope peeked out from beneath his underwear and socks. He shoved them aside and picked it up, then sat on the edge of his bed. His thoughts veered back to when he'd received it, and the calm he'd achieved was threatened by a deep, consuming rage seeping into his veins like molten liquid.

About eight months ago, he'd been on his way up to her room to check on her when the melodic chimes of the lavish doorbell stopped him. Through the peephole, he spied a burly guy wearing a ball cap with the Seattle Mariners logo embroidered on it. In his left hand, he held a clipboard and manila envelope.

Very odd, because no one ever came to their house. His mother hadn't exactly been welcoming or liked by the neighbors. Or anyone, for that matter.

He plastered on a smile and opened the door.

"Can I help you?" He kept the suspicion from his voice.

The man looked down at the name on the clipboard and confirmed he had the right person. He flipped open what looked like a leather wallet with identification on one side, a gold badge on the other. He introduced himself as a private investigator who'd been hired to locate him.

"You're a hard man to find." He held out the clipboard. "If you'll sign for this, I'll be on my way." He verified the signature, then handed him the envelope.

"Have a good one." With a tap of the pen to the brim of his hat, he turned and walked down the long path to the sidewalk, then climbed into his car.

After locking the door, he'd watched through the keyhole until the man drove off. He strolled into his mother's office and, knowing she would spit nails, settled into the fancy tufted chair behind her pretentious, oversize desk. As he sliced open the harmless-looking envelope, nothing could have prepared him for the devastating impact its contents would have on his worldview.

Inside was his estranged father's Last Will and Testament, along with a smaller, sealed envelope containing a handwritten letter. At first, all he could do was stare down at them. His initial reaction was *burn them*.

As far back as he could remember, his mother had repeatedly said what a horrible gambler his father was, what a loser, a womanizer. Many times, she'd kept him up late into the night, hammering at him about how his father abandoned them for another woman. How it hadn't helped that he was embarrassed by his own son and couldn't stand the sight of him.

He grabbed the marble lighter from the corner of the desk and rolled his thumb across the wheel few times until the flame flickered to life. The envelope dangled from his fingers, and he watched the flame dance close to the corner of the envelope.

"Dammit." He blew it out and tossed the lighter back on the desk. Curiosity would not allow him to destroy it. After a deep, fortifying breath, he opened the smaller envelope.

Dear son ...

His father wrote about how much he loved his wife but that she changed after they were married. She became mean and vindictive, manipulative and, finally, impossible to live with. He detailed steps she'd taken to keep him from his son after the divorce. How she said he hated his father and wanted nothing to do with him. Not believing her, he threatened to take her to court to gain custody. She'd packed them up and moved them to a new city. That must've been when she purchased this ridiculous mausoleum he'd grown up in. His mother had more money than God and never hesitated to spend it on the finer things.

Even as each word of the letter exposed her lies, her pure evil, it did nothing to lessen his hatred of his father. If anything, it became more deeply rooted. The man had left an innocent four-year-old kid behind to fend for himself against a vile woman he knew would take her anger out on their son.

What kind of man did that? What kind of man wouldn't burn down the world to save his only child?

One good thing came of it—he discovered his father was an extremely successful man who had amassed a fortune that put his mother's piddly millions to shame. And he'd left most of it to his only son. Guilt was a wonderful thing.

Many times, he'd been tempted to use some of his newfound wealth to stick his mother in a nursing home. But, for the first time in his life, he finally had control over her, and he wasn't willing to give that up. Even if there were times she was nothing more than a millstone around his neck.

Not anymore, he laughed to himself.

He tucked the envelope back in the drawer, tossed the towel into the bathroom and crawled into bed naked. Lying in the dark, the sheets cool against his heated body, he stared up at the ceiling, pondering his next set of moves.

Killing his mother now was an unfortunate mistake. He'd hoped to bring Emily to meet her, to rub it in the old bat's face that he *was* good enough to be with someone amazing and beautiful. Once that was done, he'd planned to give her a death much more merciful than she deserved.

He pondered his new timeline, shifting plans in his head, working out the logistical details. An all-new disguise would be needed. Something subtle that wouldn't attract unwanted attention. He'd already proven he could get close to Emily. A critical step, since the next name on his list was closer than the other two—a member of her beloved inner circle.

CHAPTER TWENTY-ONE

Van Halen blasted from the old boom box on the tailgate of the truck. The steady hum of an air compressor and occasional whine of a table saw joined the intermittent *bang* from two different nail guns.

Caleb measured and cut planks for the new front porch, then Beck and Jonathan hammered them into place. Alice wielded her own little pink hammer as she *helped* her daddy and uncle with the deck. Her sparkling pink tutu was the perfect complement to her denim overalls and unicorn T-shirt. Mason worked with Michaleen installing the amazing custom railing he'd designed as a surprise housewarming gift.

Killian and Mathias came around the corner of the house, each carrying long pieces of treated lumber atop a shoulder. Laughing about God only knows what. Mason would swear they had their own language.

He checked the time on his phone—quarter after seven, and the sun was only now starting to dip behind the tops of the tall trees. Summers in the Pacific Northwest were amazing. The days were long with temps in the upper seventies to low eighties, and the foliage was rich and green under cloudless blue skies. They easily made up for the gray and drizzle they endured the rest of the year.

"Whenever you're ready, there are sandwiches, chips and iced tea in the kitchen," Molly called from behind the screened door. Ashling was propped on one hip, holding a melting Popsicle, and Rian was cradled in the other arm. She'd volunteered to babysit while Emily, Christina and the O'Halleran wives were out at their once-a-month girls' night.

"Thanks, hon." Michaleen hung his hammer in the loop on his tool belt and tucked his work gloves in his back pocket.

Michaleen swung the door open, and Ashling thrust her Popsicle toward him. He leaned down and took a taste. "Mmm, blueberry. Yummy."

She giggled with sheer delight as he stroked his massive hand gently over Rian's tiny head, then gave his wife a lingering kiss before heading inside.

Mason found it endearing that, after more than thirty years together, Mrs. O. still blushed. The entire scene was heartwarming as hell, and he wanted that with Emily.

The twins stacked the wood neatly at the end of the porch and covered it with a tarp. Beck shut down the compressor, and Jonathan wrapped up a couple hundred feet of extension cords. Caleb cleared the sawdust from the table saw and blade, then tugged the canvas cover over it. Michaleen was a commercial and custom home builder, and he'd taught his boys how to work with their hands and how to take care of their tools and materials.

After a quick look around, certain everything was secured, they started to make their way to the door.

"You guys got a minute?" Mason yanked off his gloves and tossed them on his tool box.

They all stopped and turned back to him at the same

time. Nothing like having five sets of O'Halleran brothers' eyes trained on you all at once.

Killian looked at Caleb. "Gosh, sounds serious."

"It does, doesn't it?" Caleb agreed with a smirk.

Beck glanced at Mason. "Think he's finally going to fess up?"

"God, I hope so," Jonathan added.

"Come on, guys, let's hear the man out." Mathias, ever the diplomat, brushed wood shavings from his shoulders.

All five of them settled on one of the brand-new steps, successfully blocking the path to the porch. Beck swung Alice up in a swirl of giggles and glitter and perched her on his knee.

Mason crossed his arms, gave himself a minute to gather his thoughts, then tucked his hands in his front pockets.

"Here's the thing ... I'm in love with Emily. I think I've been in love with her since the first time I saw her." He held up his hand when it looked like they were going to interject. "Please, let me finish. I hold no illusions that I deserve her or that I'm good enough for her. But I will do whatever it takes to earn her love, and then I'll spend the rest of my life trying to make her happy."

"You done?" Beck lazily swatted a bug away from his head.

"Not yet." Mason turned to his best friend. "Caleb, I know I'm risking my friendship with you, and that sucks. I also know I'm jeopardizing my relationship with all of you and your folks." He looked from brother to brother. "But you'll just have to get used to it, because I'm not going to lie to myself, or her, anymore."

Five pairs of dark brows lifted as the brothers waited to see if he was finished.

Mason propped his butt against a sawhorse.

His best friend rose and slowly walked toward him.

Mason stood, his body tensed and ready to take a punch. He really didn't want to fight his best friend.

"It's about time." Caleb wrapped him in a hug, then held him at arm's length.

"What—"

"We've known for a long time that you were hung up on our sister." He tapped Mason on the forehead. "We were just waiting for you to pull your head out of your ass. And what the hell was all that bullshit about risking our friendship and your relationship with the family? You're like another brother to me, to all of us."

"Well, except Emily, 'cause that would be weird." Killian cringed.

"Don't be an idiot." Beck shoved him.

Mathias stepped closer to Mason. "You tied yourself to this family the second you risked your life going in after Gwen, then again when you almost died trying to save Dawn."

"What my baby brother is trying to tell you is, our parents would kick our asses if we ever made you feel like you weren't one of us. So that means you're stuck with us, dude." Killian was only a couple of minutes older than his twin but loved to harass his brother.

Mathias, ever calm and levelheaded, never took the bait.

"Good luck with Emily, Mase. You're gonna need it," Killian quipped as he jogged up the steps.

"Ignore him. We all do." Mathias reached for Alice, and she jumped into his arms. "Come on, kid. Let's go eat."

All that remained were the three oldest O'Halleran brothers. Beck stepped forward to stand right in front of Mason, his face deadly serious. As the oldest, he had taken on the role of family protector, so his opinion mattered a great deal to Mason. It wouldn't deter him from going after Emily, but Beck's objections would make it a hell of a lot tougher.

"Mason, you're one of the best men I know, so knock that shit off about not being deserving. Having said that, if you hurt her, I ..." He pointed his thumb over his shoulder. "*We* will hurt you. Got it?"

"I love her," Mason said, as if that explained everything. And it did.

"Works for me." Jonathan turned and clunked up the steps.

Caleb tossed his arm over Mason's shoulder. "It's about damn time, dude."

CHAPTER TWENTY-TWO

A ll five of them were already laughing as they headed straight for their favorite table near the back door of the Don't Know Pub. Andi had chosen it based on the strategic advantage for evasion and escape. Gwen liked it because it was close to the bathroom, something that seemed more important to her since having two children. Christina liked it because, if she sat in *just the right spot,* she had an unobstructed view of Devlin Masters, the hunky guy behind the bar. Dawn and Emily could care less where they sat, as long as they could get drinks and food delivered to them. Five women, each so unlike the other, yet, despite the differences and the distance between them, they'd become the closest of friends.

"What do you mean, Alice hid your bras?" Christina settled into her usual spot facing the bar and hung her purse strap over the back of the chair.

"I mean she hid my bras. Every single one. Nursing bras, workout bras, even the sexy ones I keep hidden at the back of my drawer. Well, at least, I thought they were hidden. When I asked her about it, she put her hands on her hips just like her father and said, "'Bwas are booby twaps and they make it so you can't feed Wian.'"

There was a split second of silence before they all burst out laughing all over again. The words, combined with Gwen's spot-on impression of her daughter, were absolutely hilarious.

Her sister-in-law talked over them. "And then, with the most serious look I've ever seen on her little face, she said, 'Daddy said it was otay fo' me to hide dem. He said it was a gweat idea.'"

"Men and boobs. Ridiculous." Andi rolled her eyes and shook her head.

"She's only three years old. How in the world did the words *booby trap* even become a part of her vocabulary?" Emily's niece was a trip.

"Well, it's not from television. She rarely watches it, and when she does, it's always *PJ Masks*. Over and over and over." Gwen set her phone on the table in front of her. "All I can think is that she must've overheard some of the guys talking about booby traps, and it stuck."

"Wouldn't surprise me. Your daughter is a little Houdini. She manages to get herself into and out of places without anyone noticing," Dawn added. She and Caleb lived near Beck and Gwen, so they spent a lot of time together.

Emily envied their closeness. Even though she griped about her brothers, she'd love it if her whole family lived in Whidbey Cove.

"Well, I think she's amazing and is going to rule the world someday," Christina said as she leaned to get a glimpse of Devlin beyond Dawn, who had the nerve to sit across from her and block her view.

"Oops." Dawn hopped up and moved to an empty chair. "Sorry 'bout that."

"I know it's silly, and I don't stand a chance with a guy like him. But he's just so ... so ... everything." Christina let loose a dreamy sigh. Her elbow landed on the table, and she rested her chin in her hand. That happened a lot around Devlin.

After his dad died, Devlin and his mom moved to Whidbey Cove to live with his Uncle Henry, who owned the Don't Know. He and Jonathan clicked, probably because they were both intense loner types, and became friends.

"He is nice to look at. But I'm still partial to a certain growly Navy SEAL." Andi lifted her hand to catch the server's attention on her way to the bar.

"What do you mean, you don't stand a chance with him?" Emily's best friend was an amazing woman. She had been through some seriously horrible stuff in her past, and she deserved all the happiness life could heap upon her.

"Yeah, he'd be lucky to have you." Gwen plucked a few napkins from the holder and wiped down the table.

"So, what appetizers do we want?" Christina grabbed the menu cards and passed them out. "We better decide quickly, or Emily will decide for us."

"Hey, I can't help it if you guys are slow." She perused the menu for the daily appetizer specials.

"Smooth subject change, by the way." Dawn checked out the options but side-eyed Christina.

"Good evening, ladies." Devlin's deep baritone cut through their laughter. "What can I get you?" He meant the question for all of them, but he was looking down at Christina when he asked it.

You could've heard a pin drop as they all watched the silent interplay between them. Devlin set his laser-like sniper's focus on her best friend, which sent the most beautiful shade of rose creeping across Christina's cheeks.

Oh, holy wow. That was some intense heat passing between those two. Emily was shocked the whole pub didn't burn down around them.

Christina finally found her voice and ordered an appetizer and a lemon drop martini.

"Ooo, that sounds good." Emily raised her hand. "I'll have one of those and an order of the number four chicken wings."

"I'll have the wings, but the number ones for me. And what the heck, give me one of those lemon drop thingies, too." Gwen looked around the table. "I'm nursing, but according to my doctor"—she indicated Dawn with a wave of her hand—"I'm allowed one drink. And anyway, it's got juice in it, so it's healthy, right?"

"Go for it. You've earned it." Andi looked up at Devlin, then tipped her head toward his office door. "Still have your Macallan stash back there?"

"Of course." He leaned a hand on the back of Christina's chair, his fingers barely brushing her shoulder. Emily thought her friend might melt right to the floor. Boy, did she have it bad.

"Excellent. I'll have two fingers, neat, and the fish tacos."

"You got it. And what can I get you, Dawn?"

"Seltzer water with a wedge of lime. Nothing to eat just yet." She went right back to scrutinizing the menu.

"Great. I'll get your food order in and have the server bring over your drinks. I'll get rid of those for you." He relieved Gwen of the wad of napkins, gave Christina's shoulder the sweetest little squeeze, then headed to the bar.

Oh, Emily was so going to be talking to her friend about that later. Right now, she had other matters to tend to.

"Hmm. No food *and* you're not having a margarita?" She crossed her arms on the table.

Dawn always *always* ordered the Don't Know's special margarita whenever they came here for Happy Hour. She had to admit, they were pretty friggin' delicious. *Shoot.* Now Emily wanted a margarita.

"Nope." Caleb's wife gathered the menu cards, straightened them and stood them up between the salt and pepper shakers and the napkin dispenser.

They all waited.

She looked at her tablemates. "What? I'm not hungry. And can't a girl order a seltzer water without everyone getting all weird?"

One of Andi's dark brows rose under her bangs. "Forgive our skepticism, but you once referred to the margaritas here as, and I quote, 'the nectar of the Gods.'"

"Oh my gosh, that's right. It was your first time here, and you had *three* of them." Emily held up three fingers. "So, okay, dish. What's going on?"

Dawn hesitated, chewed her lip, and looked at each of them.

"I'm pregnant!" She bounced in her chair as the words burst free like a pressure cooker losing its top.

Emily and Christina bounded from their chairs and circled the table. Andi and Gwen joined them, and they all wrapped Dawn in a group hug. Several heads turned their way as squeals, congratulations, and clapping filled their corner of the pub. When they finally stepped back and took their seats, they were all sniffling and smiling.

"Wow. I'm going to be an aunt again." Emily sat back in her chair.

"Me, too," Gwen and Andi said together and laughed.

Emily glanced over at Christina and could've sworn a hint of sadness flickered in her best friend's eyes. It disappeared so quickly, she thought she must've imagined it.

"That is so amazing, Dawn. I am so happy for you guys." Christina's smile seemed forced as she grabbed her expensive wristlet, which served as a wallet and phone case, and stood. "Excuse me. I need to use the ladies' room."

"Christina, wait up. I'll come with you." Emily caught up to her just as she was pushing the bathroom door open.

They took care of business, then stood side by side at the sink as they washed their hands.

Emily watched Christina in the mirror. Her usually bright and upbeat friend was definitely upset about something. "What is it?"

Christina huffed out a breath, yanked some paper towels from the dispenser and dried her hands. She tossed the paper away, lowered herself onto the wooden bench nearby. Emily joined her and waited until she was ready to share.

"I can't have kids." The words held no emotion. Like she'd practiced saying them to herself many times.

"What ... How ..."

Her head turned to Emily. "Remember when I told you about what happened to me when I was a kid?"

"Of course." How could she ever forget such horrific things being done to a child—to her best friend.

"When I was in the ER, after ... well, you know, after. I overheard the doctor tell my mom that I would probably never be able to have children of my own." Her eyes glistened with unshed tears, and her throat moved up and down. "I was pretty doped up, but I'll never forget the sound of my mother crying. My mother *never* cried."

"Could you have misheard? After all, you said you were pretty out of it."

"I asked my mom about it later. By then, her midwestern pragmatism had returned. She said a lot of women weren't able to have kids and that it wasn't the end of the world. That I could always adopt. I knew from her tone that it was the last we would speak of it."

Emily draped her arm over her friend's shoulder. More for herself than Christina.

"My dad blamed himself for what happened. Said it was his job to protect me and that he'd failed. After I came home from the hospital, he didn't know what to say to me. So he just didn't say much at all. No one did." Her voice quivered as she shared her pain. "We all just sort of moved around each other, ignoring the giant, pink elephant in the middle of the room. Except my older brother—he was determined to find the man who did it and ... well, you can imagine. Anyway, I'm pretty sure they were all relieved when I finally left home. I know I sure was because, for the first time since it happened, I felt like I could finally take a deep breath again."

Emily wrapped her arms around her friend, and there they sat, in the bathroom of a neighborhood pub, holding each other, until they were both ready to let go.

"Have you ever gotten a second opinion?" Emily snagged a couple of tissues from the counter and handed one to her friend as she sat back down. "Maybe you could—"

Dawn shoved through the door. "Man, now I understand why Gwen likes sitting close to the bathroom." She narrowed her eyes at them. "Everything okay in here?"

"Are you kidding? Everything is awesome! You're going to be a mommy." Christina hopped up and wrapped Dawn in a hug and, over her shoulder, she gave Emily a small smile.

WHAT THE HELL *are they doing in there?* He sat at the bar, staring into the large mirror in front of him. Reflected in the gaps between the bottles, he watched Emily's table and the short hallway leading to the bathrooms and back exit.

If Emily hadn't gone after her friend, he might've been able to make his move on the blond tonight. He could've grabbed her, taken her out the back door and driven off. By the time someone went to check on her, they could've been on their way to his special place in the woods.

"You're wasting your time."

He started at the sound of the bartender's voice. *Shit.* The guy moved like a fucking ghost.

"I was just—"

"You've been staring at that table since you sat down." He tilted his head toward Emily's group.

"Well, ya have to admit, they're a pretty eye-catchin' bunch." He tapped a can of chew against his palm. Tonight, he was Mutt, an auto mechanic with a thick beard and mustache and what looked like a broken nose. A blue work shirt with grease on the front struggled to contain a pot belly that hung over the waistband of his worn black jeans. A pair of wide, red suspenders was the only thing keeping them from dropping to the floor. The scuffed boots, brown eyes and brown hair underneath a trucker-style hat were his own.

The big guy with the sharp eyes rested his hands wide apart on the edge of the bar. Muscles bunched under the short sleeves of his T-shirt when he leaned in close.

"Let me give you a little advice …" His eyes dropped to the name on his shirt pocket, then back up. "Mutt. Unless you want hell to rain down on you, I suggest you focus your attention elsewhere."

"Sorry, man." He held up his hands. "I didn't mean to encroach on anyone's territory. I was merely enjoyin' the view."

The testy bartender straightened, then dropped the bill on the counter.

"Guess that's my cue." He downed the last swig of his beer, tugged some cash from his pocket and tossed a few bills on the counter.

"Have a good evenin'." He slid off the stool and headed for the door.

Even though he could practically feel the guy's eyes burning holes in his back, he risked a quick sideways glance just as Emily and the blond returned to the table and sat down.

His heart pounded in his ears as adrenaline surged through his system. He shoved open the door and took a deep breath of the crisp, night air. Keys jingled where they hung from his hand, and his boots crunched over the gravel parking lot on his way to the sidewalk. He'd parked down the street, behind a large, metal recycling container.

He climbed in, rolled the windows down and took some deep breaths.

Tonight was the first time he'd ever actually risked going inside the pub. Before, he'd waited and watched from the woods across the street.

Thursday was ladies' night, and that was when they typically showed up. Not every week, but at least once a month. One night, he'd even managed to follow Emily home.

She was pretty aware of her surroundings, so it had been tricky. When the time came to grab her, it wouldn't be easy. He'd ruled out snatching either of the two women from out of town, as well as the tall one with the short hair who carried a knife at her waist. She looked deadly as hell, and he didn't want to risk tangling with her. That left Christina. Emily's best friend and the easiest one to get to.

CHAPTER TWENTY-THREE

"What do you mean, there was a mix-up with the DNA samples?" Jonathan's voice maintained its usual calm as he spoke to the lab supervisor. He was using the speakerphone console in the middle of the table so the whole team could hear.

"It seems that ... well ... um ..." The supervisor cleared his throat. "Apparently, the wrong samples were tested."

The medical examiner found skin cells under Sandy's fingernails. He also discovered trace amounts of propofol in her system. She must've gotten a last, good swipe at her killer before she succumbed to the drug, because once it was injected, she would've been unconscious within fifteen to thirty seconds.

This could be a major break in the case, because the killer was always so careful not to leave any evidence behind. Their guess was, he never thought she would be found. At least, not so quickly.

Jonathan scrubbed his hand down his face and shook his head.

"Where are the correct samples? And you'd better not tell me they're lost."

"Oh, no, sir. They're not lost." A collective sigh of relief circled the room. "We have them here in the lab, and we've been ordered to expedite testing. Which has already begun, by the way," he rushed to say.

Jonathan scribbled a few notes on a notepad. "When can we expect the results?"

"Unfortunately, it's going to take a few days to test the sample. Once we've done that, we can run it through CODIS to see if we find a match."

DNA is maintained at the national, state and local levels, each with its own DNA indexing system. Fortunately, the Combined DNA Index System software, CODIS, integrates and connects all three of these systems. Otherwise, it could take weeks, months even, to contact every local and state lab throughout the entire country.

"Your lab received those samples twenty-three days ago. And now you're telling me we're back to square one. Is that correct?"

They all waited.

"With regard to the DNA testing, yes." The scientist's voice quavered. "I'm sorry."

Mason's teammates uttered a colorful mixture of groans and expletives. He turned to Emily, and she looked like she wanted to hit something ... or someone.

"You're sorry? Do you have any idea how badly you've fucked this up? You are aware there is a killer out there, very likely preparing to grab his next victim, aren't you?"

"Yes, sir. Mr. Burke contacted me earlier and made sure I understood completely."

Jonathan pushed up from his chair, flattened his hands on the table and leaned close to the speaker. "I want those results within forty-eight hours, or I'll see to it that your lab is shut down. Permanently." He pressed the *end call* button, and a muscle in his jaw bulged.

Mason and everyone else in the room shared his anger and frustration. They were all hyper-aware that the longer the killer was out there, the closer he got to Emily.

"This is exactly why Beck is working on getting OSI its own lab." Jonathan straightened. "He's already recruited Dr. Beatrice Parker, one of the world's leading forensic pathologists, to help get it up and operational. Her expertise will be an invaluable asset to OSI."

Leather squeaked as he lowered himself into the chair at the head of the table. "Andi, can you update us on what you've learned about the Last Will and Testament Killer?"

"Certainly. To avoid confusion, I'll be referring to the original killer as the LWT killer." She flipped open a manila folder.

"First, there are seven phases of serial murder." She ticked them off with her fingers. "Aura, Trolling, Wooing, Capture, Murder, Totem and, finally, Depression. I won't get into the details of each, because we don't have that kind of time. But I will be referencing a couple of them in a minute."

She clicked the remote to turn on the large screen, and a bullet-pointed list appeared. "I've put together a list of the inconsistencies between the eight original cases and our two. These are important to note because serial killers rarely stray from their patterns—they're part of the addiction. And yes, killing is an addiction for them."

The slide on the screen changed, and two familiar documents appeared side by side.

"The first thing is the wills. The one on the left is from one of the old cases; the one on the right is Pamela's. As you can see, the differences are quite obvious."

Andi stood and moved to the screen.

"The wills in the older cases were typed, like this one."

Her finger dragged across the screen. "Sandy and Pamela's were handwritten. We know from the handwriting and linguistic analyst that our victims' wills were written in their own words, by their own hand. The LWT killer's victims were written using legalese and were even formatted like a legal document." She pointed to the numbers running down the left margin of the older will.

"So the LWT killer had at least a basic understanding of the law. Can we safely assume he was a law student or law professor, maybe a lawyer or paralegal?" Mathias stared at the screen as he asked the question.

"Yes, I think that would be a good place to start. Another big difference between the older cases and ours is the type of victim." The wills disappeared, and photos of Sandy, Pamela, and the other eight victims popped up on the screen. "The LWT killer's victims were all attractive, had long blond hair and blue eyes, and were between twenty-three and twenty-seven years old." She pointed from the youngest to the oldest.

"As you can see, Sandy and Pamela look nothing like the other women. Another interesting disparity is, the original victims were all engaged at the time of their murders. Pamela wasn't engaged yet, and Sandy was married. The most telling difference, however, was the condition of their remains when they were found."

She moved closer to Emily, rested her hand on her shoulder and quietly asked, "You good?"

"I'm good, thanks." She shifted in her chair, and her shoulders drew back slightly.

"What I'm about to cover falls under the Totem phase. In a nutshell, this is the period immediately after they've killed. Whatever triumph the killer felt rapidly begins to fade, pushing them into the Depression phase. To prolong the high and the power they feel from the murder, they will do unspeakable things to their victims' bodies."

"This wasn't the case with Sandy and Pamela though, right?" Emily asked hopefully.

"Correct." Andi gave her a last look before she displayed the crime scene photos of the LWT killer's victims. "All eight of the original victims were missing the ring finger of their left hand, and their engagement rings were never found. All their hair had been cut off, and it was never found either."

Mason reached over and covered Emily's cold hands with one of his own. She turned one over and threaded her fingers with his.

"It's suspected that the LWT killer kept copies of their wills, also. Those, along with the fingers, engagement rings and the hair, are what experts would classify as totems, or trophies." She clicked the remote, and the screen went dark.

As one, the entire group around the table seemed to relax back into their chairs. No one ever got used to seeing the atrocities one human could inflict upon another.

"The things done to these poor women are tame when compared to what other serial killers have done to their victims. Both pre- and post-mortem," she added.

"What do these experts say is the reason for keeping totems?" Killian liked people to think he was a chill guy with only women on his mind. Not even close. He had amazing instincts and a level of street smarts that surpassed any of the other O'Hallerans. Which was saying a lot.

"According to the FBI profiler's notes in the case file, the murderer hopes that by keeping a piece of their victim, they will be able to experience the same feelings of power and glory they achieved at the moment he or she killed them. When that inevitably doesn't work—and it never does—they slip into the Depression phase and are driven to kill again. Thus, repeating the cycle." Andi returned to her seat next to her husband. He reached over, stroked his hand down her arm and left it there. She gave him a small, reassuring nod.

No matter how tough you were—and Andi was one of the toughest—an investigation like this one exacted a high emotional toll on the people working it.

"It's likely our perp is an obsessed fan of the LWT killer, and this is his fucked-up way of paying homage to him. He would have no way of knowing about the missing fingers and rings, copies of the wills, and that the original killer's victims were already dead when he buried them. These details were never released to the public." She set the remote on the table.

"So, what happens now?" Emily looked around the table. "I mean, now that we know it's not the LWT killer?"

"We'll deal with the LWT killer later. Right now, we focus on this investigation. We widen our search of people to question, and we cross our fingers that once they get the DNA tests done, there's a match in the system. If our perp has never been arrested or wasn't military, it could be a dead end," Jonathan said.

"I'll conduct follow-up interviews with some folks to see if they remember anything new." Andi flipped the file shut. "Oftentimes, right after someone has experienced a great loss, their minds are ... closed, for lack of a better term. Maybe I can coax some new information from them. Sometimes it's the little things we don't think about that can make a huge difference."

Jonathan's wife was one of the world's leading authorities on interviewing techniques, with a near perfect success rate. She'd worked on the front lines in Afghanistan for almost four years, conducting interviews of captured terrorists. Thanks to the intel she gathered, there were a few thousand U.S. and allied forces still alive today.

"Golden, meet me in my office in ten minutes. I've got a special assignment for you," Jonathan instructed.

"Yes, sir," Golden replied in his typical respectful manner.

"I think I might have something else." Emily flipped some

pages in a little spiral notepad. "I remembered Professor Tompkins saying something about Pamela and Sandy bringing him his favorite coffee. So I called and asked him if he knew where they bought it."

She checked her notes. "They both went to Brewed Awakenings. He said he remembered because he thought the name was clever. It's a little free-standing, walk-up coffee kiosk on the campus. Here's the thing: They actually have a small surveillance camera. It's focused on the tables and chairs set up out front for their customers. Pamela mentioned to some friends that a guy had been following her. Maybe someone at the shop will remember something. Or, better yet, maybe they caught him on camera."

"Did they mention how long they maintained their recordings?" Mason asked.

"It's digital and uploads to a cloud. When I asked how much storage they had, the owner was embarrassed to admit she had no idea. Apparently, her husband set it up for her and she never really gives it much thought."

Jonathan looked to the other end of the table. "Mathias and Killian, you two head down there and see what you can find out. Take photos of Pamela and Sandy with you. Also, grab an empty thumb drive and see if you can get a copy of their surveillance video. If they give you any grief, tell them you'll be back with a warrant. That usually convinces folks to cooperate."

"Great work, Emily." Pride imbued Jonathan's voice as he smiled down at her.

Andi gave her shoulder a playful shove. "Look at you, being all investigatory."

"Awesome, sis," Killian and Mathias added at the same time.

Golden gave her a big thumbs-up.

"Thanks." A warm coral color flushed her cheeks, and she busied herself with gathering her things from the table.

"Emily and I will head up to the site where they found Sandy." Mason turned to her. "Unless you'd rather not go."

"I'm going." Yeah, he figured.

"Take your helicopter. I'd prefer to have you back here before nightfall." What Jonathan really meant was, he wanted his sister close.

"No problem." Mason couldn't blame him. He wanted her close, too, but for reasons beyond just her safety.

"Okay, folks. Let's keep charging forward. The DNA is just one element of this investigation." He reached out for Andi's hand and twined his fingers with her. "That'll be all."

Emily and Mason hung back as everyone bustled out of the room.

"It's going to take me about thirty minutes to get the bird ready. Does that give you enough time to do whatever you need to do?"

"You kidding? I'm ready now." She hopped up from her chair. "Let's go."

CHAPTER TWENTY-FOUR

Emily stood on the tarmac at OSI's section of the regional airstrip, hand across her brow, shielding her eyes from the sun as she watched Mason run through his preflight check. He had on worn blue jeans and a black T-shirt that hugged against his chest, shoulders and arms yet hung loose around his narrow waist. The black, felt cowboy hat he wore wasn't just for show. It had a sweat stain around the band and fit his head like only a well-worn hat could. Add the mirrored aviator glasses and the way he moved around the helicopter with such confidence ... *Be still my heart.* Watching him drag his hand over the sleek, black fuselage sent all kinds of sensual images through her mind.

The Bell 412 was the same chopper he'd flown during the operation to rescue Gwen. That was before Mason even worked for OSI. Heck, OSI hadn't even been created yet. Back then, he'd just been a noble guy, doing a favor for a friend. He'd done the same for Caleb, when OSI went in after Dawn and Luna, and it had almost cost him his life.

Memories of that horrible time still managed to shake her to the core.

It had been around eleven thirty at night. She was brushing her teeth before going to bed when she heard her cell phone ringing on her nightstand. It was her dad letting her know he was at her front door. Since he was an early to bed, early to rise kinda guy, she knew something was wrong. She rushed to let him in, and the instant she saw the look on his face, her suspicions were confirmed. He took her hand and led her to the couch. Sitting next to her, his mammoth, work-roughened hand engulfing hers, he broke the news that Mason had been shot and that it was serious. It was as if all the air had been sucked from the room. Everything came to a screeching halt. Every sight, every sound, every breath. How could she possibly live in a world without Mason Croft in it?

Beck had arranged for a private jet to fly them to Kalispell, Montana, where Mason was undergoing surgery. One of the OSI guys picked them up at the airport, and the second he rolled to a stop at the front entrance of the hospital, Emily jumped out of the SUV and ran inside, leaving her purse and her parents behind. She flew past the volunteer sitting at the information desk calling out to her, skipped the elevators and headed straight for the stairs. She took them two at a time until she burst out onto the third-floor surgical unit. Then, for several long, agonizing hours, she waited with her family. Emily moved from her spot on the uncomfortable sofa to look down the hall so many times, her father said she'd wear a path in the floor.

Finally, *finally,* the doctor had come out to tell them it had been touch and go—*why do they always say it that way*—and that they'd almost lost him once. Bottom line, he was strong and the doctor had every confidence he'd pull through.

Emily's first question had been, "When can I see him?" And she'd sat at his bedside for several days. She was so determined to stay past visiting hours that Mason's doctor made an exception. No way was she leaving him until she knew he was really okay. To this day, she wasn't even sure he remembered her being there, and she never said anything to him about it. He'd already made his position about the two of them very clear. Why complicate things?

"Almost done here." Mason's voice snapped her back to the here and now as he moved from the other side of the helicopter.

He reached up and ran his hand along one of the long blades. The visual reminder of how strong, healthy and vibrantly alive he was helped chase away the painful memories.

She stood on her tippy-toes, cupped her hand on the window and peeked in at the cockpit.

"Holy moly, that's a lot of buttons and switches and dials and stuff." She turned to look at him. "You sure you know what all those doohickeys are for?"

Mason's hand stopped halfway to a panel next to the door, and he looked at her. "Doohickeys?"

She shrugged.

"Yes, I know what all those *doohickeys* are for." He chuckled and popped open a small compartment on the side, looked in, then closed it and turned the small metal latch to secure it.

"Okay, we're good to go." He turned the handle on the door on the left side and opened it, then gave a slight bow. "Your chariot awaits, milady."

She hesitated, chewed the inside of her cheek. Her stomach tumbled with a combination of nerves and excitement. Nerves, because she'd never been up in a helicopter before, and excitement because she would finally get to see Mason fly.

"You okay?" He stepped closer, dragged his sunglasses off and searched her expression.

"This is my first time in a helicopter." Emily had heard he

was one of the best pilots around. For that and many other reasons, she had complete faith in his abilities.

She reached up and gripped the strap by the door, but before she could pull herself up, Mason grabbed her by the waist and lifted her into the seat like she weighed nothing.

"I'm happy to be your first, Emily." He winked before he slipped on his glasses, then shut the door and circled around and climbed in on the other side.

Mason checked to ensure her harness was secure, then grabbed a headset and handed it to her. As she adjusted hers to fit, his slight twang filled her ears.

"You ready, darlin'?"

"Absolutely!" Her excitement reflected back at her from his mirrored lenses, and she spread her clammy palms over her thighs.

He flipped some switches and pressed a bunch of buttons, then the big engine fired up with a low whine. The long blades slowly began to rotate and, as the whining pitched higher, the blades sped up and the vibration reverberated throughout the helicopter. He pulled on the stick thingy and they lifted off the ground. The nose dipped slightly downward but leveled off as they started forward.

In her excitement, she let loose an involuntary, "Holy moly!"

"Quite the rush, huh?" Mason turned and smiled at her, then focused front again. "It never gets old."

It took a minute for her stomach to catch up, but once it did, she sat back and enjoyed the flight. For the next forty-five minutes, they flew over the dark, choppy waters of Puget Sound. He pointed out Fort Worden Historical Park near Port Townsend and Discovery Bay. From the air, the Olympic National Park was even more breathtaking. A sudden chill inched down her spine, as if the thickly wooded and mountainous terrain sent up icy fingers of warning—*death awaits*.

A long, rectangular, grassy clearing appeared ahead of them. Mason made a slight shift with his hand on the stick, and they swooped down over the tree tops.

Two men stood under the awning in front of a large hangar. One was tall with a bushy, dark brown beard and mustache. The other had the same basic look, only he was much shorter. They wore black tactical pants and button-up, tan short-sleeved shirts with the distinctive green and yellow U.S. Forest Service patch stitched to one sleeve.

There were two additional large, metal buildings, next to a smaller one that appeared to be the administration building. *U.S. Forest Service – Aviation* was printed on a wooden sign near the front door.

The men lowered their heads and held on to their hats. The wind from the long rotors sent grass and dirt swirling as Mason lowered the helicopter into a gentle landing.

As soon as the skids touched down, he started flipping switches overhead, pressed a couple of buttons in front of him, and the engine quieted as the chopping of the long blades began to slow. Emily followed his lead and pulled off her headset and unclipped her harness.

He turned to her with a questioning look. "Well? How did you like your first helicopter ride?"

"Are you kidding me? I loved it! It was so ... freeing!" Without thinking, she leaned across and threw her arms around him. "Thank you, Mason."

"You're welcome, Em." His hold on her tightened when she tried to pull free.

Over his shoulder, she saw the men jogging toward them, ducking as they approached the helicopter. Emily relinquished her hold, and Mason curled his hand around the back of her neck and pulled her in for a soft kiss. He slowly drew back, gave her a quick wink, then hopped out and shook hands with the taller guy.

She blinked a couple of times, stunned by what had just happened. All day, it seemed like he'd been finding reasons to touch her. Not that she was complaining. Still feeling the warmth of Mason's lips against hers, she jumped down and joined the three men.

He took her hand and drew her closer. "Em, this is Chet Rutley. He runs this station. Chet, this is Emily O'Halleran."

"Nice to meet you Ms. O'Halleran." He turned to his co-worker. "This is Butch. He's one of our park rangers, but he's also the genius who keeps all our birds in the sky."

"Ma'am." Butch actually tipped his hat to her.

"Emily, please. It's a pleasure to meet you both." She shook their hands, then turned in a slow circle, taking in the massive trees surrounding the airstrip. "Wow. You are really tucked away in here, aren't you?"

"The Olympic National Park is close to fifteen hundred square miles of land. Our job is to sustain the health, diversity and productivity of the nation's forests and grasslands. Being close in like this makes it easier for us to accomplish that." Pride radiated through Chet's words.

"Sounds like you love your work." Emily couldn't begin to imagine the mammoth effort it took to manage a park this size. Heck, she had a hard time keeping a house plant alive.

"Wouldn't do anything else." Chet pulled a map from his back pocket, unfolded it and pointed out two areas circled in red. "Okay, the burial sites are here and here. We cleared out a bunch of undergrowth right after they were found, but nature has a way of reclaiming things pretty quickly. I've sketched in some landmarks to help you pinpoint their location. ATV's over there. Helmets are in the back." He tossed a key to Mason and tipped up his chin toward the end of the hangar.

The side-by-side all-terrain vehicle was similar to the ones her parents kept at their place.

"Let me grab my pack and we'll head out." Mason slid open the side door of the helicopter, grabbed a large backpack, then dragged it shut.

"Hang on. I've got a couple of satellite radios on the charging station for you to use." Butch jogged inside and reappeared a moment later with what looked like walkie-talkies. He adjusted the settings, then handed one to Emily, the other to Mason, and they clipped them on their belts.

"Cell coverage can be pretty spotty up here. Those have GPS locators in them and are tuned to the Forest Service's frequency." He tucked his hands in his back pockets. "You'll be able to communicate directly with us and vice versa."

"Excellent. Thanks so much for your assistance, guys." Mason shook their hands again, as did Emily.

"Here, Em. You might want to put this on before we get going." As they walked, Mason tugged a big OSI hoodie from his pack and handed it to her. "It can get a bit chilly in those thick woods."

"What about you?" she asked and took a deep breath through her nose as she pulled it over her head. *Hoo boy*, it smelled just like Mason. It hung almost to her knees, and she had to roll up the sleeves several times.

"I've got another one." Mason slung his backpack over one shoulder.

The ATV was parked under a small overhang. Dried mud covered the side, and the vinyl upholstery of the driver's seat had pulled apart along the seam on one side. It wasn't much to look at, but they were enclosed in a protective cage with a sturdy roll bar, and their helmets were top-of-the-line.

Mason gave her knee a small squeeze. "You ready?"

Emily took a deep breath. "Ready." *As I'll ever be.*

The knobby tires gained purchase on the grass, and they headed into the woods. The airstrip and bright sunshine disappeared behind them as they were enveloped by the thick forest. They navigated over and around large tree roots carving across the path, testing the springs of their seats each time they bounced up and down and jolted side to side. Mud splashed, adding to the layers already there. By the time they arrived, Emily was more than ready to get out of the ATV and stretch her legs.

"According to this, we should be near the site where they found Sandy." Mason looked up from the map and scanned the area.

"What exactly are we looking for, anyway?" she asked.

"Nothing specific, really. Sometimes it helps to walk where the killer walked." His head slowly pivoted from left to right, taking in the entire area. "To experience what he experienced hiking up here. What was going through his mind? What was he feeling mentally, emotionally, physically?"

"That's the thing I can't figure out. How in the heck did he get the coffins up here without anyone seeing or hearing him? And then he comes back at least two more times with their bodies. Wouldn't he be worried about getting caught?" Emily took a few careful steps away from the ATV and pushed back branches from a bush and looked underneath.

"Andi worked with a profiler in the bureau's Behavioral Analysis Unit. Their assessment was that our killer definitely suffers from antisocial personality disorder." She gave him a questioning look. "Medical jargon for a psychopath. He's a methodical planner with a huge ego who thinks he's smarter than everyone else. A guy like that isn't worried about anything."

"I'll go this way. You look around over that way." Mason started toward the left and indicated for her to go to the right. "Make sure you can see me and that I can see you."

"Will do." She moved toward a thick patch of underbrush.

It was slightly darker, this deep in the woods, and a thin fog stole over the ground like a sheer veil of malevolence.

Errant drops of water dripped from trees high overhead. Emily would be lying if she said she wasn't a little spooked.

Something caught her attention on the other side of the small clearing. A twig snapped beneath her foot as she carefully stepped over a large fern. She held back the branch of a tree and stopped short.

"Mason," she called out as she stared at the small strip of yellow crime-scene tape dangling from where it had been tied around a tall cedar tree.

His quick steps crunched over the forest floor until he was shoulder to shoulder with her. He reached across and wrapped his fingers around the garish strip of plastic, gave it a sharp tug until it snapped, then tucked it in his pocket. It didn't belong in this place any more than Sandy or Pamela had.

Her gaze skimmed the ground, and she noticed remnants of bright orange spray paint in the shape of a large rectangle. Tiny purple wildflowers sprinkled the area, and a few bright green saplings had sprung up here and there. Snakelike vines from a blackberry bush laden with plump berries slithered along the ground, having rooted themselves into the rich, freshly-turned soil.

Mother Nature was already hard at work healing the scars left behind by evil.

Emily dropped to her knees, sat back on her heels and spread her fingers wide on the ground. Chin to her chest, she closed her eyes, and a tear tracked down her cheek.

CHAPTER TWENTY-FIVE

Mason's heart cracked wide open. He sat down next to her, scooped her up and set her in his lap. She twisted to face him and pressed her cold nose against his neck. With a desperation he'd never seen from her before, she drew her knees up, threw her arms around his neck and sobbed.

Rather than try to soften her anguish with useless words, he simply held her close, giving her a safe place to purge the sadness from her soul. He forever wanted to be Emily's safe place.

The soft sounds of her sorrow accompanied the whispers of wind rustling through the lofty trees, their needles sprinkling on the ground. Squirrels chattered and knocked loose a large pine cone as they chased each other from branch to branch. A bright crimson cardinal settled on the ground about ten feet in front of them. It called out with a low, looping whistle, fluttered its wings, then settled.

Emily quieted, then lifted her head. She swiped the sleeve of his hoodie across her eyes and stared at the bird.

"They say that when a cardinal appears, it's a visitor from heaven." She sniffled, settled her head against his chest and continued watching the bird as it groomed itself, not the least bit daunted by their presence.

For a few, wonderful, peace-filled moments, they watched it hop from spot to spot, pecking at the ground, shifting debris side to side with its beak to capture a tasty morsel.

"Thank you," she whispered.

"For what?" He tucked his chin to look down at her.

"For ... I don't know, letting me bawl all over you like a baby?" Her small hand rested on his chest, stroking gentle circles over his heart. He wasn't even sure she realized she was doing it.

"Listen to me, Emily. Crying doesn't make you a baby or weak or any of those other things I know are floating around in that magnificent brain of yours. You have every right to be sad, and I don't ever want you to feel like you have to hide that side of yourself from me." He ran his fingers through her silky hair; his fingertips massaged her scalp.

"Mason, I ..." She hesitated, and Emily never hesitated.

"What?" He searched her green eyes and waited.

"Never mind." Her chest expanded on a deep sigh and she sat up. "I guess we should finish what we came here for."

He didn't pressure her to continue. Instead, he kissed the top of her head and, in one fluid motion, stood with her in his arms.

She rolled her eyes. "Show-off."

Maybe a little. Then, with agonizing accuracy, her body slid down his front until her feet were firmly on the ground.

Mason tucked a wisp of hair over her ear. Her cheeks and nose were pink from a combination of the cooler temp in the shade of the trees and crying. Her eyes had taken on the mossy green hue of the surrounding foliage. He picked a pine needle from her hair and tossed it away, then stepped back from temptation.

"I'll do a bit more snooping around here, and you can check around over there." She brushed the dirt and debris from the knees of her jeans.

For another thirty minutes, they continued looking for anything that didn't belong. Mason stepped on something. He looked down, lifted his foot and exposed a good-size rock —about six to eight inches in diameter. He wedged the toe of his boot under it and flipped it over. Scant sunlight peeked through the trees and glinted off something. He crouched down and carefully dusted the dirt away, exposing a small hunk of silver.

"Emily, can you please grab one of those small plastic evidence bags from the ATV for me?" He took a quick picture of it with his phone and checked the area but didn't see anything else of interest.

She ran over, popped open the bag and handed it to him. "What did you find?"

"Thanks." He looked around and picked up a leaf, then used it to gently scoop the object into the bag. He rose as he sealed the bag and held it up for Emily to see.

"What the heck is that?" She looked closely, then her eyes widened. "Oh my gosh. Is that what I think it is?"

"If you're thinking it's part of a crown from someone's tooth, then yep, that's exactly what it is." Excitement practically pulsed off her as she followed him to the ATV, where he secured the bag in his backpack.

"I don't remember reading anything in the autopsy report about Sandy losing a crown." Her eyes lit up. "That means it has to belong to the killer."

"I think we've done all we can here. Let's go check out the other site, then we'll head home." Mason handed her a helmet.

After a last long look around, he waited as Emily made a vow to her friend. "We'll find who did this to you, Sandy. I promise." Then she climbed into the ATV, and they headed deeper into the woods.

CHAPTER TWENTY-SIX

"What do you mean, you're staying here?" Emily dropped her keys on the kitchen counter and hung her bag over the back of a chair.

Gary yowled and wove his body through their legs, extremely put out that they weren't giving him their undivided attention.

"I mean I'm staying here." He reached down and picked up the cat. "Hey, buddy. You want some lovin'?"

Emily resisted throwing her hand in the air and shouting, *"I do! I do!"*

"And why, exactly, are you staying here?" He had a perfectly good place of his own. And she needed space to regroup after spending an entire day with the man she was cuckoo over but could never have.

"Your brothers and I agreed that, until we find who's doing this, it makes sense for me to stick close to you." He scratched under Gary's chin. The cat looked up at him with unabashed adoration.

"You and my ..." Her jaw clenched so tight, she thought it might freeze that way. "So let me get this straight. You and my loving brothers got together and made this decision without even consulting me. Is that about right?"

"That's right." He looked down at Gary, then back at her. "Do you disagree that it makes sense for you to have someone watching your back?"

"Of course, I don't disagree. It's the way you all went about it that ticks me off." She snatched her cat from his arms. "You know how I feel about them making decisions for me, then you went and did the same thing. I wasn't even given the courtesy of being part of a conversation that directly affects me."

"Shit." He gripped the back of his neck, making his ridiculous bicep bulge. "You're right, Em. I'm sorry. We should've included you in that discussion. I can assure you, it wasn't intentional. After we got back from the burial sites, I needed to hit the heavy bag for a bit. Jonathan and the twins came in, and I told them about what we found. They asked how you were. One thing led to another ..."

Emily could certainly understand his urge to hit something after spending the afternoon where two young, vital women had spent their last, lonely moments. Which brought into clear focus why it was smart to have someone staying here. She just wasn't sure how she felt about that *someone* being him.

"Fine." She would just have to pretend he wasn't there. "You can stay in the guest room. I just need to put clean sheets on the bed."

"Not necessary. I won't be sleeping in the guest room." His fingertip brushed her forehead as he skimmed across her cheekbone.

"You won't?" She swallowed past the cotton that seemed to have lodged in her throat, her heart raced, and her belly fluttered.

"No, I'll sleep on the couch. That way I'll have an unobstructed view of the front door and the French doors." He tipped his chin toward the set of doors on the opposite side of the large, main space.

Well, that's a bummer.

Emily set Gary down and turned to grab his food from the fridge.

"Oh, well, if that's what you want." *What the heck did you think he meant?* She gave herself an internal scolding to clear her lust-fogged brain. Many nights she'd awakened all hot and bothered from incredibly detailed dreams of Mason spending the night. This wasn't exactly what she had in mind.

"That's not even close to what I want, Em." Her breath caught when his big hands slid around her waist to cover her entire midsection. His heat enveloped her and seeped into her bones.

"What I want is to scoop you up, carry you back to your room, and make love to you all damn night." His warm breath whispered across the shell of her ear.

Emily's heart skipped at least two beats, and she gave herself a few seconds to ensure she hadn't imagined the need in his voice.

"Mason, what are—" She turned in his arms.

"Listen, Em." His hands traveled a slow journey up her back, skimmed the sensitive skin along the sides of her throat and framed her face. "I thought that if I ignored the way I felt about you, it would go away. That you would go back to just being my best friend's little sister. I was wrong. But here's the thing. You're amazing and smart and I don't deserve y—"

She thumped him on the chest.

"What was that for?" He held her hand against his chest and rubbed his thumb across her knuckles.

"Because you were about to say something stupid like how you don't deserve me." She stood on tippy-toe in an attempt to bring herself face-to-face with him but came up short. "I couldn't let you do that because it's just not true."

Emily decided it was time for some tough love.

"Mason, do you know that you always keep yourself at a distance from everyone? Oh, sure, you and Caleb are best friends, and you love our family, but you always exist on the periphery, watching, never letting yourself get too close." *Physically and emotionally.* "Why?"

His hands fell away, and he stepped back from her. A sense of loss washed over her. She'd gotten too close, pushed too hard.

"You know what? Never mind." She lifted her hand. "It's obviously none of my business."

CHAPTER TWENTY-SEVEN

"I never knew my dad, and my mom was a drug addict and alcoholic." Mason leaned back against the counter, his hands gripped tight to the edge, trying hard to look like sharing the ugliness of his past with the woman he loved wasn't one of the most difficult things he'd ever done.

Emily began to close the space between them, and he automatically reached out, took her hand and pulled her to stand between his legs. He locked his fingers together against the small of her back. Loving how she leaned into him. Never wanting to let her go.

"My mother was popular with the men in town. And some just passing through town." He scoffed and shook his head. "Anyway, one day she discovered she was pregnant but had no idea who the father was. Hell, half the time she didn't even know what day of the week it was."

Emily's arms wrapped around him, and she opened her hands against his back before placing the sweetest kiss to the center of his chest.

He combed his fingers through her silky hair to calm himself as he spoke.

"The whole damn town knew I was the result of one of her many hookups. Vera May Croft's bastard kid, ya know? As far back as I can remember, I was the object of much discussion and derision because of something I had zero control over." Mason sighed and kissed the top of her head. He inhaled her soft scent, which kept him grounded in the present.

"I spent my entire childhood trying to make up for her shitty choices. Didn't matter how hard I worked to make good grades, to be a better person and lead a better life, there were always those determined to keep me down. To keep me *in my place.*" One of them had been the local sheriff, who always seemed to have had a hard-on for Mason. Years later, he found out why. Seems the crooked sheriff with the black eyes and itchy trigger finger had been one of dear old mom's regulars. He wanted to make sure his God-fearing wife and four perfect children, not to mention the rest of the town's upstanding citizens, never found out about his … indiscretions.

"Are you kidding me? How dare they treat you that way. You were just a kid, and they were the adults." Her entire body tensed with outrage on his behalf.

From her tone, he thought she might try to head down there and take on every single person she thought had wronged him.

God, how he loved this little bundle of explosive indignation.

Her voice softened. "Whatever happened to your mom?"

"Vera died a few years back." Mason had stopped calling her *Mom* the night she picked one of her boyfriends over her twelve-year-old son. "Not that she ever really lived."

"I probably shouldn't feel sorry for her, but I do." Her hands coasted up and down his back.

Of course, she did. That big heart of hers might get her in trouble one day.

"Don't waste your pity on her, Em. She had ample opportunities to change her circumstances. But she was lazy and chose to live her life that way." He'd scraped together enough money to send her to rehab twice. Both times, she'd bailed and gone straight to her dealer.

"Even with all of those awful circumstances and the horrible people working against you, you still managed to become this accomplished, wonderful guy. Most people would've taken a much darker path."

"Most people weren't lucky enough to meet Hank." Mason smiled, more than happy to move on to the subject of his old friend. "He's grouchy, gruff and most definitely suffers from undiagnosed PTSD. But he is honest, fair and tolerates zero bullshit. And, without a doubt, he is the best pilot I've ever known. And I've known quite a few."

Emily put her chin to his chest and smiled up at him. He stroked her hair back over her shoulder and kissed her forehead.

"Is Hank the one who taught you so much about planes and helicopters and stuff?"

"I learned everything I know about flying from him. Thanks to Hank, I had a place to escape to when things got too bad at home."

Considering the revolving door of boyfriends his mother had, he'd spent most of the time he wasn't in school hanging out at Hank's airfield. But she didn't need to know about that.

"I think I would like Hank, especially since he took such good care of you. Where is he now?" she asked.

"Hank would love you, darlin'." What man didn't appreciate a beautiful woman with a huge heart? "He doesn't trust anyone enough to leave them in charge of his field. But you'll meet him someday."

Mason couldn't wait to introduce her to him. He could practically hear Hank's growly voice. "*Ya done good, kid.*"

"Then we'll just have to go down there to see him." She looped her arms around his neck, pressing her breasts against him. "I happen to know this amazing guy who also just happens to be a pilot."

"Is that right?" He kissed the tip of her nose.

"Mm-hmm. And if he ever says a negative word about himself again, I just might have to kick his butt." One of her eyebrows rose in challenge. "Are we clear?"

He chuckled. "Yeah, Em, we're clear."

"Good." She started lowering her arms.

He tightened his hold, not wanting to let her go. She was his future, his hope, and he wasn't giving that up. He couldn't.

Mason lowered his head at the same time she rose up to her toes, and their lips met in the middle. Unlike the frenzied kiss they'd shared while tucked away in a dark corner, this one was slow, gliding, exploratory. Her lips were plump and soft and fit against his like they were made for him.

He speared his fingers through her hair, cupped the back of her head and took the kiss deeper. She made a soft whimper and pressed herself closer. He slid his hands down her back, curved them under her ass cheeks and lifted. She jerked her lips away, hopped up and wrapped her legs around his waist, then resumed kissing him.

For several minutes, the world slipped away and it was just the two of them.

"Bedroom. Now," she said against his mouth.

"Yes, ma'am." He was more than happy to comply.

She continued kissing him—one cheek, then the other, his nose, neck—as he carried her through the kitchen, down the hallway and into her bedroom. He used his foot to close the door behind them, turned and pressed her back against it.

Emily skimmed her nose up his neck and took a deep breath. "I love the way you smell, Mason."

"Hold on to me," he growled, then released her ass with one hand to wrap her hair around his fingers with the other. He tilted her head to the side and dragged small biting kisses from the curve where her shoulders met her neck, up the side of her delicate throat to where he licked, then kissed a spot beneath her ear.

She moaned his name and squirmed, pressing her center into him. He'd found one of her sweet spots. He made a mental note; then, hungry for more, he covered her mouth with his. She opened for him without hesitation, and his tongue dove between her lips, where it danced with hers. Soft, warm, wet and unbelievably hot.

Once again, she broke the kiss, reached down and yanked her top over her head and tossed it. Mason had to lock his knees because, *holy hell*, she'd worn a green satin bra that matched her eyes, and it was the sexiest fucking thing he'd ever seen.

He cupped her ass, turned and stomped toward the bed and set her on the edge. He crouched between her knees, splayed his fingers over her thighs and dragged them down to her ankles. He untied her boots, tugged them off, and they dropped with a *clunk* a few feet away. Next, he pulled off her socks and pitched them over his shoulder.

She leaned into him, running her fingers through his hair, kissing him on the temple, the top of his head. It would be distracting if he weren't so hyper-focused on getting her out of her clothes.

Speaking of ... He flattened one hand between her perfect breasts and gently pressed her to the bed.

"Lift." Yep, that *was* a growl.

Her hips rose, and he peeled her jeans down her legs, overjoyed to see that her panties matched her bra.

"I really like these, Em." Mason dragged one finger under the edge of her panties, from hip to hip. "They're pretty, like the woman wearing them."

She sucked in a breath and bit her bottom lip. Her hips wiggled under his touch, and her chest rose and fell with each shallow breath.

"As much as I love them, they're in my way." He hooked a finger under each side and slowly dragged them down just enough so he could lick, then kiss each of her hip bones. He continued sliding them down until they dropped to the floor.

"Mason." His name escaped on a soft breath.

"Bra's next, darlin'." He reached toward the front clasp, but Emily beat him to it.

She scrambled up, nearly kicking him in the chin, and kneeled in the middle of the bed. With quick fingers, she unhooked the front clasp and threw, yes, threw the bra to the opposite side of the room.

"Okay, *darlin'*, your turn." With a cheeky grin, she did a pretty impressive imitation of him.

Mason rose to his full height and stared down at her. Her eyes devoured him as he reached one arm over and grabbed the back of his T-shirt and pulled it over his head. Emily held her hand out and did a sort of *give me, give me* thing with her fingers. Mason complied, and she put it to her face, closed her eyes and inhaled.

Holy fuck. His dick had been hard since she'd stepped into his arms in the kitchen. Now, it threatened to bust through his fly. Time to ditch the jeans before he hurt something.

He unbuckled the belt, popped the buttons and let the whole mess slide to a pile at his feet. A second later, his boxer briefs joined the heap of denim. He stepped out of them and shoved them aside with his foot.

"Ho-ly moly. You're beautiful, Mason." Emily's eyes were wide, and her mouth hung open. Then she grabbed up a couple of handfuls of the comforter and started to cover herself.

"What are you doing?" He tried to pull the blanket away, but she gripped it tight.

"Look at you." One arm held the blanket to her chest. She extended the other, palm up, and waved it up and down in his direction. "You're so ... so ... I can't compete with all *that*."

"What the hell are you talking about?" Women could be so confusing sometimes.

"My body is, well ..." Her chin dropped, and her voice lowered. "My boobs are kinda smallish, and my hips are kinda biggish. And I'm fine with that, whatever. But you're ... geez, you're perfect."

"Okay, now you're just pissing me off." He knee-walked across the bed in all his naked perfection until he was a foot in front of her. "Come here, Emily."

CHAPTER TWENTY-EIGHT

Emily looked up from beneath her lashes, and he crooked his finger at her. She blew out a breath and rose to her knees to face him, unwilling to relinquish her hold on the comforter.

His fingers cradled her chin, and he gently lifted her face to him.

"Em, I don't love you just for your body." His blue eyes remained on hers. "I love you because you make me laugh, you're honest and kind, and you're one of the strongest people I know. You love your family and your friends without limit. And you would do anything to help someone who needs it. Even to your own detriment sometimes. Which, I'll admit, worries me."

Emily couldn't speak, as his words bounced around in her head.

"Did you hear what I said, Emily?"

"You love me?" She smiled and, thanks to the blanket tripping her up, inched forward rather clumsily, closing the scant space between them. Then she placed her hand over his heart.

"Hell, yes, I love you," he said without hesitation, then covered her hand with his and leaned in for a kiss. "Now, can we get rid of this stupid thing so I can see all of you?"

Goosebumps bristled over her skin when his finger dipped between her cleavage.

She took a deep breath and loosened her grip. He gave a gentle tug, and the comforter slid down her body to the bed.

"My God, Emily. You're beautiful." Mason's piercing blue eyes ran the length of her.

He wrapped his arms around her and lowered them to the bed. They lay on their sides, facing each other, and he flattened his hand to her back and dragged her close, tucking her front against him. Breast to chest, hips to hips, their legs entwined, and their hearts beat a powerful rhythm, one against the other.

"Hallelujah," he said on a sigh. "I've wanted to feel you against me since the first moment I saw you."

"You certainly had a weird way of showing it." Emily ran her fingers through the light dusting of hair on his impressive chest. "Until ... well, you know, the kiss, I was sure you only ever saw me as Caleb's kid sister. Which drove me crazy, by the way."

"Trust me, Em, when I look at you, I do not see a kid." He gave her a soft kiss, then turned serious. "And about what I said—that the kiss was a mistake? That was total bullshit. It was fucking amazing, blew my socks off. But it also freaked me out a bit, so I pulled a chickenshit move and hurt you in the process. For that, I'm truly sorry."

"Well, I'm not gonna lie—it wasn't fun hearing that. But I understand now why you did it. You were worried that if we didn't work out, you might lose the only real family you've ever had."

"For whatever reason, your folks accepted me from the beginning, treated me like one of their own kids. I wasn't used to anyone giving a crap about me or my life. Having a family full of buttinskis care so much took some getting used to." He chuckled. "Once I did, I was determined to do whatever it took not to jeopardize their trust in me."

"Including messing with their daughter, or sister," Emily concluded.

"*Especially* that."

"Well, I'm glad you finally pulled your head out of your butt." She kissed his chest again. "Because I've had a thing for you since the first time you came home with Caleb, about four years ago."

"What a coincidence. That's when I fell for you. I was a goner the second I saw you standing in your parents' backyard. You had on this cute little green and white checkered dress with white flip-flops and had your hair pulled up in a high ponytail. You looked so damn young. You were talking a mile a minute to some guy, and your hands were flying around the way they do anytime you tell a story. He laughed at whatever you said, and I instantly wanted to kick his ass."

"You mean Devlin? You were jealous of Devlin?" Emily never thought Mason would be the jealous type. She kinda liked it. "You *do* realize I've known him since we were kids, right? Besides, he's totally hung up on my best friend."

"I figured that out later." He kissed the tip of her nose.

"I can't believe you remember what I was wearing." She shook her head, thinking about all the time they'd wasted.

He rolled over and rested atop her. His chest hair tickled against her, and his forearms framed her head. He stroked his thumbs along her temples.

Emily's legs shifted apart to accommodate his hips, and she sucked in a quiet breath when his hard length pressed against her sensitive center. Her arms encircled him, and she splayed her fingers across his shoulder blades.

"I remember everything about every time I've ever been

near you. I would lie in bed at night, imagining you curled up next to me, and I would get hard. And being in the same room with you and not being able to touch you practically killed me."

"Please tell me this is real," Emily whispered up at him, feeling strangely vulnerable. "That I'm not going to wake up and find out this was all a dream."

"It's a dream come true, Em." As if sensing her inner turmoil, he pressed his lips softly to hers and nibbled his way from corner to corner before slowly lifting them away. "I will always be here for you. Always."

And she believed him. "I love you, Mason."

As they lay in the muted darkness, sharing their feelings in hushed tones, everything within Emily settled.

"And I love you, Emily," he whispered against her lips before stealing her breath with a kiss that was more of an unspoken vow of mutual trust and love. A love that couldn't be denied—no matter how hard they both might have tried.

She whimpered when he broke the kiss, until he lowered his head to her left nipple and those skillful lips of his drew it into his warm mouth. Her back arched for more, and she might've whimpered again. Her fingers burrowed through his hair, holding him in place, and her hips lifted against him, seeking relief from the growing need.

When he shifted his attention to the right nipple, one of his hands tickled down her ribs, skimmed her abdomen until it slipped between her legs, cupping her mound.

"Shit, you're wet for me, Em." He inched one long finger up and down her crease, spreading her slickness as he annoyingly avoided the bundle of nerves pulsing in anticipation of his touch. The man was obviously a monster.

"Mason, please." To hell with her pride. *I want him in me now.*

His head lifted, freeing her nipple with a soft *pop,* and he smiled up at her. "Glad to hear that, but I'm not done playing yet."

Oops. She hadn't meant to say that out loud.

With a twinkle in his eyes, he removed his finger and started inching his way down until his face was directly over her. He pressed her thighs apart and looked at her … *there.* Emily forced herself to be still. No man had ever studied her that way before.

"So pretty." His warm breath puffed against her and, without warning, he flicked her clitoris with the tip of his tongue.

A shock wave of sensation rocketed outward and sparked in every single cell of Emily's body. Her neck arched, and she threw her head back as she cried out. Her body grew taut, and her heels dug into the mattress as she pressed herself against his mouth, desperate for more. The fingers of one hand clenched in his thick hair, the other in the comforter now bunched beneath them.

Mason laid a hand on her lower belly and pressed her back down to the bed. Silently taking charge. A twinge of stubbornness came and went in a flash. Giving up control to him wasn't about relinquishing power. It was about trust. She didn't always have to be strong, to keep her feelings hidden from him. He was her advocate, her safety net. As much as she was his.

He dragged his tongue up and down her sex, dipping inside with a groan of approval, then back up and circling her clitoris. Her heart pounded in her chest, and she lost track of how many times he masterfully elevated her right to the edge of breaking, then brought her slowly back down again.

"Mason, enough playing." She snarled and gave a not-so-gentle tug of his hair. "Up here. Now."

"So bossy." She could feel him smile against her. Then he placed a gentle nip followed by a lick to each inner thigh, trailed kisses up her tummy to suck each nipple, then dipped his tongue into the hollow at the base of her neck and dragged it across her collarbone.

He gave her a quick kiss, then leaned over the side of the bed to grab a condom from his wallet. She'd worry later about why he carried one around.

"I put this in there the day I decided I was done lying to myself. And to you." It was like the man could read her mind. Now that they'd shared their feelings, she found that strangely comforting.

"I'm so glad you did. Quit lying to yourself, I mean. Oh, and that you put the condom there."

"Unfortunately, I only have this one, so—" He tore it open with his teeth and tossed the empty foil packet on the nightstand.

"I guess we'll just have to get creative until we can get some more." She grinned up at him.

"Works for me." He gripped his shaft.

Emily levered up, swatted his hand away and replaced it with her own, and *holy moly*, the man was blessed. She gave a gentle squeeze and one long stroke, then he shifted his hips to pull from her grasp.

"Hey!" She was just getting started.

"I want to be inside you the first time I come," he said as he rolled the condom down his impressive length.

Oh, well, then. When he put it that way ...

Mason pressed her back down to the bed and guided the head of his penis to her opening. With amazing control and gentleness, he entered her inch by amazing inch until he was fully inside her.

Emily moaned long and low, feeling him everywhere.

Mason uttered a drawn-out curse and rested his forehead to hers. "God, Em, you feel so good."

Her need rose steadily as his thickness pulsed inside her. "Mason, I … please." She absolutely could not wait a second longer.

"I love you, Emily." He lowered his head and kissed her as his hips drew back and he drove into her. He wedged his hand beneath her to lift her into him. Again, and again, and still he kissed her.

Emily crossed her ankles behind his back and met him stroke for stroke. She grabbed his tight butt cheeks and held on for her life. Sensations she'd never experienced zipped through her, sending her up and up.

"Let go, Em. I've got you." He looked down at her, love warming the icy blue of his eyes.

Emily cried out his name, and a powerful orgasm sent a series of shock waves pulsing outward from the innermost part of her, a part no one had ever touched before. She couldn't catch her breath. Boundless pleasure flashed and sizzled like sparklers through her bloodstream. Just when she was sure she couldn't take any more, he shifted his hips, bit her earlobe and whispered, "Again."

And just like that, she flew apart like a million stars being created in the galaxy. He was the only thing in her universe, the only thing that mattered.

Mason drove into her three more times and held himself there—deep inside her—and roared her name as he took his own release. He dropped atop her. His back, damp from exertion, rose and fell, and warm puffs of breath blew against her neck. He gave her two soft, open-mouthed kisses, then levered himself up to his elbows and blessed her with the most beautiful and, yes, satisfied smile.

"I am so glad you finally decided to stop being such a

knucklehead." Her fingertips skimmed lazily down the valley in the center of his back.

"Me, too." He gave her a quick kiss, then rolled off the bed and stepped into the bathroom.

Emily stared up at the ceiling, unable and unwilling to conceal the goofy smile on her face. Mason Croft loved her. *Her!* The water shut off, and he stalked back toward the bed. The man was a work of art. Not even the jagged scar on his upper left chest could diminish his beauty.

Mason noticed her looking at it and rubbed his hand over it. "It looks a lot worse than it was."

"We both know that's not true." Her stomach still bottomed out whenever she thought about how close she'd come to losing him.

"Maybe so, but it's all good now. I'm functioning at one hundred percent and am in better shape than I was before." He lay down and pulled her on top of him, then dragged his hand from her butt to her shoulders and back again.

Emily's legs dropped to either side of his hips, and she placed a long kiss to the puckered skin, reassured by the steady strength of his heartbeat beneath her lips.

"I watched you hooked up to all those machines and tubes, fighting so hard to survive and ..." She crossed her arms on his chest and rested her chin there. "I was terrified I would lose you."

"Wait." His hand stopped moving, and he gave her a confused look. "How long were you at the hospital?"

Time to fess up.

"Four days." Some of the darkest, bleakest days of her life. On the crap-o-meter, they ranked right up there with the days after Caleb was shot.

"Four days?"

"The night it happened, Mom, Dad and I to flew into Kalispell on the OSI jet. We were all there, the whole family, waiting for you to come out of surgery. Mom and Dad wouldn't leave until they saw for themselves that you were going to be okay. Once they told us you were out of danger, everyone started heading home. Except Caleb, of course."

The same time her brother's best friend had been fighting for his life, his beloved Dawn was undergoing surgery to repair a shoulder injury that occurred while being held captive.

"And you?" he added. "You stayed?"

"You're darn right I did." No way could she have left him. "They tried to pull the whole *visiting hours* thing, but Jeffrey made one call, *one*"—she held up a finger—"and they relented."

"I remember being shot, and every once in a while, I'll have flashes of being on the compound at The Farm and Caleb and Dawn working on me. Everything after that, until I woke up in the hospital, is a complete blank." He seemed to search his memory, then his brows drew together. "Except … come to think of it, there were a couple times when I could've sworn I felt the warmth of someone's hand holding mine. And someone telling me not to give up, to fight. I figured it had been a dream." He framed her face with his hands. "But it was you—wasn't it?"

She lifted one shoulder.

"Why didn't you tell me? Why didn't *anyone* tell me?" The backs of his fingers stroked her jaw, then clutched the nape of her neck. "And why did you leave?"

"The longer I sat there, the more time I had to think. In case you haven't heard, I can be a bit impulsive some-times. Anyway, I convinced myself you would wake up and wonder what the heck your friend's baby sister was doing there. That you'd look at me like some pitiful kid with a hopeless crush and would feel sorry for me. I couldn't handle that. So when you started waking up and the doctors assured me you would be okay, I came home." *Like a big fat chicken*.

"I wish you'd stayed." His fingers massaged the suddenly tense muscles at the base of her neck.

"Considering what just happened between us, it does seem kinda ridiculous now. But at the time, healing needed to be your priority." Not dealing with a bunch of unnecessary drama.

He dragged her up his body, bringing them face-to-face. "I would've loved it if the first thing I saw when I opened my eyes was your pretty face."

"Mason, you need to know that leaving you was the hardest thing I've ever had to do. Ever." She'd pestered Caleb and Jonathan constantly for updates. "And when you came home from the hospital and didn't remember me being there, I swore everyone to secrecy and never mentioned it."

He lifted his head to nibble his way up her neck until his gruff voice whispered across the shell of her ear. "I bet you would've been a great nurse."

Emily tilted her head to aid in his efforts.

"Uh-huh." That's the best she could come up with at the moment because, *hello,* who knew that area just beneath her ear was a magic libido button?

She squirmed, pressed her hands to his chest and sat up to straddle him. Her hands traveled over him, taking in every masculine inch. The tips of her fingers lightly dragged across his forehead, down the side of his powerful jaw to his neck. Her tactile journey continued down until she skimmed a circle around each flat nipple, then she leaned down and grazed her tongue over one, then the other.

He sucked in a breath and dragged his hands up her thighs to grip her hips, but he let her explore.

She kissed her way down the center of his chest, poked her tongue into his belly button and rolled her eyes up to watch him. Muscles in his jaw clenched, and he watched her with hooded eyes. Satisfied by that response, she scooched down the bed until his erect penis was within inches of her face. She trailed one finger from the base up and circled the engorged head, eliciting a small drop of fluid.

"Now, about those creative alternatives ..."

CHAPTER TWENTY-NINE

P ink and orange filtered through the sheers hanging over the wide window, reflected off the large stand-up mirror in the opposite corner, and filled the room with the soft colors of dawn breaking. Mason had been awakened by the rich, nutty aroma of coffee from the automatic coffee maker in the kitchen. His mouth watered in anticipation of downing a cup. But not as much as memories of his night with Emily.

She'd been open, honest, and sexy as fuck. When she'd taken him into her mouth, humming along the length of him, licking and sucking like he was her favorite lollipop, she'd shattered every shred of control he thought he'd mastered through years of martial-arts training. And, damn, he'd loved every single, mind-blowing second of it. If his morning wood was any indication, he couldn't wait for it to happen again.

Down, boy.

She still slept, tucked safely into the crook of his arm, curled against his side. One leg atop his, one arm flung over his abs. His girl was a bed hog, and he loved it. Once or twice she'd mumbled softly, her mind working as fiercely in sleep as it did when she was awake. Her adorable, soft snores puffed warm against his left pec, and he was gripped by a feeling of possessiveness.

Mine. He tucked his chin to kiss the top of her head.

She stirred and stretched along his side. "Mmm, good morning."

"Mornin'." His voice was raspy from a combination of disuse and the need to have her again.

She turned, bent one arm on his chest and looked up at him. "Any regrets?"

"Only that I waited so long to tell you how I felt." His hand stroked down her back, and he spread his fingers across the dip just above her butt. "You?"

"Same. I love you, Mason."

"I love you, too, Em." He lifted his head to give her a quick kiss. "And, as much as I'd love to stay right here the rest of the day—"

"We need to go talk to Mr. and Mrs. Edmonds." She blew out a breath that ruffled her bangs. "Okay, but I'm going to need another one of your earth-shattering kisses to tide me over until later."

He lifted one eyebrow playfully. "Earth-shattering, huh?"

"Well, don't let it go to your head, but, yeah." She inched her way up until they were face-to-face.

"You make me happy, Emily O'Halleran." He caressed his palm over her cheek and combed his fingers into her hair.

"You make me happy, too, Mason Croft." She lowered her face and glided her warm, wet tongue over his lips.

He growled and drew it into his mouth, grabbed a handful of hair at the back of her head and angled her to better explore. A soft sound snuck up from the back of her throat, and she pressed herself closer, letting him know she didn't mind so much when he took control. But if she wanted to run things in bed sometimes, he was totally cool with that, too. And if last night was any indication, he couldn't wait.

With each stroke of tongue against tongue, their breaths quickened and the further they were from getting out of there anytime soon.

She broke their connection and slowly lifted her lips from his.

"Wow," she whispered.

"Yeah. Wow." He gave her butt a light swat. "Okay, woman, you'd better get off me before we forget we've got places to be."

"Fine." She rolled over with a huff, then stood. Framed by the sun creeping through the window, and in all her magnificent, naked glory, she stretched her arms high overhead, no longer concerned about showing him her body.

"I love your ass, Em." He tilted his head and enjoyed the view of her nicely rounded backside.

"Seriously?" She twisted at the waist, trying to look at it in the mirror over her shoulder. "You really like it?"

"Yes, it's perfect." It truly was a work of art.

"Thank you." God, how he loved the way she blushed when he complimented her.

"You grab some coffee, and I'll hop in the shower." He glanced at the clock on the nightstand. "On second thought ... we've got time."

He hopped up from the bed, bounded across the room and bent Emily over his shoulder. He turned and nipped her ass cheek.

"Hey!" She laughed and smacked his butt.

"If we shower together, we'll save water and time. Besides, I can't be expected to go the whole day without tasting you again."

And he did taste her again ... everywhere.

A CAR DOOR SLAMMED, and the man jerked awake. Slightly disoriented, he rubbed his eyes and looked around. Ah, yes, he was outside Emily's townhouse. At some point during the night, he must've fallen asleep.

The *clack-clack-clack* of a diesel engine captured his attention. The big truck backed out of the spot in front of Emily's and headed toward him. He quickly fell over to the passenger seat until it passed, then sat up.

He waited until they turned out of the parking lot, then turned the key and put the car in gear. The asshole driving the truck was an aware motherfucker, so he maintained a safe distance before turning in the opposite direction.

"Son of a bitch spent the night," he said to no one. "The whole fucking night!"

Did he touch her? Fuck her? It made him crazy to think of another man's hands on her. *She belongs to me, dammit!*

He pounded his fist against the steering wheel and dashboard until the glove box popped open. He slammed it shut with a curse.

"This just means I'm going to have to move up my timeline." He nodded. "Yeah, that's what I'll do."

The friend, Christina, lived in the same complex as Emily, so he'd have to be very careful. He'd hoped to grab her when she left the pub, but that bartender watched her like a damn hawk.

What he needed was a diversion, something that would keep them all busy long enough for him to take her.

A slow smile slithered across his face. He knew just the thing.

"Don't worry, Emily," he said in the direction of the truck. "We'll be together soon. And you'll apologize for letting that man touch you."

CHAPTER THIRTY

Mason glanced up at the rearview mirror again. Yep, it was still back there—the same blue sedan that had been following them since they left the townhouse.

"You keep looking in the mirror. Is there someone following us?" Emily actually sounded excited.

"Possibly." He looked back to the windshield.

She unbuckled her seat belt and whirled around to her knees to look out the back window. Fortunately, it was tinted, so whoever was back there wouldn't notice.

"Which one?" She scanned the two-lane road behind them.

"See the blue car, tucked in behind the old pickup? He looked at his side mirror.

"The Honda Civic, right?" She turned to him.

"Yeah." The woman knew her cars. "I noticed him after we left your place."

She turned back to the rear window and narrowed her eyes. "Shoot! I can't see the driver or his front license plate."

"Why don't you go ahead and put your seat belt back on."

She turned and slid to her butt, then clicked her belt into place.

"Do you think it's him?" Eyes wide, she stared at the side mirror. Her hands clenched together in her lap.

"It's probably just someone on their way to LaConner." He reached over and covered her hands with his. They were ice cold. "I wouldn't worry about it."

Whidbey Cove was located just north of the Deception Pass State Park, which included the Deception Pass Bridge. To the east, on the mainland, was the Swinomish Reservation and the small fishing village of LaConner, a popular tourist destination.

Mason checked the rearview again, and the car had fallen back another spot.

"Hang on, Em." He waited until she gripped the bar above the door, then cranked the wheel to the right. The truck leaned to the left, and the big tires squealed as they sped through the turn.

The blue car didn't follow, just continued going straight.

Emily watched the side mirror, then pivoted her head to see behind them.

"Dang it!" She relaxed back into the seat with a scowl. "I couldn't get a good look at him."

"I'll have one of the techies see if any nearby business or traffic cameras might've captured a clear picture of the car and the plate." He laced their fingers together and set their joined hands on his thigh.

A few minutes later, they turned onto the long gravel road cutting through Michaleen and Molly's property. Thanks to a series of potholes and ruts, it had a well-earned reputation for being tough to navigate.

"Dad refuses to fix this stupid road." She turned to him with a pained look. "Says it forces people to slow down. Not that they get a lot of traffic here. But I understand why he did it."

"He wanted you guys to have a place you could run around and play without worrying about getting hit. And now he's got grandkids to think about." Mason respected the hell out of him for that and so many other things.

"And don't forget all the strays my mom seems to bring home. Case in point: Brownie." She pointed toward a small-ish, dark brown cow about fifty feet up the side of a grassy slope. He stared at them, ear twitching, jaw grinding back and forth as he lazily chewed his cud.

"What's the story with him, anyway?" Mason tightened his grip on the wheel when they dropped into an exception-ally deep pothole.

Emily reached up and grabbed the handle.

"Mom found him wandering through her little orchard, chomping on the apples that had fallen from the trees. She posted notices in the paper and flyers all over town. No one claimed him, so she convinced Dad to let him stay." She turned to him and smiled. "Of course, it didn't take much arm-twisting. He's pretty indulgent where our mom is concerned. He teased that she was the only person alive who could end up with a feral cow."

"Your folks are great, Em, and I want them to be okay with us being together. But ..." Mason hesitated.

"But what?" Her entire body tensed in anticipation of what he might say.

"But ..." He stopped the truck in the middle of the road, put it in *park* and pivoted to face her. "Whether they are or not, I'm not giving you up. That's not even a possibility. I'll just have to prove that we belong together. I hope you're cool with that."

She unclicked her seat belt and crawled over the console to sit on his lap. "I am totally cool with that." Her hand cradled his cheek. "But it's not going to be a problem. My parents love you."

"We'll see if that extends to me being with their daughter." He gave her a quick kiss and lifted her back to her seat. "If I start kissing you, I'm not going to want to stop."

A few brutal, kidney-pounding moments later, they rounded a curve, and the house came into view. He turned and found Emily staring at the house, tugging on her lower lip.

"What is it, darlin'?" He reached over and gently lowered her hand.

"Is it silly that I'm a little nervous about seeing Sandy's mom and dad?"

"It's not silly at all. Questioning people who've lost someone they love is very difficult and requires a special touch." He lifted her hand and placed a kiss to the back. "You've got this, Em."

"Thank you." This time, she kissed his hand.

"You're welcome." Mason parked next to a white four-door parked next to the large driveway, cut off the engine and started to get out. Emily grabbed his arm, and he turned back to her.

"I love you," she said.

"I love you, too." He would never let a day pass without making sure she knew how he felt about her. "Ready?"

She took a deep breath, blew it out. "Ready."

He rushed around and helped her out of the truck. She placed her much smaller hand in his, and they walked up the flagstone path to the large, hand-carved front door. Another one of Michaleen's masterpieces.

Emily shoved open the front door and called out to her folks. "Mom? Dad?"

"Hey, you two." Molly walked through the open triple-wide sliding door that led out to the backyard and headed toward them. She slowed her pace and glanced down at their joined hands, then up at them with a huge smile.

Arms spread wide, she closed the space between them and wrapped them up in a joint hug. "So nice to see you two together."

Mason relaxed into her hold, the way he always did, happy that, so far, one of Emily's folks seemed happy to see them together. The toughest was yet to come, because everyone knew she was Michaleen's baby girl.

As soon as her mom stepped back, Emily wrapped her arm behind his waist at the same time his went around her shoulders.

Molly waggled her finger between him and Emily. "This makes my heart happy."

"Mine, too, Mom." Emily grinned up at him.

"Everyone's out back. It's just too beautiful of a day to sit inside."

"How are they?" Emily leaned around her to look toward the backyard.

"As well as can be expected. They've taken comfort in knowing OSI is working on Sandy's case. You kids go on out." She shooed them away and went into the kitchen.

Mason leaned down and gave Emily a soft kiss. She looked up at him, her emerald eyes sparkling, and he tucked her close to his side. She blew out a breath, and they headed outside.

They stepped onto the patio, and Michaleen turned to them. Quick as a flash, his eyes took in the way they held each other. He pushed back his chair, stood and sauntered toward them, moving to Emily first.

"Hey there, honey." He gave her a hug, kissed the top of her head and released her.

"Hi, Dad."

Mason actually tensed when Michaleen stepped in front of him.

Emily's dad pulled him in for a massive bear hug and whispered next to his ear. "Glad to see you finally came around, son." He clapped him on the back and released him with a wink. "I'm going to leave you folks to your business. If you need anything, just let Molly know. I'm headed off to finish up a project."

With that, he turned, headed toward his company truck and drove away.

Mason rubbed the back of his neck and caught Emily giving him a private little grin. She spent the next few minutes making introductions and sharing hugs, then sat next to Patricia Edmonds.

"We were so happy to hear you were all working on Sandy's case." Bob Edmonds lowered himself into a chair on the other side of his wife. The poor man seemed to have aged a decade since learning of his daughter's fate.

"And it means so much to us that you're involved, too, Emily." Patricia patted her hand. She was thinner than she'd been at the funeral, and her color was a bit pallid.

"Let's hope you have better luck than the rest of those useless cops did." Mark McMahon, Sandy's husband, looked at each of them and sighed. "Sorry. My therapist says I'm entering the anger phase of my grief. Only three more phases to go."

He reached out a shaking hand and grabbed a glass of what looked like tea. The ice tinkled and condensation dripped from the bottom when he brought it to his lips for a long swallow.

The guy had every right to be angry over how the investigation had been handled. The agencies working the case initially had wasted a lot of valuable time arguing over jurisdiction.

For the next several minutes, Mason and Emily gently guided them through a series of questions—some new, some they'd been asked before.

"Did Sandy ever say anything about someone following her? Maybe showing up at some of the same places she happened to be?" Emily used just the right combination of sympathetic understanding and professionalism as she questioned them.

"There was one time, ten days before she disappeared." Mark tugged his phone from his back pocket, tapped the screen a few times and scrolled through a long text stream.

"Here ..." He set the phone on the table and slid it over so Mason and Emily could see the screen, then pointed at a message from Sandy.

Guy at the coffee place just asked if I wanted to have coffee with him sometime. I told him I was married and, get this, he called me a bitch and walked away. WTH? He seriously needs to work on his technique. LOL!

Emily shifted in her chair and shared a sideways glance with Mason.

"When I asked her about it that night, she laughed and blew it off as no big deal. She thought it was funny, so I sort of let it go and forgot all about it. But this morning, knowing I was going to be talking to you, I decided to go back through our text conversations, just in case I might find something, anything that could help in the investigation. That's when I came across that message." He picked up the phone and stared down at the text in disgust. "I should've followed up. Maybe gone to the coffee shop with her or something."

"It wouldn't have done any good." Mason leaned his forearms on the table and clasped his hands together. "The guy doing this is smart. He likely assumed she would say something to you about the encounter."

"Mark, can you tell me the date and time you received

that text?" Emily scribbled the information as he related it. "And you're sure that's the only time she mentioned him?"

"I'm positive. If she'd ever mentioned him approaching her again, you can be damn sure I would've done something about it." He turned to his in-laws. "Did she ever mention anything to you guys?"

They both shook their head.

"No." Bob looked at his wife.

"Not a word." Patricia dabbed a tissue to the corner of each eye.

"Do you know what coffee place she was referring to?" Emily asked.

"I'm pretty sure she only ever went to Brewed Awakenings. They have a punch card that lets you earn a free coffee drink of your choice. The woman loves ... loved freebies. Hang on, I've got one." Mark pulled out his wallet and slipped a business card from the main pocket and handed it to her. There was a large coffee cup graphic in the center and three holes punched along the bottom.

Emily looked at it, then handed it to Mason.

"May we keep this?" He tapped the edge with his finger.

"Sure. I'll never use it again." Mark tucked his wallet back in his pocket. "Did you have any other questions for us?"

Emily looked at Mason, and he shook his head.

"I think that's it for now. Thank you so much for taking the time to do this." Emily stood and hugged each of them. "I'm not going to pretend that I know what you all are going through. But Sandy was my friend, and I want you to know that we will not stop looking until we find the person who took her from us."

CHAPTER THIRTY-ONE

"What are the chances both of our victims had the same prof, went to the same coffee shop and had a strange guy approach them?" Emily might be new at investigating, but even she realized three coincidences had to mean something.

"The chances are pretty damn slim." Mason turned onto the two-lane road that circled the bay. "Why don't you give your brothers a call and see if they've had any luck at the coffee shop?"

"Oh, good idea." She dug her phone from the bottom of her bag and placed the call.

"Here." Mason pushed a few buttons on his display screen and connected her phone to his truck's Bluetooth.

"Wow. You let me hook my phone to your truck's Bluetooth. That's quite a commitment, buddy," she joked.

"You think that's a commitment. Just wait until you hear what else I have planned for you," he teased.

"What—"

"Hey, squirt. What's up?" Killian's voice interrupted.

Mason winked at her but offered no further explanation for his cryptic statement.

She narrowed her eyes at him, then focused on the call.

"Did you guys have any luck at the coffee place?" Emily looked out over the bay. Sailboats with bright, multicolored sails stretched taut by the strong breeze dotted the small inlet. They were headed out to the open waters of the Puget Sound and would have to navigate the powerful, churning currents beneath the Deception Pass Bridge.

"Actually, we did. Hang on a sec. I'm driving, so I'm going to give the phone to Matty, and he can put it on speaker." Killian was the only one who referred to his twin by that nickname.

"Hey, sis. Mason, you there, too?" Mathias asked.

"Yep." Mason leaned an elbow on the center console.

"Okay, good. We showed Sandy and Pamela's pictures to the coffee shop owner, and she recognized them immediately. Said she was so upset when she found out what happened to them. Apparently, they were regulars, coming in three or four times a week." He took a swallow of something. Probably coffee.

"She said neither one of them ever mentioned being approached by a guy while they were there, and she's always so busy, she never noticed. When we asked about the surveillance video, she was more than happy to let us have it but didn't know how to access it."

"Seriously?" Emily groaned.

"But," Mathias continued, "she called her husband, who was able to log into the business account, and he sent it to my work e-mail."

"That's great. You guys headed back to the office?" Mason asked.

"We are," Killian said. "Will we see you two there?"

"Yeah." Mason reached across and wrapped his fingers around her hand. "We just left a meeting with Sandy's parents and husband. He showed us a text that Sandy sent him ten days before she disappeared. A guy at the coffee place got a little nasty with her when she wouldn't accept his invite to have coffee with him."

"I've got the time and date of the text," she said.

Mason lifted her hand and kissed her knuckles. "We can use that date to narrow down the search on the surveillance video. What time do you guys expect to be back?"

"We're pulling up to the ferry terminal now, but the next one doesn't leave for another fifteen minutes." Killian thanked the ticket agent. "We should be back in about an hour and a half."

"Andi is doing some follow-up interviews today, but the rest of us can meet in the strategy room to start looking at those surveillance videos." Mason flipped on his turn signal and pulled into the parking lot of the Don't Know Pub.

"Sounds good. I'll touch base with Jonathan," Mathias said. "See you there."

"Ciao!" Killian called out, just before his twin hung up.

"What are we doing here?" She looked around the empty lot. The pub didn't open until three in the afternoon.

"I want to talk to Devlin. Give him a heads-up about what's going on." He turned off the engine and walked around to open her door. "He's a Marine recon sniper and is trained to notice things. Nothing wrong with having someone with his skill set keeping an eye out."

Mason lifted her from the seat and held her against him. Her feet dangled off the ground, and she wrapped her arms around his neck.

Emily tilted her head. "What?"

"Nothin'. Just thought I'd tell you again how much I love

you." He kissed the tip of her nose, then pressed a soft kiss to her lips.

"I love you, too." She kissed him back. "I'm so glad we can finally say that to each other."

He set her down. "Okay, we'd better get inside before I change my mind and take you to my place and ..." He stopped.

"Take you to your place and what?" Emily wrapped her arms around his waist and smiled up at him.

His arms circled her. "Emily, I ... I bought the Landers place." He hurriedly added, "I had no idea you wanted it. If I'd known, I wouldn't—"

"Mason, you don't honestly think I didn't already know about that, right?" She chuckled. "You know how fast news travels in Whidbey Cove."

"You're not upset?" His lips brushed across her forehead. "Your mom said you've wanted that place for a long time."

"I'll be honest—at first, I was a little disappointed. After all, I've loved that place since I was a little girl. But it was too much for me to handle by myself." Emily had pretty much given up on the idea of buying the property when her foot fell through not one, not two, but *three* of the rotted steps leading up to the porch.

Sure, she could have asked her dad and brothers to help her, but she'd always had an issue with asking them for help. She worried it fed into their image of her as the helpless little sister, unable to do for herself.

"I'm glad you bought it, Mason. You deserve to have your own place, your own *real* home." She went up on her tiptoes and kissed his chin.

"Funny, your mom said something very similar." He narrowed his eyes, and one corner of his mouth lifted in that adorably devilish way she loved so much. "I have the perfect compromise."

"Which is?" Emily asked.

"Move in with me," he stated succinctly. "When I first got the place, I could see you in every room or sitting next to me on the porch swing I hope to hang one day soon. I imagined you picking out paint colors and bringing home swatches of fabric for ... well, whatever the hell swatches of fabric are for."

"Mason, I—"

"Look, I know it seems like I'm moving fast on this, but it feels like I've waited a lifetime for you, and dammit, I don't want to wait anymore." His hand cradled the side of her face, and his thumb caressed her cheek. "Thoughts?"

For the first time ever, Mason looked nervous.

"My thought is ..." She turned her face into his hand and kissed his palm. "I love you, and I don't want to wait anymore either. Let's do it."

He picked her up and, right there, in the middle of the parking lot of the Don't Know Pub, they kissed like their lives depended on them being attached at the lips. When they finally pulled apart, they were both breathing heavily and Mason's eyes had taken on a sexy heavy-lidded look she recognized from the night before.

"It isn't ready for human habitation quite yet, so that gives you plenty of time to pick the cabinets, flooring, appliances and all the other finishes you want." Mason slowly lowered her to her feet but kept his hands firmly on her butt. "In the meantime, we can take Gary with us when we go out there so he can get used to the place."

Emily felt tears building.

"Hey, hey. What's the matter, darlin'?"

"You're worried about my cat."

"Well, yeah." He looked totally confused.

"Not many people would've given him a thought. But you

did." She threw her arms around his neck. "I love that you love my grouchy old cat."

"Gary's my bud. Of course, I want to make sure he's comfortable at his new home."

"You two just gonna stand out here making out all day, or are you coming in?" Devlin stood on the top step, one hand on his hip, the other holding the door open. He wore an old, brown Indian Motorcycle T-shirt and had a bar towel draped over one shoulder.

Emily could definitely see why her best friend was hung up on the guy.

Mason took hold of Emily's hand as if he'd been doing so for years and led her into the pub. Devlin pulled the door shut and locked it.

"Can I get you guys anything to drink?" He took his usual spot behind the bar. "Kitchen's not open yet, but I can probably throw together a couple sandwiches."

"Nah, I'm good. Em?" Mason looked down at her.

"Ice water would be great." All that kissing was making her thirsty.

You'd think, after growing up with five brothers, Emily would be immune to a man's arms at work. Apparently not. Because when Mason reached down and pulled out one of the unique and very heavy tractor seat barstools for her, she couldn't take her eyes off him. Her insides fluttered, and she wanted to jump his bones. Seems the man had unleashed a latent sexuality Emily never knew she possessed. She kinda liked it. She kinda liked it a lot.

"What's up? You said you needed my help with something." Devlin set a glass of ice water in front of them.

"Yeah, it's this case we're working on." Mason took the seat next to her.

"Okay." Devlin grabbed a small knife and a couple of limes from behind the bar and started cutting them into wedges.

"Dev, do you remember Sandy Edmonds?" Emily took a sip of water.

"Yeah, you guys used to hang out together when you were little." He dumped the lime wedges into a divided tray, next to a bunch of shiny, bright-red maraschino cherries.

"She was kidnapped, and her body was found buried up in the Olympic National Park."

Devlin cursed under his breath. "I heard about it on the news but didn't know it was her they were talking about. Didn't they find another woman up there?"

"Yeah, a few months prior to that. Her name was Pamela Wescott. We're working her case, too." Mason curled his fingers over Emily's thigh.

"Christ." Devlin grabbed a few lemons and started slicing.

"Here's our problem—Emily knew both of our victims."

"You know about Sandy," Emily said, "but Pamela lived in the same dorm I lived in at the U."

Devlin's hand stopped, and he slowly set the knife down.

"General consensus is that he'll be coming after me soon." *Lucky me.*

Mason rotated her stool to face him. "That is *not* going to happen, Emily."

"What do you need me to do?" Devlin yanked the towel from his shoulder, wiped his hands, then tossed it in a bin under the bar.

"We just need you to keep your eyes open for anyone or anything that seems suspicious. Anyone close to her could be on this guy's radar. Our expert says he's about power and being in control, so he'll likely only target women."

"Including Christina." Devlin's entire demeanor changed.

"She is my best friend, Dev." Which put her near the top of the list.

Before he could respond, Mason's phone rang.

"Croft." He gave her an indecipherable look. "Yeah. Okay, we'll be there shortly."

"What's up?" Emily knew from his expression that, whatever it was, it wasn't good.

"Devlin, thanks for helping us out on this." They shook hands.

"I assume you guys have someone on Christina? If not, I can—"

"Relax. She works in one of the safest buildings in the world." Mason helped Emily down from her stool. "And we've got someone watching her place in the evenings."

Emily's brows slammed together, and she turned to him. "Since when?"

"Since we first made the connection." Mason circled his fingers around her elbow and guided her to the door.

Devlin walked with them, tugging keys from his pocket.

"Ya know, there was this one guy." He looked at Emily. "He was sitting at the bar the last time you were all here for ladies' night." He turned back to Mason. "He spent a bit too much time eyeballin' their table, so I warned him off and he left."

"Can you describe him?" Mason knew if anyone would remember, it would be Devlin.

"About six-foot, heavyset, brown hair, brown eyes, beard and mustache. He had on a trucker hat, dark jeans, suspenders and a grimy work shirt. If I had to guess, I'd say he was a mechanic or something like that. There was a name on the shirt pocket." He hesitated, then snapped his fingers. "*Mutt.* That was it. Oh, and he chewed tobacco."

"That's great." Mason looked at Emily. "We'll get our folks working on trying to identify him."

"Who's watching Christina?" Devlin twisted the lock on the door.

"Golden is parked out in front of her place every night."

Mason must've sensed the other man's hesitance. "He's one of our best guys, Devlin."

"Good." He shoved the door open without further comment, though it was obvious he wanted to be the one watching over Emily's best friend.

CHAPTER THIRTY-TWO

"Does Christina know Golden is lurking around outside her house every night?" Emily accepted Mason's help into his truck and fastened her seat belt.

"First off, he's not *lurking around*. He's parked at the end of the parking lot, sitting in his SUV. Secondly, yes, she knows. She wasn't totally happy about it, but she understood why." He gave her a quick kiss, hurried around the front of the truck, climbed in and fired up the engine.

"Why didn't she tell *me*? I'm her best friend." She propped her elbow on the open window and tugged on her bottom lip.

"She was worried you would blame yourself." He risked a quick sideways glance in her direction. "Which, it seems, is exactly what you're doing."

"I can't help it. Because of me, some psycho is out there, planning to hurt someone else that I care about."

Her hands dropped to her lap, and her head fell back against the headrest. Typical of Emily to be more concerned for her friend than for herself.

"We're going to get him, Em." He reached over and threaded their fingers together and gave her hand a quick squeeze. "We are. I will never stop looking for this guy until I know you're safe."

"Nor will I. It just ticks me off." She rolled her head to face him. "So, what was that phone call about?"

"Jonathan has some information he wants to share with us." He pulled out of the parking lot, his eyes checking the mirror but seeing no sign of their buddy in the blue sedan.

About ten minutes later, they pulled up to the OSI building and, after passing through the security protocols, entered the elevator.

He stepped in front of her and placed his hands on her shoulders. "You okay?"

"Yeah, I guess. It's just ... so frustrating." Her forehead fell to his chest. She stepped into him and wrapped her arms around his waist.

One hand cradled her head, and his arm circled her body and he held her tight until the elevator dinged. The door opened with a *swoosh*. He kissed the top of her head, took a deep bracing inhale of her sweet scent, then they stepped into the long hallway and walked down to the strategy room.

Jonathan, Killian and Mathias glanced up at the new arrivals, and three sets of deep blue eyes dropped to the couple's joined hands.

Emily's chin lifted and she moved closer to Mason's side, as if daring them to say anything. Mason stifled a grin and pulled out a chair for her, then took the empty seat next to her.

Jonathan spoke without looking up from his notes. "Nice to see you two finally decided to stop dancing around each other." His eyes rolled up to look at Mason, then Emily, and one side of his mouth twitched.

Killian and Mathias snickered from the other side of the table.

"Wait? You all knew?" Emily looked at her brothers.

"Duh," Killian offered.

"Okay, let's get to it." Jonathan clicked the remote, and a familiar face appeared on the screen. "We may have found our first viable suspect."

Emily gasped.

Killian's gaze trekked from the screen on the wall to his sister.

Mathias narrowed his eyes, then turned to her. "Isn't that the guy you were going out with?"

"WHY DO you have a picture of Richard?" Emily's back stiffened, and she turned to Jonathan. "Were you snooping into his background?"

"Before you tear into your brother, it was my idea to dig into the guy's past," Mason said. "So if you're going to be pissed at someone, be pissed at me."

"Mason called me after your little ... encounter with Evans the other day. We *both* decided we needed to know more about him." Jonathan sifted through a stack of files.

"Wait a minute." She turned and speared Mason with a look. "You told him about that?"

"What encounter?" Mathias and Killian said together as they looked from Jonathan to Emily to Mason.

"Hell, yes, I told him. There is a sicko out there who is fixated on you, Em." He pointed at the screen. "And this asshole just happens to show up in that parking garage at the exact same time you and I are there investigating the kidnapping of a woman you knew?"

Well, when he put it that *way ...*

"You're right. I'm sorry." She shook off her umbrage. "I never thought about it that way."

"No apology necessary." With a quick wink, he smoothed his hand down her arm.

Emily had grown up being overprotected by her brothers. Not just from perceived physical threats but emotional ones as well. Mason treated her like an equal, like she was strong enough to handle anything. To hear anything. She loved that about him.

"What. Fucking. Encounter?" Killian ground out between clenched teeth.

Speaking of overprotective.

"He grabbed my wrist, I gave him a shot to the junk, and he dropped to his knees on the ground like a little baby. No big deal." And that was all she was saying about that particular topic.

"Moving on ... Here's what we found out." Jonathan flipped open a file folder. "Richard Clyde Evans, age thirty-five, works at Naval Air Station Whidbey Island." He gave Emily a quick look. "However, he does not work at the flight desk and is not in the Navy—never has been."

Emily slowly sat forward and crossed her arms on the table, shocked by what she was hearing.

"He works for a company called Base Grounds Management. They hold the government contract to maintain all the natural spaces on base. Areas around the secured points of entry, parks, playgrounds and landscaping adjoining base housing, those sorts of things. Evans has been with them for just under fifteen years. His supervisor says he's a satisfactory worker with a decent attendance record." He rubbed his hand down his neatly-trimmed beard. "I'm moving him to the top of our list of suspects. Not that we have any others."

"What kind of car does he drive?" Mason asked.

Jonathan scanned the page. "Blue 1998 Honda Civic, sedan."

Mason cursed.

Emily's fingers dug into her upper arms, so she forced a deep, quiet breath, then loosened her grip.

"What?" Jonathan looked at them both.

"I'm pretty sure this asshole was following us when we left Emily's this morning." He turned to Emily. "It was a Honda, right?"

"Yeah, light blue with a dent on the left, front-quarter panel, just above the wheel well." A girl doesn't grow up with five brothers and not learn a little something about cars. "We turned right at Lancaster Drive, and the Honda kept going."

"Hang on a sec." Jonathan reached out to press a button on the speaker console in the center of the table. A few seconds later, a woman's voice answered.

"Comms, this is Sammy." She was the only female who worked in the communications center.

"I need you to pull all the video footage from within a five-mile radius of Emily's place, as well as the church where Sandy's funeral took place. Every traffic camera, every security camera, all of it."

"On it." Computer keys clicked in the background. "Anything else?"

"Yeah, have Golden run over to Richard Evans's place. I want him to pay him a little visit."

"You got it, boss." Sammy had the instincts of a bloodhound. Once she found the scent, there was no stopping her.

"I thought Golden was watching Christina?" Emily hated the idea of her friend being vulnerable.

"As long as she's here, she's safe," Jonathan reassured her.

"What about a social life? Does Evans have friends he hangs out with? Does he ever go out after work to grab a couple of brews with his co-workers? What about other women?" Killian gave her an apologetic look. "Sorry, Em."

"Okay, enough. I was not hung up on this guy, all right? We only went out a few times, and right from the beginning I was very clear I wasn't interested in anything besides friendship. Am I ticked that he lied to me? Heck, yeah. But that's just because I feel stupid for not seeing through his bull. Got it?"

She wanted to make sure everyone was clear on that. Especially the man in the chair next to her whose body grew more tense as each of Richard's lies was revealed.

Jonathan continued his briefing.

"Evans's co-workers know nothing about his personal life." Jonathan set his fancy gold pen on the table. "Emily, did he ever talk to you about his family, friends? Anything that might be useful?"

She thought back over their conversations.

"He talked about how being active duty made it tough for him to see his family. Which we now know is a big fat pile of steaming bull dung." The jerk had even tugged on her heartstrings about how much he missed them and how lucky she was to have her family so close.

"Did you ever go to his place?" Mason spun his chair to face her. "Does he have roommates?"

"I've never been to his place. Come to think of it, the topic never even came up. I guess I assumed he lived on base or something. Again, we only saw each other a few times."

Emily was becoming very concerned about what other secrets Richard was hiding.

"We went to dinner twice and bowling once, but I always met him there." She liked having her own car, just in case she wanted to leave early. "He always escorted me to my car and waited for me to drive off." Her thoughts turned inward for a moment. "Come to think of it, I never even saw his car. That's weird, right?"

"Under normal circumstances, probably not. But with everything else we've learned out about him ... it could be another red flag." Jonathan flipped the folder closed, sat back with his elbows on the arms of the chair and steepled his fingers together.

The speaker in the center of the table beeped. Mason pressed a button to answer the call.

"Okay, boss. I pulled some of the videos around Emily's place and at the church, like you asked and am shooting them to you now. The rest of the traffic cams will take a bit longer." She told him the times to look for on the videos and hung up.

Jonathan clicked the remote a couple of times, then fast-forwarded through the different videos. Richard had driven by her house at least twice every day since she'd last seen him, including late at night. He'd also been parked near the church where Sandy's funeral had taken place.

"Okay, this proves the guy has definitely been watching Emily." Mason did not sound pleased. "It also shows him and one other vehicle exiting the townhouse parking lot shortly after us. The other car turned right, but Evans turned left and ended up behind us."

She examined Richard's driver's license photo, searching for any clue that he could be capable of kidnapping two women, then burying them alive. Could she have been that gullible? Or was he just that much of a psychopath?

"Emily, if you hear from him or you see his car again, you let us know immediately."

She gave a quick shake of her head and forced her gaze away from the screen. "Sorry, what?"

"I said, if you see him or hear from him, let us know immediately."

"Ya know, I could just call him and—"

"No!" She flinched as four male voices rang out like an angry chorus.

"You just crushed the guy's nuts and blew him off. Don't you think it would be a bit suspicious for you to contact him now? More importantly, he's been lying to you from the beginning." Jonathan gave her his most serious look. "Stay away from him. Don't call him. Don't text him. Nothing. The guy could be dangerous."

"Don't worry. She'll be with me. And as soon as I can get it habitable, we'll both be moving into the new place." Mason held his hand out to her.

Emily took it and looked at each of her brothers.

"Sounds good." Jonathan grabbed his cell phone and dialed. "Hey, can you join us in the strategy room? We're getting ready to go through the videos from the coffee shop." He waited. "Thanks, babe."

He pressed the screen and tucked it in his pocket. "Andi's on her way down."

"Speaking of your place, Mason. Dad and some guys from his crew got the roof done today. I'll head over there tomorrow to finish up the flooring in the kitchen." Mathias leaned back in his chair. "Once you get your cabinets, we should be able to get them and your appliances installed in one afternoon."

"I'll go over with you, Matty. I want to secure those new built-in bookcases in the great room." Killian clasped his hands behind his head. "Front and back porches are all done, so they're safe to walk on again. Windows are replaced and the bedrooms are done. The only thing left to do in the bathrooms is to paint the walls, install the cabinets and hook up the plumbing."

Mason gave Emily a questioning look. "Did you know that's where your dad was going earlier?"

"I had no idea." She shook her head. "I just assumed he was going to one of his job sites."

"He didn't have to do that." Mason turned to Mathias and Killian. "And I certainly never expected you guys to do as much as you have." Mason seemed genuinely gobsmacked by their kindness.

"It's no big deal, really," Mathias said. "We started working on Dad's sites the day we could lift a nine-pound hammer."

Emily squeezed his hand and made a vow to herself. Never again would this amazing man feel undeserving.

"You're family," Killian stated without hesitation. Simple. Succinct. To the point.

Mason gave her a confused look, and she smiled at him. Yeah, he was going to have to get used to someone having his back for a change.

"Thanks. Seriously, that means ... it means a hell of a lot to me." His hold tightened slightly and he kissed the back of her hand.

"Let's watch some movies." Andi blew into the room in her typical take-no-shit way, then plopped down in the chair next to Jonathan's.

CHAPTER THIRTY-THREE

"We'll use the date of Sandy's text as a jumping-off point." Mason grabbed the portable keyboard and accessed the file with the video.

Emily walked over to flip off the overhead light, then returned to her seat next to him. "If we can get a look at the guy who approached her, then we can go back through the video to see if he ever approached Pamela."

Jonathan's cell phone rang.

"Hey, Viking. Hold on while I put you on speaker." He tapped the screen, then set the phone in the middle of the table. "Okay, the rest of the team is here with me. What's up?"

"I'm at Evans's place. His car's not here, and there's no answer when I knock on his door." Golden's footsteps could be heard in the background. "I tried looking through some windows, but all the blinds are down."

"Talk to the neighbors. See what they have to say about him. Ask if they've noticed any kind of suspicious activity coming from his place," Jonathan continued. "And Viking ..."

"Yes, sir?"

He grinned at his team. "Smile so you don't scare the shit out of anyone."

"Roger that." Golden chuckled, perfectly aware that his size could be intimidating. But only to those who didn't know him.

Jonathan hung up and indicated for Mason to continue. He fast-forwarded to the correct date and clicked *play*.

There was no audio, and the image quality was not the best. The camera did have a fish-eye lens, which gave them a wide-angle view of the area directly in front of the walk-up window, as well as a decent section of the parking lot.

Initially, they couldn't see much, since Brewed Awakenings opened at 5 a.m. and the sun hadn't come up yet. A few minutes into the video, lights flickered on, and the owner began moving around inside the shop.

"She must've come in through the back door." Andi stood and moved closer to the screen.

The owner turned on machines and poured water into their reservoirs, counted money into her small cash register, lugged the small tables and chairs out to set up in front.

Mason sped up the video and, as the sun began to rise, they could see cars arriving, people beginning to line up. The place looked to be extremely popular.

"Stop!" Emily bounded up from her chair and rushed over to the screen.

"That's Sandy." She pointed to a woman walking across the parking lot. "I'm sure of it."

The entire group inched forward in their seats and narrowed their focus to that one woman. She stood at the end of the line, with seven people in front of her. Too far away to make out details or to confirm her identity. With each step closer to the window, the quieter they all became.

When a person ordered and moved aside, her features became clearer. It was definitely Sandy. She was now second in line, and the customer in front of her finished placing their order. By now, they could tell that she had on a short denim jacket over a T-shirt tucked into a flowy skirt. Sandy stepped up to the counter and smiled, then placed her order. She slid her punch card and credit card across the counter. The owner ran the credit card, punched the coffee card and handed them both back to Sandy, who moved to the side to wait for her name to be called.

"Whoa, whoa. Where the hell did he come from?" Andi turned back to Mason. "Rewind to when she finishes ordering."

Mason punched a couple of keys, and the video reversed in super slow motion.

"Right there!" Emily pointed at a guy with the hood up on his jacket.

Like a wraith, a man materialized from around the side of the small building. He loomed over Sandy as he talked to her. She shook her head and gave him a tight-lipped smile. His body language changed, became more aggressive. He pointed at her face, said something, then turned and moved out of camera range. Sandy blinked a few times, shook her head, then turned to the pick-up window and grabbed her coffee. She glanced around as she walked back to her car, got in, but didn't drive off right away.

"That must be when she texted her husband about what happened?" Arms crossed, Emily stared at the screen until Sandy's car drove off. She turned back to the group. "We're going to watch that again, right?"

"We are," Jonathan said. "This time, we'll watch it in half speed."

"Em, why don't you come over here, and I'll show you how we make that happen." Mason knew it was important to keep her focused on the investigation and not her feelings about her friend.

Her eyes lit up, and she hurried to sit next to him. After a couple of basic instructions, he let her handle the video playback.

"Notice how he stays in that blind spot." Andi stepped closer to the screen. "Even when he's giving her shit, he's really careful not to move out of it."

"He knew about the camera," Jonathan said.

"Hell, the owner had a sticker on the window just below it that said, *Smile! You're on Camera.*" Killian rolled his eyes and shook his head.

"I don't think that's the only way he knew." Mason thought back to how well concealed the cameras in the parking lot were. "He's too smart to take any chances. I'd bet he checked the place out, just like he did the parking garage before he grabbed Pamela."

"Okay, we're not going to be able to do much more with this right now. Let's time-stamp it and move on to Pamela." Jonathan made a note.

EMILY FLIPPED ON THE LIGHT, and everyone groaned and blinked their eyes.

They'd been sitting in the dark for a couple of hours analyzing grainy video images. As tedious as the task was, it had paid off. They now had video footage of Pamela and Sandy being approached around the same time of day, in the same manner, by what appeared to be the same person. Unfortunately, whoever it was, he'd done a heck of a job concealing himself. Best guess: He was about six feet tall, average build with dark hair. Black, brown, dark blond? They weren't sure, since the video was in black and white. He could be one of a million people ... including Richard Evans.

"Mason, go ahead and send those two segments to Jimmy

and see if he can do anything to clean them up a bit." Jonathan gathered up his files and shoved up from his chair. "Have him run the plates on every single vehicle parked in the lot or driving by on the street. And I want names for the other customers. One of them might have gotten a better look at our perp."

"Done." He closed the video, and with a click of the remote, the large screen on the wall went dark.

Jimmy was their main tech genius. He worked at the compound in San Francisco. The guy practically lived there and resented having anyone else in his space.

Andi stood and raised her hands high overhead in a big stretch, then tilted her head side to side. Jonathan reached over and massaged the base of her neck. Mathias and Killian rose from their chairs and rolled them back into place.

"Kill and I are going to grab some dinner at the Don't Know. Anyone care to join us?" Mathias checked his phone, then tucked it back in his pocket.

Mason turned to Emily.

"Sure." She grabbed her bag. "Let me go see if Christina wants to join us. I hate the thought of her having to hang around here until Golden gets back."

"Good idea." Mason took her hand and gave her a kiss.

"Well, well, well. This is new." One of Andi's dark brows lifted, and she waved her finger back and forth between them. "And it's about damn time. Jesus, it was painful watching you two pussyfoot around each other."

"Ain't that the truth," Jonathan added under his breath as he tugged his wife to his side. "You guys have fun. I promised Ashling we would watch her favorite Disney movie together."

"She's only watched it a thousand times." Andi shook her head, but her love for their daughter came through in her big smile.

"We'll see you guys there." Killian gave them a lazy wave, and he and his twin turned to leave the room.

Jonathan's phone buzzed. He looked at it and held up a hand. "Hold up, guys." He swiped his finger over the screen. "What's up?"

Mathias and Killian returned to stand by the table as Jonathan put the call on speaker.

"The neighbors were a dead end, and Evans hasn't returned," Golden said.

Jonathan and Andi shared a long look, then she said, "Think you can get inside?"

"Yes." Golden was a big dude, but he was resourceful.

"Do it. Get in, get out, leave no trace. Got it?" Jonathan instructed. "Do not take any unnecessary risks."

"Yes, sir," Golden responded. "I'll be in touch."

Emily couldn't imagine how difficult it must be to give an order that could send someone into a potentially dangerous situation. And for someone to follow that order without question. Her respect for the people supporting the OSI mission grew with each day she was privileged to work with them.

"Let's go see our daughter." He tucked his phone in his back pocket and wrapped his fingers around his wife's wrist.

"You kids don't do anything I wouldn't do." Andi smirked over her shoulder as Jonathan led her from the room.

CHAPTER THIRTY-FOUR

S tep one of his plan had gone better than he could've hoped and had given him plenty of time to make it back to Whidbey Cove. He'd backed into a spot next to the gas station down the road from OSI, in hopes he could carry out the second part of his plan tonight. His patience had finally paid off when the big truck cruised past him. To be safe, he'd let a few cars get between them, then pulled out to follow.

They rolled into the left turn lane just as the light turned red. Looked like they were on their way to the pub. *Excellent.*

Now, for step two.

He went straight through the intersection, looking away from them as he passed, then pulled over and parked alongside the curb. The pub was only two buildings down, so he yanked his keys from the ignition, jumped out of the car and ran down a side street. He ducked into a dark alcove just as the beam of their headlights sliced across the front of the buildings.

Chest heaving, he tucked back into the space and watched the truck, then an SUV turn into the lot and park alongside each other. The bright overhead light gave him a perfect view of the two guys getting out of the SUV. They were the twins he'd seen at the funeral.

The asshole who'd been spending too damn much time with Emily climbed out of his truck and walked around to the passenger side.

"Hey, Croft," one of the twins shouted over the hood of the SUV. "If I remember correctly, you owe Mathias and I a round of drinks."

"Not sure I remember that, but sure, I'll get the first round." He opened the back door and helped Christina out, then moved to the front. He leaned in and, when he turned around, the son of a bitch's arms were crossed under Emily's ass, holding her against him.

Intense pressure built in the watcher's head, flooding it with the sound of his own pounding heartbeat.

"Mason! Put me down." Her tinkling laughter sailed across the parking lot, and she wrapped her arms around his neck and kissed him.

A loud, high-pitched ringing sliced through his brain like a hot knife. His mother's voice joined the cacophony. *She's laughing at* you. *You're a joke, and she knows it.*

He squeezed his eyes shut and slammed his palms over his ears. The ringing increased, threatening to shatter his eardrums. His fingertips dug into his scalp until his nails bit into flesh. It was just enough to jerk him back to the moment. Bit by bit, the noises quieted and his body relaxed. He slowly opened his eyes and peered across the street. There was no sign of Emily.

The episodes seemed to be lasting longer. *I just need to be with Emily.*

Over the next hour or so, he remained hidden as more cars and trucks filled the parking lot. Music and the sound of people having a good time spilled out the door each time someone opened it.

He looked up and down the empty street. *All quiet.* His soft leather soles were silent on the blacktop as he casually walked across the street. He cut between parked cars and trucks until he reached the dark, narrow, three-foot-wide strip of land between the pub and the building next to it.

With the shadows hiding his movement, he fought through the tall weeds and overgrown brush on his way to the rear of the old brick building. Thorny branches caught and snagged the sleeve of his cardigan and slapped against his khaki pants as he cautiously made his way through the darkness. The slick bottom of one shoe hit a soggy patch of leaves, but he managed to keep from falling on his ass. Good thing—getting muddy would've ruined everything. Finally, he reached the end and settled his back against the wall. He cast a quick look up at the night sky, held his breath and risked a peek around the corner.

A big mercury light at the top of a pole lit the space up like it was the middle of the fucking day. He'd bet his entire fortune there was a camera rigged up there, too. An old beater truck was parked next to the back door. An alley ran behind the pub and dumped out onto the street two buildings down. Right where he'd parked his car.

Now that he had a feel for what to expect, he returned to the parking lot. Before stepping out into the open, he bent over to brush off his pant legs, then licked his thumb to rub dust from the top of his loafers. He adjusted the collar of his button-down and tugged on his cuffs. His hand ran down the sleeve of his sweater, and a finger tangled in a loose stitch. He patted his shirt pocket, and it was empty. *Shit!* He squatted down and ran his hand over the ground until he felt the familiar shape of a syringe. It must've fallen out when he was fixing his pants. With a relieved sigh, he stood, blew a burst of air over it to knock the dirt off and tucked it back into his chest pocket. *Crisis averted.*

He smoothed his hair to the side and pressed lightly against his mustache and goatee to secure it. The blue contacts and a pair of trendy glasses, and he was just another average guy stopping for a brew after a hard day at the office. The genius was in the simplicity.

An older couple was just heading to the door, and he tucked in behind them. Once inside, he squeezed past them and moved over to the corner. He did a double-take when he realized he was standing next to a stuffed black bear wearing a top hat. He hadn't noticed it when he was in here before. Then again, he'd been pretty focused on Emily. He lounged against the wall and surveyed the large space.

To his left, a couple of guys played pool. Some of their friends cheered them on while others talked trash. The dance floor was shoulder to shoulder with people dancing to an old swing song from the forties. Every stool at the bar was taken, and behind them, the crowd was two deep waiting for drinks. Servers held trays high overhead as they swerved around tables and bodies. There wasn't a seat to be had in the entire place.

Perfect.

He craned his neck over the crowd and spotted Emily's group at the same table near the back. The guy he now knew as Mason Croft sat next to her, his arm over the back of her chair. His damn fingers were caressing the side of her neck. The bartender joined them and sat next to the blonde.

"Hey, I didn't see you over here." He flinched when a server appeared in front of him. "Can I get you anything?"

"I'll take a light beer." Definitely something an average guy would order.

"Draft or bottle?" She tugged a pencil from over her ear.

"Bottle is fine. And here, let me save you a trip." He pulled cash from his wallet. "Keep the change."

"Thanks, I appreciate it." She smiled and hurried back to the bar.

He looked her up and down. She wasn't ugly, but she wasn't Emily, either.

A few minutes later, beer in hand, he watched the goings-on at the back table. The bartender and Croft got up and walked into a room behind the bar.

Now was his chance. He tipped the bottle to his lips and held it there as he weaved his way through the crowd. Each step closer to *her* had his heart rate soaring. He lowered the bottle slightly for a better look when he passed their table, and Emily actually looked up at him for a moment, then gave him a polite smile. His steps stuttered with the urgent need to stop, but he forced himself to continue to the men's room. *Soon,* he told himself. *Very soon.*

CHAPTER THIRTY-FIVE

"I'll be right back." Mason kissed Emily and followed Devlin to the bar. "I know you're slammed, but you got a minute?"

"Sure, hang on a sec." He flagged a server down to help the other bartender. "Let's talk in my office."

They passed through a storage room lined with shelves. Paper products, condiments, mixers, bottles of alcohol and several other things a restaurant and bar would need were neatly organized. Stainless-steel kegs of varying sizes stood in a row along one wall. It was the neatest storeroom he'd ever seen.

Devlin pulled out his keys and unlocked a door at the back, and they stepped inside. He closed it and moved toward his desk.

Mason looked around, struck by how tidy Devlin's office was, too.

"What can I say? I like everything in its place." Devlin relaxed against the edge of his desk and crossed his arms. "What did you want to talk about?"

Mason provided a brief update on what they'd learned about Richard Evans.

"You're pretty sure he's your guy?" Devlin asked.

"Right now, he's our only suspect, and we've not been able to locate him. Golden's going through his place now." He was hoping to get a call from him soon.

"What the hell? I thought he was going to be watching Christina?" Devlin's voice held a note of censure. He rose and made a move toward the door.

Mason stopped him with a hand around his upper arm. "Relax. Mathias and Killian are with them." He released him. "And she's been at work all day. Believe me, no one could get to her there. If Golden isn't done by the time we're ready to leave here, she'll stay with Emily and me."

"No. I'll watch over her." Devlin was the right man for the job. He was more than qualified, and he was personally invested in her welfare.

"That'll work." Mason felt the same way about Emily.

"So, you two together now? You and Emily."

"Yeah, we're together." And they were staying that way.

"Congrats, man. I know you've been hung up on her for a while." Devlin crossed his arms. "I've known Emily a long time. She'll keep you on your toes."

"I'm counting on it." Mason never felt more alive than when he was with her. "What about you and Christina? You ever going to make a move?"

"When the time is right." And with that cryptic answer, he headed to the door.

Mason's phone vibrated in his pocket. He tugged it out and checked the caller ID.

"It's Golden. Mind if I take it in here?"

"Only if you put it on speaker and let me hear what he has to say," Devlin said.

"Hey, Viking. Hold up a sec." He looked Devlin in the eye. "Nothing leaves this room, agreed?" He trusted the man completely, and Jonathan had been trying to hire his old friend since opening the PacNW office. But it needed to be said.

"Agreed." Devlin nodded.

"Vike, I've got Devlin here with me, so I'm putting you on speaker." Mason held the phone between them. "Go."

"I just finished at Evans's place. He had candid shots of Sandy and Pamela tacked to the wall in his bedroom." Mason and Devlin shared a look. "Sandy coming out of a hair salon. Pamela walking into what looks like a medical building. Their necklaces were hanging next to them. I took a couple of pictures and am sending them to you now."

Totems. Andi's briefing had been spot-on.

Mason's phone pinged, and he opened the photo of Pamela alongside the necklace.

"That's definitely Pamela's." He was certain of it.

Her mother had provided them with an appraiser's photo of the custom-made pearl and diamond pendant she'd inherited from her grandmother. It was an incredible, one-of-a-kind arrangement.

He opened the second photo. "And that appears to be Sandy's."

Hers was a very popular design from a national jeweler. But finding it and Pamela's in the same place, together with their photos, was all the proof he needed.

HIS PLAN WAS to move into a stall if someone came in and move back to the door after they left. He'd tugged his rubber gloves on, prepared to wait all night if necessary, but it would seem luck was shining down on him. Not five minutes later, she appeared at the opening to the hallway, backlit by the lights in the bar area.

She laughed over her shoulder at something someone in her party said, then pushed open the door and walked into the ladies' room.

His grip tightened on the handle and he tensed to pull the door open when a guy started heading toward him in a hurry. There was no time to hide in a stall, so he moved to the sink. He turned on the faucet and remembered that he'd put his gloves on. *Shit!* No time to take them off now. He'd just have to be careful the guy didn't notice.

"S'up?" The man tipped his chin up at him, stood in front of one of the urinals and took a leak.

He didn't respond, just continued rinsing his hands and watching the other man's back in the mirror.

The rasp of a zipper and the flush were his cue.

Instead of using the hand dryer, he plucked several paper towels from the dispenser and did the best he could to disguise the gloves.

The guy washed his hands, popped out a few paper towels to dry them and headed out.

He blew out a huge breath, and his chin dropped to his chest. He chucked the paper towels into the bin and hoped he hadn't missed his chance to grab her. The sound of the hand dryer in the ladies' room vibrating against the wall assured him he hadn't. He slipped the syringe from his pocket, used his teeth to drag the top off and tucked the small piece of plastic back into his pocket. The dryer quieted, and he cracked the door open.

She stepped out of the bathroom, and he pounced on her from behind. His left hand slammed over her mouth, and he jabbed the needle into the side of her neck with his right. He wrapped his right arm around her waist, pulled her back against him and lifted her off the floor. The noise of the pub drowned out her muffled screams. Frantic breaths puffed out through her nose and over his hand. The clip in her hair dropped to the floor, and her light-blond hair tumbled around her shoulders and against his face. Her wallet dangled and swung from a strap on her wrist as she dug her nails into his fingers. Her legs kicked feebly against his shins, then stopped altogether, and her hand fell away as the drug took her under.

He carried her the few feet to the exit door and shoved against it with his hip. The alley was still empty. He flipped her to face him, leaned over and folded her over his shoulder and straightened. Her arms hung limply, and her wallet slipped from her wrist and dropped to the ground. He noticed it held her cell phone, so he squatted down to pick it up. His quads burned and his legs quivered as he stood. After a last look around, he took advantage of the lack of lighting behind the other buildings and hurried toward his car.

───

"Christina's gone!" Emily charged into Devlin's office, gripped by a sickening combination of fear and panic.

"She went to the bathroom and was in there for a really long time. So I got worried and went to check on her, but she wasn't there. No one was in there. She was just gone." Words poured out of her uncontrollably.

Devlin was already running from his office. She and Mason followed. They rushed past Mathias and Killian, who stood at the entrance to the hallway.

Devlin charged through the door to the ladies' room. He banged open each stall door and practically plowed Mason over as he shouldered his way around him.

"Found this on the floor." Mathias held up Christina's favorite purple hair clip.

"Is this door always open like this?" Killian had moved to the exit door.

"Son of a bitch!" Devlin bounded outside with all of them behind him.

Emily caught a glimpse of her friend's light blond hair just as she was being dropped into the back seat of a car.

"There!" She pointed.

Devlin sprinted down the alley.

The familiar Honda lurched into traffic, a horn honked when he almost hit another car, then he sped away.

"Oh my gosh! Was that Richard's car?" Emily noticed the dent.

"Sure looked like it." Mason spun back toward her brother. "Killian, call this in to the Command Center. Then I want you to stay here and see if anyone saw anything."

"Got it." He grabbed his phone and stepped away to make the call.

Devlin jogged back toward them and headed to his old truck. "I'm going after her."

"I figured, but let's take my truck," Mason said.

"Fine. I need to grab my weapon from the safe in my office." He disappeared into the pub.

Mason took Emily's hand and led her, with Mathias at their back, through the crowd and out the front door.

"Mathias, take Emily back to your place. I'll wait for Dev."

"Come on, sis." Mathias held open the door of his SUV.

She crossed her arms and dug in.

"Now is not the time to be stubborn, Emily." Mason unlocked a box bolted under the front seat and slid open the drawer. With the skill of a man used to handling weapons, he pulled out a .45-caliber, semiautomatic handgun. He confirmed the magazine was full and a round was in the chamber and tucked it into his waistband.

"I'm not being stubborn. I'm being practical. You need Mathias's help on this." She stepped up to him and placed her hand on his chest. "I'll take his car and go straight to the office. You know I'll be safe there."

And she could park her butt in the comms center and listen to what was happening.

Mason cradled the side of her face and looked like he was going to argue.

"I promise." She leaned into his warm touch.

"Mathias, call your older brothers and let them know what's going on." He tossed out his instructions without looking away from her.

"Will do." Mathias handed her his keys, grabbed his phone and climbed into the back seat of Mason's truck to give them some privacy.

Mason opened the door of the SUV for her and waited until she was secured inside. She lowered the window. He bent at the waist and wrapped his fingers around the nape of her neck.

"I want you to let me know the second you get to the office," Mason said.

"I will." As much as she'd like to go with them, she wasn't properly trained and would be a distraction for Mason. Which could easily get someone she loved killed.

Tears welled in her eyes, and her chin quivered. "She's my best friend, Mason."

"We'll find her, Em." His thumb swiped the tear from her cheek.

Devlin came running from around the back of the building carrying a brand-new Mk 13 Mod 7 sniper rifle with a Nightforce scope. The same setup was used by Marine Corps snipers. She recognized it because they were a part of OSI's arsenal.

"Let's go." He climbed into the front seat of the truck.

"I love you. Please be safe." Her heart physically ached at the thought of him getting hurt again.

"I love you, too, Em."

CHAPTER THIRTY-SIX

The bartender charged down the alley, heading straight at him with murderous vengeance darkening his features. He stomped on the accelerator and shot off down the street, thankful when the guy faded from sight. He jerked the wheel to the left. The tires squealed over the pavement and the back end fishtailed before straightening, then he sped toward the road that would lead to his destination.

He glanced at his cargo in the backseat, her face obscured by her long hair. She'd be out until he got to his place in the woods. Stupid bitch put up a good fight until the drug set in. Normally, he'd be all about that, but standing in that hallway, with all those men less than twenty feet away, was definitely not the time for it.

The syringe! He ran through the last few minutes in his mind and realized he must've dropped it in the hallway. Fortunately, he never handled one without gloves, so fingerprints weren't an issue. Leaving it behind was not ideal, but nothing could be done about it now.

One hand on the wheel, he reached across and unlocked

the glove box. He grabbed the burner phone and dialed the only number programmed into it.

"Detective Harden. How can I help you?" He'd gotten the guy's name and number when he appeared on the news.

"Um, yeah, are you the fella workin' on that case with them girls that was buried up there in the woods?" he asked.

"Yes, sir. How can I help you?" He sounded distracted, and it sounded like he was shuffling through papers or something.

"Well, ya see, I's up here in Anacortes, pickin' through some garbage bins, lookin' for aluminum. Ya know, 'cause I can get money fer it? Anyways, I heard a car door shut, which is very unusual because there ain't never anyone around here this time of night. And I coulda swore I saw a feller headin' into one of the warehouses down here at the marina." He was rather enjoying this accent.

"I'm sorry, sir. I'm not sure what that has to do with our case."

"Well, when I looked over, there was this little blue four-door sittin' there, and he was carryin' a woman over his shoulder." There, that ought to capture his attention.

"Did you say a woman?" A chair squeaked, and he could practically feel the detective's excitement rippling through the phone.

"Yep. I knew it was a woman 'cause I seen long blond hair hanging down. And I recall seein' that same feller carryin' a bunch of lumber in there a few days ago. At the time, I didn't think nothin' of it." He hesitated for the sake of drama, then went in for the kill. "Didn't y'all say he buried them girls in wooden coffins?"

"Give me that address again?"

"Don't got an address." He gave him the cross streets for an old, derelict warehouse in Anacortes, hung up and ripped the battery out of the phone.

He lowered the window and tossed the pieces out one at a time. Even if someone found them, it would be too late.

"I DOUBT the guy's gonna stick around." Mason had been zigzagging the streets of Whidbey Cove for about forty-five minutes, hoping to come across the familiar blue Honda.

"There are only two ways off the island. South on Highway Twenty toward the ferry terminal, or north, across the bridge and around until he hits Interstate 5." Mathias scanned left to right from the backseat.

"He's not going to risk getting stuck in a line waiting for the ferry," Devlin added.

The Bluetooth jingled through the truck's speaker. Mason pressed a button on the steering wheel to answer the call.

"What have you got, Sammy?"

"Detective Harden with Seattle P.D. called. He just got an anonymous tip from a guy in Anacortes. Said he saw a man carrying a woman with blond hair into a warehouse down by the marina. He said he'd seen the same guy carrying a bunch of lumber into the building before."

Mason snuck a glance at Devlin. "Did he say anything else about the woman?"

"No, but he did say the man was driving a blue four-door."

His eyes connected with Mathias's in the rearview mirror, then he looked over at the angry, worried man in the seat next to him.

Devlin turned his way. "That's gotta be him."

"Sammy, send me those GPS coordinates." Mason flipped on his blinker and turned at the next street.

Anacortes was about fifteen minutes north on Highway Twenty.

"Done. Beck and Caleb are monitoring from San Fran;

Jonathan, Killian and Golden are en route in the quick response unit. Anacortes P.D. has been contacted but given orders to stand down and watch the building until our team arrives." Sammy clicked away in the background. "Okay, you should have the coordinates. Kick ass and stay safe."

"Thanks." Mason hung up. "We'll get her, Dev."

"He's a dead man." Devlin's voice teetered on the knife's edge of rage.

Mason thought about how he would feel if it were Emily and didn't waste a second arguing with him.

ANDI PACED the limited space of the comms center. Emily opted to sit next to Sammy. The room was dark, cold and wide enough to hold several pieces of high-tech equipment. The main wall was covered with different-size flatscreens.

Emily shivered. Her shoulders drew up, and she wrapped her arms around herself. She should've stopped by her office and picked up the sweater she kept on the back of her chair. But her only thought had been to get to the comms center.

"Okay, here we go." Sammy sat forward, her fingers flew over the keyboard, and the large center screen flashed to life.

Andi stopped in her efforts to wear a path in the carpet, moved over and stood next to Emily.

"This is live from the drone Jimmy's got hovering over the warehouse. It's equipped with a thermal imaging camera." She used her mouse and dropped a red circle around two white spots in front, then another two behind the building, and one more on the roof of the building next to it.

"That's Killian and Mathias getting into position in the back, Mason and Jonathan in the front." Andi pointed at the two sets of moving white images.

"That one, up there on the roof, is Devlin with his sniper rifle. You know why he's set up in that spot?" Andi looked down at Emily.

"Because it's the best vantage point to see anyone coming or going from the front or the back. Right?" Emily had watched Golden and a few other guys work on their sniper skills at the range.

"Exactly." Her sister-in-law walked over to an empty chair by the wall and rolled it up next to her and sat. "He's pissed because he wanted to go in after Christina. Can't say as I blame him."

"Why didn't he?"

"Technically, he's not even supposed to be there. Maybe once this is over, he'll finally take Jonathan up on his offer to come work with us," Andi said.

"Where's Golden?" Emily asked.

"He's monitoring on-site from the tactical van." Sammy dropped a circle around the van, hidden behind a nearby eighteen-wheeler.

"No sign of the car." Jonathan's low voice crackled through the speaker.

"Do you think he took her somewhere else?" Emily felt sick at the thought of not finding her friend in time.

"Place is pretty big. Maybe he pulled it inside?" Sammy said.

Earlier, she had shown them an image of the warehouse. The place was massive, but it was also run-down to the point it looked like it might collapse in on itself. Yet another thing to worry about.

"Heading in," Jonathan said.

"It's go time, folks." Sammy increased the volume.

All four of the white images moved toward the nearest door.

Emily scooched to the front of her chair. She tugged on her bottom lip as the fingers in the other hand dug into her palm. A cold sweat broke out along her temples and forehead, and her heart beat so powerfully in her chest, it was almost painful.

"Breathe, Emily." Andi watched the screen as she gently rested a hand on her shoulder.

She hadn't realized she was holding her breath, and air burst from her lungs. She shook out her hands and watched her brothers and the man she loved head straight into danger.

"On my mark." Jonathan's voice was a mere whisper. "Three, two, one."

Emily stiffened in anticipation of hearing a door being blown in or, at the least, kicked open. None of that happened —it was eerily quiet.

"Their strongest weapon is surprise," Andi explained.

"Oh, so they picked the locks." Made sense.

"First floor rear, all clear. Heading up the back stairs."

"That was Killian," Sammy said.

"How could you tell?" Most people thought Killian and Mathias sounded alike.

"Their mics are voice-activated. Any time one of them speaks, their name appears right here." Sammy circled the bottom right corner of the screen.

Emily had so much to learn.

"First floor front, all clear." Jonathan's name replaced Killian's on the screen. "Heading up."

Ice settling in Sammy's large insulated cup, the hum of the computers, and the air-conditioning blowing down on them were the only sounds in the room. The silence from the guys was deafening, and Emily almost couldn't stand it. Then Jonathan reported in.

"On the second floor, but there's—" There was a loud crash, then static.

Emily jolted, and Andi shoved up from her chair.

"Shit!" That was Mason's voice.

Emily stood and moved closer to the screen. As if she'd be able to see them better.

"Report." Sammy was the picture of calm. "I say again, report."

Minutes passed with no response.

"Why aren't they answering?" Emily's eyes flashed over the screen, waiting, hoping to see someone coming out of the building.

Mason's name appeared in the corner of the screen, but all they could hear was grunting and scraping noises.

Andi picked up a headset and placed it over her ears, then pressed a button on the console next to Sammy's. "Report now, dammit."

"We're all fine. The floor gave out." Mathias spoke for the first time. "Jonathan managed to keep himself from dropping through to the first floor, but his mic is toast."

Andi's head dropped forward for a couple of seconds, then she looked back at the warehouse. "Did you find anything?"

"Nothing." Mason's frustration was palpable. "No one's been in this place for years."

There was a rustling sound, followed by muffled voices, then Jonathan's voice filled the room. Emily looked down at Killian's name in the corner and realized they'd switched mics.

"Sammy, we're heading back to H.Q." He coughed a couple of times and muttered under his breath, "Fucking dust."

"Roger that." She typed something. "We'll continue overwatch until you guys are clear."

Emily's phone buzzed. She yanked it from her back pocket. Her mouth dropped open, and she stared wide-eyed at the name on the screen.

"Wait!" She turned to Sammy. "Record this."

Andi stepped up to Emily. The tech hit a few keys, then gave a single nod.

She took a deep breath, then answered. "Christina?"

CHAPTER THIRTY-SEVEN

He checked the *Favorites* list on the phone. Sure enough, Emily's number was there at the top. He tapped the screen and tried to calm himself in preparation for hearing her voice.

"Christina?" Her voice was hopeful, yet tinged with suspicion.

His thumb pressed the bezel on his watch to start the timer.

"Hello, Emily." Thanks to a handy little device he found online, she wouldn't recognize his voice. "I've missed you."

"Richard, is that you?"

"You'll find out soon enough, my love." He smirked.

"What have you done with Christina?" she shouted.

"Tsk, tsk, Emily. Yelling isn't nice." He disliked being the cause of her upset, but he would not tolerate such behavior.

"I'm sorry. I'm sorry. I'm just worried about my friend." The softness and concern in her voice warmed him. She was such a good person to care so much for her friend.

"That's better. And don't you worry your pretty little head about your friend. She will be just fine, as long as you do exactly what I tell you to do." Complete lie—he never left anyone alive. No sense sharing that detail just yet.

"What do you want me to do? Anything. Just tell me what to do." Her desperation to save her friend was the thing he counted on most.

"Get in your car and start driving north on Highway Twenty. Do not tell anyone. I will call back using this phone with more information." He needed her on the road before they figured out the warehouse was a dead end.

He checked the timer.

"Where am I going?" Emily's voice no longer shook.

"You'll find out soon enough. And Emily, if you tell anyone, I *will* kill your bestie, and I promise you, you will never find her body." As threats went, that was a pretty powerful one.

"Why are you doing this?" she asked. "Why do you want to hurt her?"

He watched the second hand work its way around the face of his watch.

"Emily, you naughty girl. Are you trying to keep me on the phone so someone can trace this call?" Of course, she was. He'd be disappointed in her if she hadn't thought of it.

"No! I swear, I'm not doing that!" she rushed to say. "Please, just ... don't hurt her, okay?"

"Well, that depends on you following my instructions, doesn't it?"

"How do I know you haven't already killed her?"

The second hand *click-click-clicked* its way to the twelve.

"You don't." He hung up and turned the phone off.

MASON ENTERED the comms center and headed straight for Emily. She rushed to him, and they wrapped their arms around each other. All the dusty gear strapped to his chest didn't seem to bother her.

Over her head, he said to Andi, "Jonathan said to meet him in the gear room."

Andi darted from the room.

Emily tilted her chin up to Mason. "You heard?"

"Yeah, Sammy patched the call through to us."

She buried her face against him.

"He's going to kill her, Mason, I just know it. I could hear the crazy in his voice." Her body trembled, and her words were muffled against his protective vest.

"We're going to do everything we can to make sure that doesn't happen." He squeezed her tighter.

"Got him!" Sammy frantically clicked away at her keyboard. "He's at the Walker Valley ORV, east of Interstate 5 near Mount Vernon."

"ORV?" Emily looked over her shoulder at the comms tech.

"Off Road Vehicle," she said. "It's land in the Walker Valley Forest that's been set aside for dirt bikes, ATV's and mountain bikes."

"How did you find her?" Emily lowered her arms, and he held her hand.

"All OSI employees have trackers installed in their phones. It's a cool, tiny little device Caleb and Luna invented. That kid's a freakin' genius, by the way." Sammy's excitement built as she warmed up to her topic. "What's great about it is, the tracker works independently of the phone. Even if the phone is turned off and the battery is removed, the device continues to send a signal." She pointed up at the satellite image on the screen. "See that pulsing red dot? That's Christina's phone. And when I scroll my cursor over it, the latitude and longitude appear."

"Let's just hope he didn't ditch the phone." Mason was

legitimately concerned about that. After all, this guy was no dummy.

"I don't think he would do that. You heard him. He said he would be calling me back on that phone and that I'd better answer." Emily looked up at him, and the worry and fear in her eyes pissed him off and made him want to kill the man who put it there.

"Sammy, send those coordinates to everyone on the team." He pulled Emily into his side. "Tell them to meet me at the airstrip."

"Roger that." She turned back to her console.

"Emily, you—"

"I'm coming with you." She pursed her adorable lips and held up her hand. "Don't even bother arguing with me, Mason Croft. His instructions were very clear. He is going to call me to give me more details."

"Not happenin', Em." Hands on his narrow hips, he leaned down so they were nose to nose. "It's too dangerous."

There was no way in hell he was letting her anywhere near this psychopath.

Sammy whirled in her chair to face them. "Hate to interrupt your little ... disagreement, but Anacortes P.D. just found Evans's car."

"Christina?" Emily hurried over to her.

Sammy shook her head.

Without a word, Emily turned on her stubborn little heels and stomped out of the room.

Mason looked down at Sammy, who shrugged. He tossed up his hands and went after his woman. Again. He caught up to her in the gear room, along with the rest of the team. She was just reaching into the large closet to grab a protective vest.

Jonathan stopped as he was loading his magazine. "Care to tell me what the hell you think you're doing?"

Everyone glanced up to take in the exchange.

"She thinks she's coming with us." Mason loomed over her.

She didn't say a word, just pulled the vest over her head and started securing the Velcro straps. She turned toward the open door of the massive safe, and he stepped in front of her.

"Out of my way, Mason." Her hands clenched at her sides, and he was pretty sure she wanted to deck him. Thinking back to how effectively she took down Evans, he kept a close watch on her knees.

She stepped around him and approached her brother.

"Jonathan, he's going to be calling me with more instructions. *Me*. If I don't answer, he'll know something's going on." She heaved a sigh and lowered her head. "Look, I know we have his location and that you guys are going to do your thing. But, until then, we have to play along. We can't give him any reason to become suspicious."

"You can do that from here, where I know you'll be safe." Mason looked to Jonathan for backup. "Help me out here, man."

"He's got a point." Jonathan slammed the magazine into place and slid his gun into his thigh holster.

"What if she goes with us but stays with the helicopter?" Andi slid extra magazines through loops on her vest. "She'll be safe there and, if something happens, she's a hell of a shot."

"I agree with Andi." Mathias was the first to speak up, and he looked at the men around him.

Killian, Golden and Devlin all nodded their agreement.

Mason wanted to punch every single one of them in the mouth.

Jonathan narrowed his eyes at her, and she lifted her chin in challenge. Yeah, *dammit*, his girl was a fighter.

"Shit." Jonathan shook his head. "You can go. But ... you will stay with the helicopter and don't move. Understand?"

Mason cursed under his breath.

"I understand." She pivoted and stepped up to him. "Mason, she is my best friend, and I am a part of this team."

His eyes traveled over her, taking in the determined set of her chin and the way the protective vest drooped off one shoulder. But it was the look of confidence and trust in her eyes that convinced him. Confidence in her skills and trust in his and the team's ability to keep her safe and have her back.

"You'll need a vest that fits properly." He lifted it over her head, grabbed a smaller one and held it out to her. "Here, put this on while I get your weapon ready."

She smiled and threw her arms around his middle. He curled his free arm around her and burrowed his nose into her hair.

"I love you," she whispered.

"I love you, too." *So fucking much.*

"Time to go." Decked out in all his black gear and loaded down with flash-bangs, multiple handguns and a big bowie knife, Jonathan looked like the badass Navy SEAL he was trained to be.

Mason gave Emily a quick kiss, then grabbed her weapon. He checked it while she secured her vest, then handed it to her. Her thumb pressed on the mag release button, and she double-checked it was full, then locked it back in place. She made sure there was a round in the chamber and tucked it into her holster like a pro.

He tugged on her vest, made a couple of adjustments. "You good?"

"I'm good." She smiled up at him. "Thank you, Mason."

He hated every fucking thing about this idea.

CHAPTER THIRTY-EIGHT

On their way to the airstrip, Emily's phone rang again. Everyone in the van exchanged a glance and went silent.

"Go ahead." Jonathan said.

Her hands shook as she pulled the phone from a pocket on her vest.

Mason's long fingers curled over her knee. "You got this, darlin'."

She took a nice deep breath and blew it out. "Hello?"

"Emily, my love. Oh, I do love the sound of your voice." The creepy voice effect made the hairs on her arms stand on end. "It sounds like you're on the road, as instructed."

"I am," she said.

"Good. Are you ready for your next set of instructions?"

Not even a little bit. But her friend needed her to be strong.

"Hang on, let me write them down."

Andi snapped her fingers a few times, and Mathias handed Emily a small notepad and pen. Mason clicked on a small flashlight and held it over her.

The kidnapper rattled off the instructions, and she scribbled them down as quickly as she could, listening to see if she recognized Richard's voice or for any sounds in the background that might prove helpful.

"When you get to the dirt road, you'll see an old hollowed-out tree stump. Inside is a burner phone with Christina's number programmed into it. I want you to turn the burner phone on, then destroy yours. Then you will call me for further instructions." She heard a door slam and what sounded like chain rattling. "And Emily, I will be watching you from the moment you pick up the burner phone. If you don't show up, or if I see anyone else with you, your friend dies. See you soon, sweetheart."

Emily hung up, her hand dropped limply to her lap, and her head dropped back against the wall of the van. She swallowed back the bile burning her throat.

"You did great, Em." Mason kissed her on the temple. The warmth of his kiss soothed her tattered nerves. "What did he say?"

She told them about the phone exchange and how he would be able to see her.

"I have to go pick up that phone. If I don't, he's going to kill her." So much for her staying with the helicopter.

Devlin growled, and his nostrils flared.

"Okay, here's what we're going to do." Jonathan laid out their revised plan.

"I don't like it," Mason objected. "That puts her too fucking close to this guy."

"We'll be in place before she ever gets there," Jonathan said. "Mathias, get on the phone with Sammy. Have her arrange to have a truck waiting for us near our landing point. Nothing new or flashy."

If anyone could materialize a truck out of thin air, it would be Sammy.

The new plan swirled around in Emily's head as they

pulled through the gate at the airfield and sped down the dark runway toward the OSI hangar. Only two other people kept small planes here, so there shouldn't be any curious lookie-loos this time of night. Emily was already in the middle of negotiations with the owner to purchase the prop-erty. Before long, the entire airstrip would belong to OSI.

The tactical van pulled to an abrupt stop in front of the large building, and everyone jumped out the back. Mason and Killian jogged over to roll up the hangar door. It rattled up, revealing several aircraft. Tonight, they would be using the same helicopter they took to the Olympic National Park.

Mason climbed into the pilot's seat, and a minute later, the platform with the helicopter sitting on it began rolling outside. About fifty feet from the building, it stopped, and the entire thing lowered until the skids settled on the ground. What looked like clamps around the skids opened and retracted, and the entire thing rolled back into the hangar.

Fascinating.

While he was doing his pre-flight check, everyone else dragged huge duffel bags full of who knows what from the back of the van.

"Here, Emily, take this and come with me." Andi handed her one of the smaller bags, slung another larger one over her own shoulder and started toward the helicopter.

Mathias and Golden slid open the side doors and began loading gear into the back of the helo. Emily handed her duffle to her brother, and he added it to the mix. Killian started up the van and drove it inside the hangar, then dragged the door down and secured it. Devlin stood several feet away, rifle in hand, silent as a stone, scanning the darkness.

She leaned close to Andi and whispered, "Is he okay? He's being awfully quiet."

"Eh, snipers. They get like that." Andi pulled out her

flashlight and ran the beam over their cargo. "He's in his head, focused on the mission."

"Saving Christina?"

"That and killing the man who hurt her." She clicked off her flashlight and tucked it in a pocket, tugged on a pair of black gloves and climbed into the helo. The words had been tossed out so casually, like it was a foregone conclusion.

Criminy. Emily took in the group around her and knew without hesitation she was *way* out of her league. Her place was working behind the scenes, making sure they had everything required to successfully complete their missions and come home alive. Jonathan was right—that's where she was needed. Where she belonged.

As soon as Christina is back home, safe and sound.

Mason walked toward her in that relaxed way of his—a façade that disguised an intense, dangerous man underneath.

"You ready?" He raised his brows and waited. Probably hoping she'd changed her mind.

"I am," she said.

"All right, then. Up you go." He took hold of her waist, lifted and set her inside the helo. "Jonathan's up front with me. I'd like you to take the seat directly behind him and put on the headset."

"Yes, sir." Emily saluted and settled into her seat.

"Smart-ass." He grinned and helped secure her harness. "Hold on, darlin'. This ride's gonna be a bit different than your last one."

With those ominous words hanging in the air, he slid the door shut and secured the latch. He jogged around and climbed into the pilot's seat and pulled on a helmet with night-vision goggles attached. Then he made sure his microphone was positioned in just the right spot in front of his lips.

"ICX check." The sound of his deep baritone rumbling in

her headset tamed the razor-winged butterflies wreaking havoc with her insides.

She looked around as, one at a time, they each responded, "Lima Charlie."

Emily tapped Golden on his arm. "What does that mean?"

"It means we can hear him." He tapped his headset.

"Lima Charlie!" she blurted out much too loudly and could hear muffled laughter coming from her teammates.

Mason smiled and swung his NVGs, night-vision goggles, into place. A second later, the interior went pitch-black, the exception being the green light glowing from the gauges and sneaking out from behind his goggles.

They slowly lifted off the ground, spun 180 degrees and surged forward. Emily looked out the window as the airstrip fell away and faded from view. Lights from Whidbey Cove twinkled below until they, too, blinked out of sight.

The sensation of flying at night was completely different than during the day. The bright moon overhead was the only thing keeping her from becoming disoriented and confused about what was up and what was down.

Mathias, Killian and Golden chatted quietly with each other. Andi smiled down at her phone as she scrolled through a bunch of photos of Ashling and her daddy. Devlin, who was tucked away in the back, had his arms crossed, head back against the wall, and looked like he was sleeping.

Her insides were flipping around like a carnival acrobat, and they all looked like they were riding on a city bus, not headed into a dangerous situation.

Sammy had sent them satellite images of the area where they'd picked up the signal from Christina's phone. They'd studied them in the van, on the way to the airfield. There was a partially overgrown fire road that led to an old building of some sort. It was the only structure anywhere nearby, so they surmised it had to be where he was holding her.

The plan was to land a mile or so away, then the team would make the quick hike in and surround the place. Emily would wait a specific amount of time, then she would drive to where the kidnapper had hidden the burner phone. Her job was to try to grab the phone, get back in the vehicle, and then call him. She was also supposed to draw him out into the open, if possible. She had a plan for that and just hoped he fell for it.

Her stomach jumped to her throat and she grabbed the edge of the seat when Mason suddenly dropped into a small clearing. He gently set the helo on the ground and began shutting everything down. The side doors slid back, and everyone started piling out. The rasp of duffle bag zippers being dragged open joined the low sounds of the blades cutting through the air as they slowed.

Emily stayed in her seat—out of the way—and watched in awe.

Devlin and Golden slung their rifles over their backs and took off into the woods. They would split up, scout the area and communicate their findings to the rest of the team. Mathias, Killian and Andi began pulling gear from the duffle bags and securing it in various pockets. Mason and Jonathan joined them, and within five minutes, everyone was loaded up and ready to execute their plan.

They stood in front of her, decked out in their black tactical gear, reviewing the aerial photo of the shack and going over their plan one last time. Emily was proud of the part she'd played to ensure they had all the equipment they would need to safely carry out this mission.

She turned at the sound of tires crunching through the underbrush.

Mason jumped into the helicopter with her while

everyone else scattered. They took up positions behind the chopper or flat on the ground, their guns aimed toward their incoming target.

A few anxious moments later, an older model pickup truck—its headlights off—appeared through the edge of the tree line and headed directly toward them.

"Move to the back," Mason whispered against her ear.

She did, making sure she could peek through the side window.

The truck pulled to a stop several feet away, and the driver's door swung open. An older man groaned as he stepped out, then slammed the door. His white hair curled out from under a green John Deere hat.

"My granddaughter called and said you guys needed a vehicle?" He stayed where he was, his hands casually raised in the air.

"You Bud?" Jonathan called out.

"Yeah, that's me." He lowered his hands, leaned to the side and spit, then walked over to them.

Emily would swear she could *feel* the tension ease as everyone holstered their weapons and joined Jonathan and their new arrival. They all shook hands.

"So, Sammy's your granddaughter, huh?" Jonathan asked.

"That's right." He turned, spit again, then tugged a red bandana from his back pocket and mopped it across his chin.

Lovely.

He handed Jonathan a single key. "The clutch can be a bit persnickety, so you have to let her know who's boss."

"We appreciate this, and we'll arrange to get it back to you."

"Don't worry 'bout that. I'll get her back from Sammy." Bud's eyes traveled across the group. "She didn't say what you were doing up here, but I might be able to help. See, me and my brother grew up playing in these woods when we were kids."

"Really? Well, maybe you can tell us about that old building up the way." He pointed his thumb over his shoulder in the general direction.

"Shoot, that old place has been empty for thirty years, at least. These days, it's nothing but a place for kids to hang out and party." He bent over and grabbed a stick, then squatted down. "Here, let me show you what to expect when you get up there."

He drew out the old, square building. Said it had wooden clapboard siding. One door in front, another in the back, a single window on each wall. Half of the old stone fireplace had collapsed. He sketched out the location of two large boulders about twenty feet from the front door, as well as a couple of good-size trees nearby that would provide good cover, should the need arise.

"There's a loft and a basement, but the place is small." He lifted off his cap and used fingers on the same hand to scratch his head, then put it back on. "You need to be careful in that old place. It's being held together by nothing more than termites and memories of days past." He stood and tossed the stick aside.

"Good luck to you." He started walking back toward the woods but stopped when Jonathan called his name.

"Bud, you going to be okay getting out of here?"

"Yep." Then he stooped under a small opening in the trees and disappeared.

CHAPTER THIRTY-NINE

Mason checked out the truck and had Emily start it and shift through the gears. Bud was right—they were gummy, but she slammed her foot on the clutch and wrestled them into submission through sheer stubbornness and willpower. The thing was solid as a tank and she should be safe, as long as she stayed in the cab. He was still heavily conflicted about the idea of sending her up there on her own but knew it was the only way this whole fucking thing would work. Fortunately, the drop point for the phones was at least a half mile from the old building.

Assuming that's where the asshole is.

"Son of a bitch." Jonathan crammed his phone into his pocket. "The lab called. They finally got the results of the DNA test and were unable to find a match in the system."

"Considering everything we've discovered about Richard, aren't we pretty confident it's him?" Emily stood in front of Mason, his arms around her shoulders, holding her back against his front.

"Once we get him, we'll have his DNA tested to confirm it matches." Jonathan looked at her. "Okay, squirt. It's time."

Everyone moved away, leaving just Mason and Emily. She turned in his arms and clenched the front of his vest with both hands.

"I'm going to be fine." Her face tilted up to him.

"Tell me the plan again." Mason fussed with the straps on her vest ... again.

"Mason, we've been over it a dozen times."

"Humor me." He wanted it ingrained in her brain to the point she didn't have to think about it.

She sighed. "I drive up, leave the truck running and get out and grab the phone. Before I destroy my phone, I press one button to send this text to let you guys know." She showed him the pre-written text message with the word '*go*'. "Then I destroy my phone, get back in the truck and call him using the burner phone. You guys will make your move while I have him on the phone."

"Excellent." He cupped his hands on the side of her face and brushed her cheeks with his thumbs.

"What if he hurt her, Mason?" Moonlight shone off the tears pooling in her eyes.

"One thing at a time, Em." He kissed the tip of her nose. "Let's get her out of there first."

"You're right." She sniffled and took a deep breath.

"I love you, Em." He pulled her closer, trapping her folded arms between them.

"I love you, too, Mason." She rose up on her toes, and he bent his head to kiss her.

He threw everything he had into that kiss, making sure she knew she was his world, that he couldn't survive without her. She slowly dragged her lips from his and opened her eyes.

"I'd better go." She climbed into the truck, fired up the grouchy old engine, and he watched her drive away.

Mason rushed back to the group. Since he and Jonathan

were the only ones wearing NVGs, they would be taking point, leading the group through the dense trees.

"Windows are covered, but there's some dim light coming from inside." Devlin kept his voice low as he reported in. "Haven't seen any movement."

There was a cracking and rustling sound, then he said, "I'm in position up a tree about one hundred feet out from the southwest corner of the building."

"Emily's on her way up. Can you see the old tree stump from there?" Mason asked.

"Yeah, I can put eyes on her." Devlin had an incredibly powerful night vision scope on his rifle.

"We're moving out, D," Jonathan said.

"Roger that."

"Let's go." Mason flipped down his goggles and headed toward the evil bastard who'd caused so many people so much pain.

The terrain was challenging—dark as a mine, gouged up by gullies, roots everywhere, fallen trees blocking their path. Andi, who could destroy their wooded obstacle course, almost slipped into a small ravine. By the time the building was in sight, they all had cuts and scrapes on their faces from random branches and thorny brush.

Jonathan held up a fist, and they all stopped. He circled one finger in the air, and everyone split up and silently made their way toward their designated spot.

"K, in place," Killian whispered through their earpieces.

"M, in place," Mathias did the same. Then Golden, Andi, Jonathan and Mason.

Mason squatted behind a large boulder in front of the building and each minute ticked by with the speed of molasses.

"She's in place," Devlin murmured.

Emily was going to try to draw the kidnapper outside by

making him think she had a bad connection on the burner phone. It was a long shot, but it was the only hope they had.

"Shit," Devlin cursed. "Someone just jumped in the passenger side of the truck. They're headed your way."

Fuck! Fuck! Fuck! Why hadn't they considered that possibility?

The rumble of the old truck grew louder until they cruised right past the spot where Mason lay hidden and parked in front of the old shack.

The passenger door swung open, and someone stuck their head out for a quick look and ... *What the hell?* He wore a mask of some kind that covered his entire head.

He ducked back into the truck and, from where Mason hid about twenty feet away, he could hear him talking to Emily.

"Come on, sweetheart. We'll only be here a short time, then I'm going to take you home to meet my mother." He was no longer using the voice modulator. Not a good sign.

The dick stepped out and dragged Emily from the truck. She tumbled out and landed on her knees. She jumped to her feet and made a move to run. He grabbed a handful of her hair and still, she resisted, digging her feet into the gravelly dirt, thrashing her body and striking out with her fists.

"I don't have a clean shot," Devlin whispered in Mason's earpiece.

The kidnapper wrapped his arms around her, trapping hers at her side. He lifted her off the ground and headed up the three narrow steps leading to the front door.

Mason was preparing to make a move when Emily tilted her head forward, then brought it back and smashed it into the guy's face.

Cartilage and bone crunched, and blood poured down his face. He yelled and loosened his hold, and they tumbled down the steps. Emily landed on her back, him on top of her.

He tightened his fist in the front of her shirt and yanked her to her feet as he stood. "You bitch," he roared, drew back his hand and smacked her across the face.

Dark red hair flew; her head whipped to the side. She gave a quick shake of her head, then slowly lifted her face. Moonlight glinted off the blood on her lip.

Everything inside Mason went black, and he gave himself over to the killer within.

The guy wrapped one arm around her throat, the other around her middle, lifted her off the ground and turned his back to carry her inside.

"Shit." Devlin cursed because he still didn't have a clear shot.

Mason could not let him take her inside that building. He lifted his goggles off his head and set them on the ground, then army-crawled, using the shadows to move closer.

He slipped his knife from the sheath. With the stealth attained from years of martial arts, he silently closed the distance between them. He was a foot away when the killer began to turn his way.

Mason didn't hesitate. He lunged across the few feet and slashed his blade across the back of one of the man's thighs.

The kidnapper howled in pain and collapsed to the ground, taking Emily with him. She screamed and wriggled and shoved him off her, then crab-walked backward away from him.

"You okay?" Mason gave her a quick look and noticed the monster bruise forming on her cheek.

"She's mine!" The man let out a manic scream and lifted his gun.

Mason threw himself over Emily with his body, drew his weapon, turned and fired. Sparks exploded from the end of the barrel, and the kidnapper's body jerked. At the same time, the distinctive *thwip* of a suppressor came through his earpiece, and the killer's head lurched back. A hole appeared in the mask's forehead, and dark crimson expanded in a vivid bloom across the front of his dress shirt.

Wide, shocked eyes stared out through large holes in the rubber, the gun dropped from his lifeless fingers, and he slumped to the ground.

Their teammates burst into the clearing from all directions and rushed over to the body. Jonathan picked up the revolver, emptied the rounds from the cylinder and shoved it all in a pocket. The guy's Freddie Krueger mask was askew, and his clothes were covered with dirt, dead grass and other debris. Killian bent over and yanked off the mask.

"Holy shit," Andi said. "Who the hell is that?"

"Well, it's not Richard Evans." Jonathan squatted down and placed his fingers to the side of the man's neck. A formality, really. "Killian, Golden and Mathias, check out the house. And be careful."

Killian went around back. Mathias and Golden headed in through the front door.

Jonathan patted the dead man's pockets and pulled out a set of keys. "No identification. Not that I expected to find any."

Mason stood and reached his hand down to help Emily up.

"Why did you do that?" Emily slapped at his chest, then glared up at him.

"Hey, what was that for?" He wrapped his fingers around her wrists because he wasn't sure if she was done hitting him.

"Why did you cover me like that? He could have killed you, and I can't be on this earth without you, you big ... stupid-head ..." Tears welled in her eyes. She blinked, and they trailed down her cheek. Her forehead fell against his chest. Her shoulders shook as she sobbed into his vest.

He circled his arms around her and let her cry.

"Darlin', I'm not going anywhere. I plan to be around for a very long time." He tilted her face up to him. "But you need to understand that I will always do whatever is necessary to keep you safe. So you might as well get used to it."

Her proud little chin quivered. She quickly swiped the tears from her cheek and cleared her throat. He tugged a bandanna from a pocket on his pants leg and gingerly dabbed it to her lip.

"You kicked his ass, Em." He was so fucking proud of the way she fought.

She pulled her head away and tried to step around him. "We need to find Christina."

"The guys are already on it. I'd like you to wait over here with Andi while I help them inside." Mason gave her the cloth, put his arm around her quivering shoulders and led her past the body.

Emily glanced down at the man on the ground and gasped. She took a step closer. Her forehead crinkled, and her brows drew together.

"I ... I know him. He was a janitor in the psych building." She looked up at Mason. "Remember? I told you about the guy that replaced the older janitor when he retired?"

"This is the guy?" Mason pointed down at him.

"Now that I think about it, he did comment on my necklace." She reached up and rubbed the green jade pendant between her fingers. "He said he'd never seen anything like it and how he liked the way it matched my eyes. I thanked him and went to my next class."

"Guess that explains why he kept Pamela and Sandy's necklaces," Andi added.

Devlin, his rifle strapped to his back, crashed through the woods like a bull, blew past them and charged straight into the shack.

"Christina!" he called out.

"Son of a ..." Jonathan tossed the keys he'd found in the kidnapper's pocket to Mason. "Go after him."

The other exterior door stood open, directly across the room from the front door. The only things inside, other than empty beer cans and booze bottles littering the main space, were a card table and two chairs. The room was connected to a tiny kitchen with bare plumbing, no sink, cracked and yellowing laminate countertops, and a small set of cabinets, their doors broken or missing.

"All clear." Killian climbed backward down the steep stairs from the loft. "Nothing up here but empty bottles and garbage. Oh, and a crap-ton of rat shit."

"All clear here, too." Mathias stepped into the hallway from the small bathroom. A smashed-up toilet was next to a rust-stained sink and an old metal shower with a sapling growing up through the drain.

Golden shut the door of a small closet in the hallway. "Empty."

"Here!" Devlin shouted.

They ran into the kitchen and found him in a small pantry. There was a door at the back of the space, and he shone his light on a huge, pristine deadbolt.

Mason squeezed in next to him with the keys.

"No time for that." Devlin lifted his foot and smashed his boot against the door, right above the lock.

The corroded hinges ripped from the rotted jamb. The door flew off and slid partially down a flight of decaying wooden stairs. It was like looking down into a mine shaft. The tangy, metallic smell of copper—of death—poured from the opening and chewed its way up their nostrils and into their sinus cavities.

"No, no, no, no, no." Devlin shoved the broken door out of the way and pointed his flashlight and weapon downward as he descended into the abyss. The beam of his light slashed from side to side.

Mason flipped the light switch, but nothing happened.

"She's here!" Devlin bellowed from the dark.

Mason, the twins and Golden hurried down the wobbling steps, one man at a time. Dreading what they might see.

Christina lay in the fetal position, eyes closed, her bloody wrists shackled and chained to a ring in the wall.

Mathias and Golden shone their lights on her while Devlin gently lifted the strands of hair from where it was stuck to her muddy face. He placed two fingers to the side of her throat, hesitated, then blew out a breath.

"She's alive." His lips close to her ears, voice soft, he said, "Christina, honey. Can you hear me?"

She didn't respond, didn't twitch an eye, nothing.

He supported her wrists in his palm. "Mason, please get these fucking things off her," he whispered, as if afraid to disturb her.

Devlin cupped his other hand over her head and stroked his thumb across her temple as Mason worked his way through the keys. Finally, the padlock popped open, and Mason gently removed the metal shackles to reveal her torn and bloody wrists.

Mathias cursed under his breath, squatted down and checked to make sure it was safe to move her. "Okay."

Devlin gingerly slid his arms beneath her, curled her into his chest, stood and headed for the stairs.

"Found Evans." Killian squatted next to a body in the far corner. His light traveled over the body. "Gunshot wound to the center of the chest."

"Think he was working with the guy out front?" Mathias dragged the beam of his flashlight around the room, over the walls, the ceiling where a broken bulb swung from a wire.

"Who the hell knows." Mason needed to see Emily. "Let's get the hell out of here."

They carefully navigated the old set of stairs and shuffled out into the fresh night air. The scent of blood would linger in their noses for days.

Mason walked over to where everyone congregated around the bed of the truck. Devlin climbed in back and sat with his back against the cab, Christina unconscious in his lap. Worried faces hovered around them. She was important to every single one of them. She was family.

Golden dug in his pocket and pulled out a small silver packet. He tore away the cellophane and shook out an emergency thermal blanket and draped it over Christina. Emily checked her for injuries, then Mason helped Emily down from the bed of the truck and wrapped her in his arms.

"How's she doing?" His lips moved against the top of her head.

"There's a bruise around a small puncture wound on her neck." She levered back and looked up at him. "And her wrists are a mess."

"The son of a bitch had her shackled like a wild animal." He pressed a soft kiss to her forehead.

"Mason, she's already been through so much, and now this." She sucked in her bottom lip and cast sad eyes upon her best friend. "It's just not fair that this happened to her because of me."

"Huh-uh. Nope. I am not going to let you blame yourself for something a fucked-up psychopath did. None of this is your fault, do you hear me?" He bent his knees to bring them eye to eye.

"You're right." She rubbed her hand down his back.

"Come on. Let's get her to the helo." He held her hand. "Jonathan, call Sammy. Have her contact Skagit Bay Memorial and let them know we'll be inbound. ETA, less than fifteen minutes."

"You got it." He slipped his phone from his pocket and stepped a few feet away.

An indistinguishable sedan sped up the dirt road, its headlight blinding them. Everyone whirled, weapons drawn, ready to take down the potential threat. The car rolled to a stop next to the truck. The headlights went out, and Detective Harden lifted his burly frame from his car, hiked up his pants and started toward them.

Jonathan walked back to his team. "At ease, folks." Then he walked over and shook the detective's hand.

"I've got four patrol cars at the bottom of the mountain, waiting for my orders to come up." He looked around at the intimidating group guarding the truck. "I suggest you take advantage of that time to make yourselves scarce."

"We appreciate you working with us on this." Jonathan rubbed the back of his neck. "We'll make sure your department gets credit."

"I could give a shit about that." The detective looked around him at the body. "I'm just happy you guys got the son of a bitch."

"As I mentioned when I called you, there's another body in the basement." He crossed his arms over his chest. "It's Richard Evans."

"I'll take care of it." They shook hands again, and he stepped around Jonathan and headed toward the shack.

"Let's load up." Jonathan climbed in and fired up the old engine.

Andi yanked open the passenger side door and slid across to the center of the bench seat. Mathias got in next to her and pulled the door shut with a metallic bang. Everyone else climbed in the back with Christina and Devlin.

Jonathan executed a three-point turn and headed down the hill to the chopper.

After backing the old truck into the bushes and leaving the key in the glove box, they hurriedly stowed their gear and took their seats. Jonathan let Emily sit up front, and he sat next to his wife. The long blades began chopping through the chill air, and they lifted into the night sky. Below them, flashing blue and red lights snaked their way up the side of the small mountain.

Mason reached across, laced his fingers through Emily's and kissed the back of her hand. She smiled, turned their joined hands over and returned the favor.

EPILOGUE

Emily stood back to admire her work. She'd picked dark teal for the walls in the bigger of the two guest rooms —a color that was way outside her comfort zone. Seeing it now, she was happy she'd listened to her gut. She was also glad this was the last room that needed any work. It felt like she'd been painting ever since they moved in a month ago.

"Perfect." She bent over to set the paint roller in the pan.

"Yes, it is."

She spun around, her hand to her chest. "Criminy, you startled me."

Mason casually leaned one shoulder against the door frame. His yummy arms were crossed over his equally yummy chest. She hadn't decided which she liked best. Who was she kidding? She liked every single thing about him equally. Heck, just looking at him never failed to send her heart rate soaring.

"Sorry, darlin'." He shoved off the jamb and moved toward her like a powerful cat. "I didn't mean to scare ya."

Oo, the man was sinister—he knew the effect that sexy Texas drawl had on her.

"So, what do you think?" She turned back to the wall and spread her arms wide.

He came up behind her, wrapped his arms around her middle and pulled her against him. His delicious body curled over hers, and he rested his chin on her shoulder.

"I think it's great." He tugged aside her collar and nibbled his way across then up the side of her neck.

"You're not even looking at it." Her eyes drooped shut, and she tilted her neck to give him better access. She stretched one arm up and stroked her fingers over the back of his neck.

His big hand splayed over her left breast, and he flicked his thumb over her nipple. He spent the next few minutes dragging his tongue around the edge of her ear, kneading her breasts, whispering filthy, wonderful things to her. Generally, getting her all heated up.

"Mason, I ..." She inhaled a quick breath when he placed a gentle bite to her neck.

"What's that, Em?" His voice had grown rough and husky. Yeah, he was as worked up as she was.

"Everyone's going to be here soon, and I still have to shower."

"MAYBE I'LL JOIN YOU." Mason ground his crotch against her ass, torturing himself further.

She turned in his arms and grinned up at him. "If you do, we'll never make it to our own party."

A week after Emily ordeal, they'd moved into the house together. That was exactly one month ago today.

"Knock, knock, knock." Molly's voice was accompanied by the sound of a knuckle rapping on the screen-door frame.

"Your folks are here," he murmured in her ear, then continued to plant sucking kisses to the magic spot on her neck and down to her shoulder.

She hummed. "Hmm?"

He smiled against the soft skin beneath her chin. "I said, your folks are here."

She groaned and dragged her hands down his chest, then tugged her phone from her back pocket and checked the time. "Shoot! I had no idea it was this late."

"I'll take care of things out here. You go shower."

"Are you sure?" Her arms circled his waist.

"Yes, but you'd better get in there before I change my mind and decide to join you." He turned her toward the door and swatted her butt.

She gave him a stern look and pointed. "You'll pay for that later, mister."

"I look forward to it." He left her to her shower and jogged to the front of the house.

"Hey, come on in." Mason held the door open for Michaleen and Molly.

As usual, their arms were loaded with platters and dishes of food.

"Here, let me take those for you." He relieved Molly of her burden and led them into the kitchen.

"That blue one needs to go in the fridge." She hung her purse on a hook in the pantry. "The other one can just sit out on the counter."

"Where would you like these, sweetie?" Michaleen held up the ones in his hands.

"Right here is fine, honey." She patted the counter and turned to Mason with arms open wide. "Okay, now I want my hug."

He gladly obliged, then it was Michaleen's turn.

"Emily will be out shortly. She was painting and lost track of time." He turned and shifted things around in the fridge to make room for the dish. It was like a game of food Tetris.

"Why don't y'all go ahead out back and make yourselves comfortable? I'm going to make sure the Pack 'n Play's all set up for Rian." Never in his wildest imagination did he think those words would ever come out of his mouth.

"I think that is so sweet that you guys bought one to keep here." Molly's eyes twinkled. "Perhaps someday soon you two might have use for it?"

"Good grief, woman. Leave the boy alone." Michaleen pretended to scold his wife and turned to Mason. "Need some help with that, son?"

Son. At long last, Mason had a loving father figure he could admire, respect and emulate.

"Thanks, but it's already set up. I just want to make sure it's secure." He rubbed the back of his neck. "The first time I set it up was a bit hairy, but I finally got it figured out."

He could tear down the engine on an Apache helicopter and put it back together, but he had to pull out the instructions to figure out how to unfold a portable crib.

"Been there, done that." Michaleen clapped him on the back and let loose one of his big, hearty laughs.

"Okay, honey, let's go pick a good spot to sit where I can see everyone." Molly kissed Mason's cheek, and they headed to the backyard.

He went down the hall toward the second guest room and halted his steps at the sound of the shower running in their large, walk-in master bathroom. He visualized water and soap bubbles trailing down Emily's sweet, curvy body, her head back as she rinsed her hair, her perfect tits all shiny and waiting for his mouth ...

Shit. He took a moment to carefully adjust himself. Last thing he wanted to do was walk into the middle of a family gathering with a raging woody.

They were hosting a casual barbecue with family and close friends to celebrate them moving into their new home together. What Emily didn't know was, he was planning to ask her to marry him today.

They'd talked about it quite a bit, and he knew she was totally on board with the idea. Still, he hadn't been this nervous since he was twelve years old and Hank let him fly solo for the first time. Probably didn't help that her entire family would be here to witness the event. But it just seemed *right* for all of them to share in this moment. Unfortunately, he wasn't able to convince Hank to join them. He'd wished Mason luck and grumbled something about needing to get back to work because "that engine wasn't going to fix itself."

Mason had covered all the bases and done everything by the book. He'd sat down with Molly and Michaleen and told them how much he loved their daughter and how she would always be his number one priority. Molly had cried, Michaleen had told him to take good care of his little girl, then they'd happily given him their blessing. He'd even gathered all of her brothers together via teleconference at Jonathan's place. They'd busted his chops for several minutes with things like, *You sure you know what you're getting into?* and *She can be kind of annoying, you know.* They'd also warned him that if he ever hurt her, they'd never find his body. You know, typical overprotective big-brother bullshit. Knowing he didn't scare easily and that he truly did love their sister, they'd finally relented and given him their approval.

Not that he would've let anything stop him from being with Emily.

Molly had given him some insights regarding a ring, and he'd taken that information and had one made especially for her. Said ring was currently burning a hole in his pocket.

He headed toward laughter coming from the backyard.

He stepped out onto the back porch, and warmth filled him as he took in the group of people that had begun to gather. His family.

Molly and Michaleen, their fingers laced together, lounged in a couple of handmade Adirondack chairs. They smiled and watched all the activity around them.

Next to them, on a blanket spread out under one of the big shade trees, Gwen sat cross-legged next to baby Rian, who was sprawled out like a starfish and sleeping soundly through all the noise and activity going on around him.

Gary sat at the edge of the blanket, yowling and hissing at anyone who dared get too close. Seems he'd taken quite a liking to little Rian and had assumed the role of protector. It was hilarious to watch.

The old cat had grudgingly accepted the move to the house. Though he still wandered from room to room yelling at absolutely nothing. Emily joked that maybe he could see ghosts.

Beck stood next to the blanket with Jonathan, Andi, and Jeffrey Burke, smiling as they watched Ashling and Alice tearing around the yard with squirt guns.

The gate at the side of the house creaked, and Mathias and Killian walked through, each holding a handle on a huge cooler.

"Hey, Mase." Killian stopped at the base of the steps and looked up at him. "Where do you want this?"

"You can set it up here, in the shade." He pointed to a spot behind him on the porch.

"You got it." The twins responded in unison and started up the stairs.

He jogged down and high-fived them on his way by. He did a quick visual check of his new grass as he walked across the yard toward the group gathered under the tree.

"Thanks for coming." They exchanged handshakes and hugs. "Emily will be out shortly."

"The place looks great," Jonathan said, and everyone looked at the house.

As he took in the finished project, he had to admit, everything had turned out better than he'd ever imagined.

"I couldn't have done it without y'all's help." Hell, he'd probably be sleeping in a tent out front had they not butted in and pretty much taken over.

The twins sauntered over, hands loaded with bottles of beer that they passed out to everyone.

"It's cool the way you repurposed some of the old wood to make a playhouse for the kids." Andi smiled. "Ashling loves coming over to her Uncle Mason and Aunt Emily's house to play."

Uncle Mason. He would never get tired of that moniker either.

"Seemed a shame to let it go to waste. Your dad was a huge help." Mason had a great time working on the project with him and learned so much.

"I have to admit, it's the smallest house I've ever built," Michaleen said.

Gwen patted Beck's calf and smiled up at him. "Alice keeps harassing her daddy to make one for her. She actually said that: If he really loved her as much as Uncle Mason did, he would build her a playhouse of her own."

"I'm tellin' ya, that girl is a master at emotional manipulation, and she knows I'm an easy mark. And this one thinks it's hilarious." Beck reached down and gave a playful tug on his wife's long braid.

"Because it is." Gwen laughed, and Beck kissed her.

Alice ran over and stood in front of Burke.

"Unca Jeffwey, wiw you come pway wif us?" She flattened

her palms together and fluttered her eyelashes at him. "Pwease! Pwease!"

Burke was Ashling's godfather, but he had a soft spot for all the O'Halleran children. Not that anyone would ever tell him that to his face. The guy was intense.

"Sure, honey." He didn't even hesitate, just reached down and took hold of her little hand.

They all stood and watched one of the most dangerous men in the world get dragged away to go play with two little girls.

"See what I mean." Beck shook his head. "She's a master."

They all laughed, albeit amongst themselves, at the sight of the powerful head of the NSA sitting cross-legged on the grass, having a tea party.

The gate creaked again, and Luna held it open while Caleb walked through carrying a cornhole set. Dawn, looking a little green, was right behind him holding a six-pack of ginger ales in one hand and a box of soda crackers in the other. Caleb said that she never went anywhere without them. Apparently, she'd been suffering from extreme morning sickness that didn't have the decency to stick to mornings. She'd assured him there was nothing to be concerned about, but that didn't stop him from worrying. Didn't seem to matter that she was a doctor who should know what she was talking about.

Mathias rushed over and grabbed one of the backboards and helped him set it up. Killian ambled over and challenged his twin to a game.

Dawn settled on the blanket next to Gwen, who draped an arm over her shoulder in solidarity.

"Ugh" was all Dawn said as she dug her hand into the box of crackers.

"Gwen, honey, would you like me to take Rian in and put him down? I have it on good authority that the Pack 'N Play is set up and guaranteed to stay that way." Molly winked at Mason.

"I think that's a great idea. Are you sure you don't mind?" Gwen moved to her knees and gently lifted her son.

"I don't mind one tiny little bit." She started to rise, and Michaleen stood and offered her his hand. "Thank you, honey."

Gwen transferred Rian to his grandmother's arms, and Molly tucked him to her chest. She shared a sweet kiss with her husband and took the baby into the house. Gary trotted alongside her, meowing and looking up at Rian, as if making sure she knew what she was doing.

Michaleen smiled with incredible tenderness at his wife as she walked across the yard, up the steps and into the house. The door slapped shut, and he turned to Mason.

"Mind if I dip into your tools? I'd like to check the bolts on that playhouse, make sure they're good and tight."

"Absolutely. You know where they are."

He headed off to double-check his own work. The man was a perfectionist.

Emily appeared at the top of the steps wearing that cute little green and white sundress she had on the first time he saw her. She waved over at their group, held up one finger in a sort of *just a minute* kinda way and walked over to say hi to Jeffrey.

"How's she doing?" Beck turned suddenly serious as he watched his little sister pretend to sip tea from a tiny plastic tea cup.

"She's doing pretty well. I think moving in here and doing stuff around the house helped keep her mind occupied. She is worried about Christina, though." Mason didn't share with them about the couple of times she'd been awakened by nightmares.

"Yeah, I've been concerned about her, too." Andi crossed

her arms. "She spent one night in the hospital, just long enough for the drug to leave her system, then she insisted on going home. I couldn't believe it when she showed up to work the next day, her usual bright and cheerful self. Like nothing happened."

"I tried to convince her to take some time off, but she refused. Said there was too much to do and that she didn't want anyone messing around with her system." Jonathan took a sip of his beer.

"You know that's not normal, right?" Andi's concerned expression said it all.

"Yeah, I know." He draped his arm over his wife's shoulder and kissed her temple.

Just then, Christina walked out the back door with a large covered dish propped on one hip. She looked out over the yard, gave them a big smile and lifted her hand in a casual wave. The bright sun bounced off one of the brushed silver cuff bracelets she'd started wearing the day the bandages were removed. She set the food down on the table and joined the tea party.

"She's been over a few times, helping Em paint or hang curtains or whatever. One night they had a few too many margaritas, and she crashed in the guest room." Though Mason could hear her across the hall, tossing and turning all night. "When she's ready to open up, Emily will be there for her."

"Devlin watched over her at the hospital," Jonathan said. "He told me that, as she was dozing off, she mumbled something like, 'He shouldn't waste his time on damaged goods' or some nonsense like that. The next morning, he asked what she meant, and she laughed it off and blamed it on the drugs. She's been avoiding him ever since, and it's driving the poor guy nuts."

"Is he going to be here today?" Dawn held her hand over her eyes and squinted up at Mason.

"No, he has to work at the pub tonight." He tucked his hand in his front pocket and brushed his fingertips over the ring.

"His skills are being wasted behind that bar." Andi joined Gwen and Dawn on the blanket.

"Any movement on him coming to work for OSI?" Beck tipped back his beer for a long swallow.

"Not much, but after getting a taste of the action again, I think he's closer. I'll keep working on him," Jonathan said.

"Detective Harden called earlier. Said he was promoted to the major crimes division," Beck said. "Which means there's a pretty good chance we'll work with him on future cases."

"He's a decent cop, but he's hamstrung by a system with too many fu—" Andi glanced over at her daughter. "Darn rules."

"Good save, Mom." Jonathan winked at his wife.

"I'm just glad the lab didn't screw up the evidence. Dr. Parker assured me that what happened there will never happen in OSI's lab." Beck and Jeffrey were extremely impressed with her.

Emily recognizing the killer as the janitor from school helped narrow down their search for his identity. As an employee of a state university, he was required to provide fingerprints, which were then input into AFIS, the Automated Fingerprint Identification System. Their search came back with the name Roger Wheeler. They also matched his DNA to their sample and the piece of the silver crown from Sandy's burial site.

People he went to elementary through high school with said he was a weird, quiet loner who stared at some of the girls a bit too long, but he never made a move on any. On the rare occasions anyone saw his mother she was always very well put together—hair perfect, expensive clothes, high-end jewelry—and incredibly stuck up. Several remembered over-hearing her putting him down, calling him names. They always felt a little sorry for him. She also controlled all the money, depositing substantial funds into her son's account each month. They figured he took the job as a janitor simply to spite her. After he inherited a shit-ton of money from his estranged father, he quit his job and sort of dropped off the map.

"They searched Wheeler's house and found a bunch of photos of Emily, going way back to when she was at U Dub. There were also a couple of her with Richard Evans at the bowling alley." Mason wanted to destroy every photo the psychopath took of her but knew it wasn't an option. "He killed Evans because he got too close to her and planted the necklaces in his apartment to send us on a wild goose chase. That's why Emily and I think his obsession with her must've started the day he chatted with her about the green jade necklace she got for her sixteenth birthday."

"After Evans's photo showed up on the news, two other women came forward and said he'd lied to them, too. When they confronted him about it, he told them he did it to impress them. Instead of leaving them alone, he started stalking them," Jonathan said.

"Wheeler was one sick puppy." Andi shook her head. "He killed his own mother, then lived in the house with her dead body while he went about his business."

"Harden said they found a stack of news articles about the Last Will and Testament Killer in the guy's closet," Beck said. "He must've been quite the fan, because they were in pristine condition. They also found a bunch of wigs, makeup, latex and other stuff like that."

"Yeah, I looked at the photos and recognized a dark wig and suit from Sandy's funeral. He'd disguised himself as an old man and actually had the balls to bump into Emily." Mason was still pissed the demented piece of shit had gotten that close to her when he and her entire family were nearby.

"Well, Roger Wheeler is the devil's problem now." Gwen took a small sip of Beck's beer. "Oh, gosh, that's good."

"How 'bout I fire up that new barbecue grill of mine and get some burgers started?" Mason rubbed his hands together and walked over to their brand-new outdoor kitchen.

A few hours later, everyone was sitting around on blankets and miscellaneous lawn chairs, sharing conversation, stuffed to the gills with great food and drink. Other than the Adirondack chairs Michaleen made for them, Mason and Emily hadn't had time to pick out patio furniture.

Ashling and Alice had finally run out of steam and were crashed on an air mattress inside the playhouse. Rian was cooing and gurgling, letting loose adorable deep-bellied baby giggles, safe in his daddy's arms.

A deep orangey-pink lit up the horizon, then blended upward into a deep blue, where stars had already begun to sparkle. This was Mason and Emily's favorite time of day. Each night, they would sit on the back porch until the sky grew dark, Emily on his lap in one of the chairs made especially for them by her father.

He glanced around at the people assembled and knew this was the perfect time. He stood with Emily in his arms, turned and set her back in the chair.

"Where are you go—" She gave him a curious look.

He reached in his pocket and knelt in front of her.

Her eyes widened, and she clapped her hands over her mouth.

"Emily, I want to spend the rest of my life listening to you laugh. I want to share in your happiness, and I want to be the one to wipe away your tears when you're sad. I'm your biggest fan, and I want to grow old with you. So ... Emily Ann O'Halleran, I'm asking you in front of the people who mean the most to us, will you do me the great honor of marrying me?"

"Yes! Yes, I'll marry you, silly!" She squealed, jumped up and tackled him to the ground.

"It's not official till the ring is on your finger, squirt," Jonathan called out over everyone's laughter.

"Oh my gosh, you're right." She crawled off Mason, sat back on her heels and held out her left hand.

Mason slipped the platinum ring on her finger.

"Oh, Mason, it's perfect." She smiled down at the oval-shaped emerald surrounded by smaller diamonds, then threw her arms around his neck.

He turned to Molly and mouthed the words, "Thank you." And she blew him a kiss.

Everyone gathered around, waiting their turn for hugs and handshakes and to get a look at the ring. They all wished them the best of everything and welcomed Mason, once again, to the family.

As they were all packing up their belongings and gathering up their children, he pulled Emily aside.

"You've made me a very happy man, Em." *Happy* seemed like such a lame word to describe how he felt.

"I love you, Mason. And I can't wait to spend the rest of my life with you." She stood on tiptoe and circled her arms around his neck.

"I love you, too, Em." He tucked his hands in her back pockets and held her close.

Never in his life did he imagine he would have a woman like Emily who loved him unconditionally or a life filled with laughter and people who cared about him.

Mason would never take Emily and her family—their family—for granted.

Watch for Deadly Secret, Deadly Disciple *and* Deadly Deception, *books 1, 2 and 3 in TJ Logan's O'Halleran Security International series.*

DON'T MISS OUT!

Sign up at https://www.tjloganauthor.com/subscribe-to-newsletter to receive the "COVERT DETAILS" newsletter. You'll receive advance notice of release dates, get the first look at book covers, have access to exclusive content, and be eligible for fun giveaways.

You can also find TJ on ...
Facebook: https://www.facebook.com/tjloganauthor/
Covert Commanders Private Facebook Group:
https://www.facebook.com/groups/238241904179626o/
Twitter: https://twitter.com/TJLoganAuthor
Instagram: https://www.instagram.com/tjloganauthor/
Website: https://www.tjloganauthor.com/
https://www.tjloganauthor.com/blog

BOOKS BY TJ LOGAN

O'Halleran Security International Series

Deadly Secret

Deadly Disciple

Deadly Deception

Deadly Judgment

Deadly Apprentice – *Coming Soon*

Deadly Resurgence – *Coming Soon*

DEADLY SECRET

HE STEPS INTO THE SHADOWS TO PURSUE A KILLER...

F.B.I. Special Agent Beckett O'Halleran values Family, Honor, and Loyalty. A botched undercover assignment results in the brutal murder of his partner. When the killer is set free by a Deputy Director on the take, Beck walks away from the Bureau. He vows to stop at nothing to avenge his partner's death, including using an innocent woman.

SHE IS DRAGGED INTO THE SHADOWS BY HER MOTHER'S PAST...

A deadly secret from the past threatens Gwendolyn Tamberley's life. Thrust into the crosshairs of a merciless psychopath who will destroy anyone who threatens his empire, she becomes the center of a firestorm between the Russian mafia, the F.B.I. and a former agent hell-bent on retribution.

WILL DEADLY SECRETS DESTROY THEM?

Gwen's only hope is the man who's been deceiving her. And Beck must choose between his obsession with vengeance and the woman who's come to mean everything to him.

DEADLY DISCIPLE

AN HONORABLE MAN DRIVEN BY THE NEED FOR RETRIBUTION...

Caleb O'Halleran is a Tactical K9 Specialist with the FBI's elite Hostage Rescue Team. Finding the traitor responsible for his K9 partner's death is the only thing that matters ... until he meets an enchanting, strong-willed doctor.

A NOBLE DOCTOR DETERMINED TO HELP OTHERS...

Dr. Dawn Pannikos is a busy ER doctor with a surly teenage sister to raise and a past that has taught her not to trust love. There's no room in her well-ordered life for an irresistibly charming ladies' man with shadows around his heart.

TWO INNOCENT WOMEN DRAGGED INTO A NIGHTMARE...

Dawn and her sister become prisoners of a psychopathic cult leader and are plunged into the middle of a dangerous FBI operation. Will Caleb and his new K9 partner, Jake, find them in time, or will he be too late to save the woman who owns his heart?

DEADLY DECEPTION

A WARRIOR DEVASTATED BY AN UNIMAGINABLE LOSS...

Navy SEAL Jonathan O'Halleran's world is upended by tragic loss. Civilian life as a single father and hunting down the traitor responsible for bringing death to his family's doorstep are only temporary distractions from his grief, anger, and guilt.

A TOUGH AS HELL WOMAN WHO DOESN'T KNOW HOW TO TRUST...

Andréa Swain is a brilliant, stubborn NSA Interrogations Tactics Specialist with serious daddy issues. She is yanked from the front lines in Afghanistan and ordered to work with a surly Navy SEAL who blames her for his friend's death.

WILL DISTRUST AND HEARTACHE STAND IN THE WAY OF THEIR FUTURE?

Andi risks her life to save Jonathan's daughter from a man desperate to fulfill his destiny in the White House. Jonathan finally lets go of the past and embraces a future with Andi. Will he get to them in time, or will history repeat itself?

ABOUT THE AUTHOR

TJ Logan is an award-winning author of romantic suspense anchored by strong themes of family, honor, and loyalty. Her writing journey began one day, back in 2012, when a bunch of strange voices popped into her head. Hoping to exorcise the craziness, she started typing, which simply ushered in more— as if she'd cracked open some sort of portal for fictional characters to charge through.

Those random voices morphed into the O'Halleran family. The family grew with the addition of lovers, friends, neighbors, and co-workers. Voila, the first six books of the O'Halleran Security International (OSI) series was born.

TJ grew up in a military family, lived all over the country and was surrounded by five brothers ... and, amazingly, lived to tell about it. She was also a key member of a team who managed a secret program for one of the world's top defense companies. All of these things have given TJ an interesting perspective on life. And every bit of it goes into her writing!

Family, Honor and Loyalty aren't just words in a tagline to TJ. They are everything.